CLAY BRENTWOOD SERIES
BOOK SIX: THE CHAMELEON

I0592497

Creative Texts Publishers products are available at special discounts for bulk purchase for sale promotions, premiums, fund-raising, and educational needs. For details, write Creative Texts Publishers, PO Box 50, Barto, PA 19504, or visit www.creativetexts.com

CLAY BRENTWOOD: BOOK SIX: THE CHAMELEON
by Jared McVay
Published by Creative Texts Publishers
PO Box 50
Barto, PA 19504
www.creativetexts.com

ISBN: 9780692084854

THE CHAMELEON
By
JARED MCVAY

An imprint of Creative Texts Publishers, LLC
Barto, PA

Thank you to all my readers. Your reviews and requests for more Clay Brentwood books is an inspiration to me. I'll keep writing them as long as you keep requesting them...

Jared McVay

ALSO BY JARED McVAY

Other works by Jared McVay

Jared McVay is an award-winning author who writes, Westerns: A western series: Historical Fiction: Action/Adventure: YA: Children's books: screenplays: teleplays: Short stories, and also does storytelling.

NOVELS:

Clay Brentwood western series:

Book 1 – Stranger on A Black Stallion

Book 2 – Unjust Punishment

Book 3 – Hammershield

Book 4 – Cinch Mountain

Book 5 – The Storm

Book 6 – The Chameleon

Historical Fiction: The Legend of Joe, Willy & Red – award winner

Historical Fiction: Silent Runner, Guardian Warrior

Western: Hacker's Raid – award winner

Action/Contemporary - Not on My Mountain – double award winner

CHILDREN'S BOOKS

Bears, Bicycles & Broomsticks – 11 short stories

Randal Gets A Hit

Santa's Magic Ring

SCREENPLAYS

The Hobos

Jared & the Warden

Talltree

Santa's Magic Ring

TELEVISION PILOT SCRIPTS

McClusky [6 episodes] - Drama/Comedy

ACT Acute Care Transport - Drama/Comedy

Melinda: Award winning short story

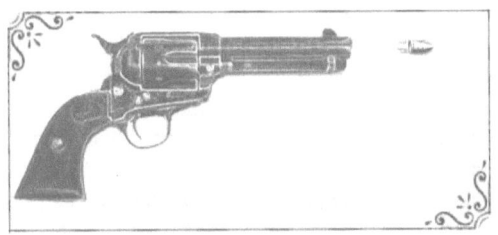

CHAPTER ONE

Death sometimes comes when we least expect it and from a direction that leaves folks a might slack-jawed.

The town hall in Waco, Texas was alive with activity. Nearly every citizen, except for the sheriff, the bartenders and the men who preferred whiskey to politics, turned out to hear Senator Rodney P. Morgan discuss his plans for building a university of higher learning just outside of town. This was a big-ticket item for the people of Waco and they had high hopes for the new school. Good schools were few and far between out here, especially universities. The good ones, like Harvard and a few others, were all back east and very expensive.

Henry Lowe, owner and pharmacist of the Corner Drugstore, set up a table near the front of the town hall where he handed out free bottles of his newly invented soda pop. He was still working on a name for it, but claimed it was a real pepper upper. The new drink was a big hit with the women and children, along with a few of the men. Not many, but a few. Most of the men preferred beer or whiskey, or even coffee to this sweet tasting non-alcoholic beverage. Two of the men who tried it said they enjoyed buttermilk over the sweet soda. Undaunted, Henry declared it a big success. Being a widower, Henry was also a big hit with many of the widow ladies in Waco and proclaimed his new soda drink would make him rich and famous.

Senator Rodney P. Morgan, a large man in his fifties with a strong jaw, steel blue eyes, and mutton chop whiskers, stood on the stage looking out across the room filled with people. He had no doubt the idea of a university of higher learning would garner him the votes he needed to help get him elected for a second term. Whether he could actually raise the money, or build the school was of no consequence. If he could make them believe this was of a prime interest to him and he was trying to do as he promised, he was guaranteed to win their votes and that was why he was here. That's what political campaigns were all about, winning votes, not actually getting anything done.

If he'd learned anything during his first term, it was to make the voters believe you were looking after them and their interests. And, if he did actually get something passed that was important to them, they would say, "He did exactly what he promised to do and you can't ask more than that."

He chuckled to himself as he adjusted the flower on the lapel of his suit jacket. One of the women, an attractive widow in her late forties, had given it to him and had actually made eyes at him as she placed the stem through the buttonhole on his suit jacket. He knew the look and reached up and squeezed her hand just enough to make her giggle like a young schoolgirl.

"Maybe a bite to eat, later at the hotel?" he asked, raising one eyebrow - his steel blue eyes holding the hint of a suggestion in them that caused her to blush.

She looked around to see that no one was near, then suggested in a whisper, "Maybe it would be better if you came to my house."

"I was hoping you would suggest that," he'd said, squeezing her hand lightly again and smiling broadly.

After giving him directions, she walked back to her seat with a little more bounce in her step.

Rodney watched with admiration. It would be an eventful night all the way around.

People would believe anything you told them as long as it was what they wanted to hear and a university of higher learning was exactly what all the women and some of the men wanted. Oh, he would make an attempt so he would look good to his constituencies, but if he failed, oh well - at least he'd tried and that was all he'd promised to do. But if he succeeded, his position as senator would be set for life.

The senator was in his glory. He was like an evangelist leading his flock to the alter, and knew just how to handle them. He held their attention with his grand oratory and by their reaction he was sure he would get every vote there was to get in Waco, Texas.

Before becoming a senator, Rodney P. Morgan had gone by his real name, which was, Leonard Gustafson. During his younger days, he'd been a flim-flam man and made a lot of money weaseling funds from innocent people's bank accounts, which was against the law and he found out quickly the protectors of justice frowned on such dealings. On several occasions he had been only one step ahead of watching the sun come up from inside prison walls.

Being a man who could see what would eventually happen if he didn't find a new way to swindle people out of their money, he changed his name and turned to politics, which paid better, and he wasn't always only one or two steps ahead of the law.

Raising his hands for quiet, he watched as they settled down, and after clearing his throat, he began.

"You good folks of Waco have my word that I will do everything in my power to bring higher learning to the great state of Texas. I will do my best to establish a university right here in Waco that will stand side by side with any other university in the country."

There was a great deal of cheering and loud clapping. They were under his spell, just the way he knew they would be. He raised his hands and waited for them to quiet down. He wasn't finished. He was about to deliver what he believed to be the clincher to his speech when he heard a commotion at the front door and he looked in that direction.

To everyone's surprise the governor of Texas, Cramer Lovington, came walking in, smiling and nodding at people as he made his way down the aisle toward the stage.

Senator Morgan's eyes were wide and his mouth was hanging open. For the first time that he could remember, he was speechless.

During the short time Rodney P. Morgan had been in politics, he and the governor had never seen eye to eye. They had always been on opposite sides of the fence on just about everything. The governor was straight laced and believed all that hogwash he dished out and was well liked. He'd even gotten several political promises passed.

Suddenly, an idea flashed in Rodney's brain and he grinned broadly.

As Rodney watched the governor make his way down the aisle, he decided this would be a good time to add justification to his position as senator. He would elicit the governor's endorsement for this university thing. It would be a feather in his cap and the governor was sure to back him, it was just the kind of thing the governor would support.

What a stroke of luck. This was turning out to be his night for good things to happen he thought, thinking of the widow lady who had given him the flower.

When the governor reached the stage, he stopped and looked up at the senator for a moment, then reached into his topcoat and pulled out a forty-four pistol and shot the senator dead center in his chest, three times, then turned and walked out the side door, disappearing into the night without a word.

The blast of the big forty-four pistol was overpoweringly loud inside the room. Not only had the senator been killed instantly, but the impact from the bullets slamming into his chest, knocked him backward to the center of the stage, where he lay staring at the ceiling with non-seeing eyes.

For several minutes, the hall was empty of sound. The smell of burnt gunpowder filled the room. The people were in total shock, not quite sure what they'd just witnessed. It couldn't have been the governor who did this. He was a highly respected man who was looked up to. There was just no way he could have done such an evil deed as this. He was the governor of the state of Texas, for god's sake, and a highly respected man.

But the reality was, every person in the room had witnessed him do it and if called onto a witness stand, they would have to say he was guilty. The eyes don't lie, and what they saw had been right there in front of them, as plain as day, but even so, every man and woman in the room had a hard time making themselves believe it was true.

Doctor Wallingford Overholster was the first to come to his senses and climbed the steps to the stage and knelt down next to the body, checking the senator's throat for a pulse, but found none. He turned his head toward the anxious faces of the people and shook his head.

Amos Speck was sitting at the back of the room, and when the initial shock wore off and he regained his composure, he stood up and darted through the front door and down the twenty front steps in two leaps. His heart was pounding, his mind in a whirl.

Amos raced the two blocks down the street to the sheriff's office where he found Sheriff Billy Miles behind his desk doing paperwork.

"What're you so all fired up about, Amos?" the sheriff asked when he looked up and saw Amos standing there, panting like he'd been running from a band of Comanche Indians.

"The senator's been shot, and accordin' ta Doc Overholster, he's dead," Amos gasped.

The sheriff leaped out of his chair and grabbed a shotgun from the gun rack. He knew the senator was speaking down at the town hall, but never expected anything like this.

"Don't suppose you'll need that scattergun, Sheriff. The shooter just walked in and shot the senator three times in the chest, then like he was takin' ah stroll, he left through the side door. Reckon he's long gone by now."

Since the sheriff never carried a sidearm, he kept the shotgun anyway and asked as they ran down the sidewalk in the direction of the town hall, "Anybody get a look at the shooter?"

"I reckon most everbody in the room got ah good look at him," Amos said with an air of authority. "He smiled and nodded ta all of us as he walked down the aisle."

"He did what?" the sheriff asked, finding this bit of information hard to believe.

"You heard me right. He walked down the aisle, smilin' and noddin' his head ta all of us, and when he got down ta the edge of the stage, he looked up at the senator for just ah second or so, then with no more effort than if'n he was straightenin' his tie, he pulled ah hog leg pistol out of his coat. Looked like ah forty-four ta me. And then without ah word, he shot the senator in the chest three times; then walked out the side door like he just happened ta be passin' through."

"And nobody tried to stop him?" the sheriff asked not believing this could happen.

"Reckon we was all in shock," Amos said, shrugging his shoulders as though that told the entire story.

"Did you or any of the others happen to recognize the shooter? Was it somebody we might know?" the sheriff asked as they approached the town hall building.

"Did," Amos said.

The sheriff stopped dead in his tracks and looked at Amos and asked, "Did what?"

"Recognized the shooter," Amos told him as they started up the steps.

"So, if it isn't too much bother, do you suppose you could tell me who the shooter was?"

"Sure," Amos said with a big smile. "It was the governor."

The sheriff's jaw dropped and his eyes got wide. "You been drinking? If this is some kind of a prank..."

Amos Speck was the hostler and owner of the livery stable, along with being the towns sometimes veterinarian for the past three years since the real one had passed on after being kicked in the head by a mare during a difficult birthing.

Amos stood six foot five and weighed two hundred and fifty pounds and in all of his forty-six years, he'd had only one drink and that had been to celebrate his sixteenth

birthday. It made him sick and he'd never had another drink since. "You know I don't drink, Sheriff, and this ain't no prank. Ain't no doubt about it, it was Governor Cramer Lovington who shot and killed the senator... Me and everybody in there saw him do it," he said, pointing toward the top of the steps.

The sheriff hurried into the town hall and up to the stage.

Sheriff Billy Miles was a good sheriff for the most part, as long as the town stayed quiet. You couldn't actually say he was lazy, but on the other hand he was no whirling dervish, either. If there was one thing he hated, it was when folks upset his daily routine, and if what Amos had just told him was true, this time his daily routine was shot all to hell.

"Dead. Three bullets dead center to his heart," the doctor said when he saw the sheriff climbing the steps to the stage.

"Did you happen to see who the shooter was?" Billy asked, cautiously, wanting to know if the doctor had seen the same person Amos Speck thought he saw.

"I know it's going to be hard to believe, but everyone in this room will tell you the same thing, it was Governor Lovington."

Billy was overwhelmed by the doctor's blunt statement. This couldn't be happening. The governor was a good man and didn't go around shooting people. He'd heard about the friction between him and Senator Morgan, but he wouldn't allow himself to believe the governor would walk in and shoot the senator; at least not in plain sight and in front of the whole town. Suddenly, he felt as though the weight of the whole world had been dropped on his shoulders.

"You'll see to the body?" the sheriff asked of the doctor as he turned and headed back down the steps without waiting for an answer. His mind was whirling, trying to figure out what he was going to do next. A couple of drunken cowboys having a shoot out was one thing, but this... this was all together different.

At the bottom of the steps, the sheriff looked at the crowd and saw the faces he was searching for. "I want the town council to follow me to my office right now," he said as he headed for the front door.

-

Back in his office, Billy sat looking at the ten men of the Waco town council, studying the face of each man, then asked, "You're all positive it was the governor who shot and killed Senator Morgan, and you would swear to that on a stack of bibles?"

Conrad Bains, president of the bank looked at the sheriff and said, "The governor and I grew up together; went to school together. I've known him all my life and I can't imagine in my wildest dreams him doing such a thing. As far as I ever knew, Cramer detested firearms. Stunned as I am, I would have to swear that without a shadow of doubt it was my dear friend, Governor Cramer Lovington, who shot and killed the senator, and I'll testify to that in court if I have to."

Billy could see the tears welled up in the bank president's eyes and knew how hard this must be on him, knowing he'd just witnessed his best friend murdering someone.

After he'd taken statements from the town's ten most prominent men, and they'd left, the sheriff poured himself a cup of coffee and laced it with a large dollop of whiskey to help calm his nerves. His hand was shaking as he lifted the cup to his lips.

He couldn't just walk into the capital building and arrest the governor for murder like he was some ordinary cowboy; he was the Governor of Texas, which made him the most powerful man in the state.

Billy was beginning to get a headache and he was in need of another whiskey-laced cup of coffee.

-

When the sun came sneaking over the rooftops of the buildings, Sheriff Billy Miles was still sitting at his desk, blurry eyed and trying none too successful to sort things out. The whiskey he kept putting in his coffee hadn't helped his thinking much, but had dulled the throbbing in his head a little. He was tired from trying to understand how a thing like this could happen in his town and what he was going to do about it. There would be a city meeting and the townsfolk would want to know why he hadn't been at the town hall attending the senator's speech to make sure something like this didn't happen. Which was ridiculous since he didn't have a clue that something would happen, and for damn sure he didn't in his wildest dreams think the Governor of Texas would walk in and shoot the senator.

And second, they would want to know what he was going to do about it? He knew he had to tell them something, but what that would be, he had not the foggiest idea. His throat was raw from the whiskey and Billy could feel his headache coming back and his stomach was growling from lack of food, along with his body aching from lack of sleep.

Billy was sitting at his desk with his elbows propped on the top of it and his head in his hands when Carl Speck, Amos Speck's son came sauntering through the door.

"Mornin' Sheriff. Figured out what you're gonna do about goin' after Senator Morgan's killer?"

The sheriff looked up and said, "I can't just go up to the capital and arrest the governor like he was some ordinary run of the mill killer, but on the other hand, I reckon I can't just sit here and do nothing, either."

Billy felt like he was between a rock and a hard spot and if Carl didn't have something constructive to say...

"Twas me, I'd pass the job on to somebody else," Carl said easy like, while picking his teeth with a piece of straw.

Billy looked up at Carl and shook his head. "And just who would you pass it to? You got any suggestions as to who you think might want to do the job? How about you? Think you could arrest the governor and bring him back here to be tried for murder?" Billy asked, rubbing his temples.

Carl held up both hands, palms forward. "No sir, not me. I ain't never had no hankerin' ta do law work; it's too dangerous. But I got ta thinkin', if'n I was in your boots, I'd sure be lookin' for some way ta get outta bein' the one who arrested the governor, especial like if he's innocent, and that's when it struck me."

Billy looked up at Carl, anticipation on his face, and when Carl just stood there picking his teeth with that piece of straw, Billy asked, "Well, are you gonna tell me or not?"

Carl dropped the piece of straw on the floor and grinned like a little boy who had stolen a piece of pie and gotten away with it.

After a moment Carl said, "Bill McDaniel, head of the Texas Rangers, up in Austin. Ain't they supposed ta be the most powerful law enforcement in the whole state? I heard they ain't afeered of nobody. Yup, was me, I'd pass it on ta him."

Billy looked up at Carl for a long moment. If it would have been appropriate, he would have jumped up and kissed him. Why he hadn't thought about doing that was beyond

him. He guessed he was too caught up with the idea that the governor was a murderer to think straight, and the whiskey hadn't helped any.

Billy stood up and reached out his hand. "That's the best idea I've heard lately. And you say it came to you, just like that?" Billy asked, snapping his fingers and making a loud pop.

Carl stood there for a moment, considering Billy's question before he grinned and shook his hand, saying, "Yup, I reckon that's just how it happened. I just knew I wouldn't want ta be the one ta tell the governor he was under arrest fer murder. Reckon I'd quit my sheriffin' job and go ta wranglin' cows, or somethin', first. But then it hit me, if'n I could pass the job onta somebody else, well sir, I'd be in the clear and not have ta be worrin' bout the town council or my job."

"You had breakfast, yet?" Billy asked, grinning from ear to ear.

"No, sir. I was in too much of ah hurry ta come tell you my thinkin'," Carl said, shaking his head.

"Well I think you need to be rewarded for doing your public duty and coming in here. I'm gonna take you down to the hotel and buy you the biggest breakfast they have," Billy said, slapping Carl on the shoulder and guiding him toward the door.

"You think I could have steak and eggs, and maybe some flapjacks?" Carl asked.

"You can have whatever you want, and it's on me," Billy said as he closed the office door and started toward the hotel.

A few years back, Carl slipped and fell off a wagon and hit his head on a rock while helping his father unload some sacks of grain. Since then, folks assumed Carl's brain had been scrambled because he was a bit slow in his way of speaking and thinking, but not this morning. He definitely was not slow this morning; at least not in Billy's way of thinking, no sir, not by a long shot.

This idea of turning the case over to the Texas Rangers was a stroke of genius as far as Billy was concerned. It would solve all his problems. It would satisfy the town council and at the same time get him off the hook. Now all he had to do was to figure out why it would be the Texas Ranger's case and not his.

Several cups of hot, black coffee and some breakfast in his belly would help him think a little straighter and maybe help him get rid of his headache.

While Billy's stomach would tolerate only about half his breakfast, Carl ate a double helping of flapjacks, a large order of bacon, six eggs, a large steak, and then scraped what was left of Billy's breakfast onto his plate and devoured that too.

Billy sat staring out of the window; wondering how such a thing could have happened? It just didn't make sense that the governor would commit murder.

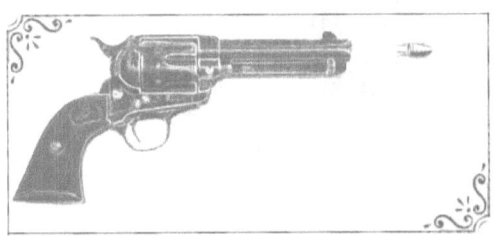

CHAPTER TWO

By the age of thirty, Horace Libersky had been run out of every decent acting academy in New York and several other cities along the eastern seaboard, which didn't deter him one iota. He had been born in Queens and raised in New Jersey. Both his mother and father had been actors and had made a decent living at it. They were real thespians and true to their calling, along with being liked by directors and other actors all up and down the eastern seaboard.

Horace believed he had inherited his parent's acting skills, which for the most part was true. His ability to impersonate other people was phenomenal and he could memorize his lines easily. He believed he was an outstanding actor and couldn't understand why other people didn't realize that.

What he didn't understand was, being kicked out of acting academies had nothing to do with his acting skills. It was his personality that always got him into trouble. He thought he should always get top billing along with top money in every show he did whether he had a lead role or not. Horace had a gigantic ego and as far as he was concerned, all the other actors and directors were beneath his status and he frequently reminded them of such, which earned him a bad reputation with the end result being, no one wanted to work with him.

Being blackballed in almost every theater on the east coast, Horace decided to relocate to Chicago to allow the audiences there to witness his greatness. And at first, he was successful, but then his offensive personality caught up with him and he found himself once again, out of work and being blackballed by every director he'd ever met and even some he hadn't.

While he was in Chicago, he met a makeup woman by the name of Luella Burnside, who could make him look identical to any of the people he impersonated on stage, and they became a team. She was drop dead gorgeous and knew it. She had a dominant personality and loved to control men. She inflated Horace's ego by complimenting him often on how great an actor he was, which made him easy to manipulate.

Luella had a wild streak a mile wide and ten miles long. Nothing was beyond her nerve. She seemed to need adventure on a grand scale and would do anything to get it. One Sunday afternoon she convinced Horace to stand on the corner of State and Grand and take shots at people with a derringer pistol in each hand as they passed by while she yelled obscenities at them.

It wasn't long before they heard the police coming and made a quick exit. Fortunately, no one had been injured and the police hadn't pursued them with much enthusiasm.

Later, in the apartment they shared, they were laughing loudly over the ordeal. Luella was drinking a glass of wine when an idea seemed to explode in her head.

"What if you had actually shot someone?" she asked Horace, who was looking out of the window to make sure the police weren't still chasing them.

He turned and stared at her with a questioning look in his eyes. "That would make us fugitives; outlaws with a price on our heads," Horace said, looking back down at the empty street, wondering why she would ask such an insane question?

"What if you could shoot someone and get away with it?" she asked, raising one of her eyebrows as she poured more wine for both of them. "And what if we were paid to do it?" her eyes dancing with an excitement Horace had never seen before.

"You mean like assassins for hire?" Horace asked as he reached for the glass of wine she was holding in his direction.

"Paid assassins. Yes, I like that," she said, her mind whirling with ideas. "We could get rich and travel the world. We could go to Paris, London, or anywhere we wanted to go."

She seemed to be in her own world, far beyond anything Horace could understand; yet something inside him stirred as his mind tried to explore the idea.

"While that sounds intriguing, it's not very realistic," Horace said, sipping on his wine, trying to control his own imagination, envisioning himself shooting someone.

Horace had never thought of himself as a killer for hire, but the idea actually intrigued him to distraction. He was tired of being looked down on by what he considered inferior people. But to actually kill someone and get away with it was mind-boggling. Maybe he would start with all the petty directors he hated and then some of the reporters that had written bad things about him.

Taking a long swallow of the wine, he shook his head. This was all foolishness, just a pipe dream. Luella had to know it was just an exercise in futility. Besides, who would hire him to kill all the directors and newspaper writers who had written bad things about him? Yet, the idea had been planted in his head and wouldn't go away.

"We'd never be able to get away with it," he said, secretly wishing she would argue with him and come up with a foolproof plan, convincing him otherwise.

Luella lit a small cigar and paced the floor, puffing on the cigar between sips from her glass of wine.

Finally, she sat down at the table and said, "Sit down, Horace. I think I have a way, but it will take both of us to make it work."

Horace couldn't believe she was still considering doing something like this but he was intrigued and curious. Horace sat down across from her and also lit a cigar; only his was the large Cuban kind. He took a puff and waited.

"I'm good with makeup, don't you think?" she asked, her face dead serious.

"The best," Horace conceded, wondering where this was going.

"And you're as good an actor as anyone, right?"

"One of the greats," he boasted.

"So... what if we made you up to look like somebody else? What if a lot of people saw you kill someone, but thought it was someone they all knew? Think about it, you wouldn't even have to hide or wear a mask, and whoever you look like would get the blame! You could pull it off, Horace! I know you could! You're the best actor I know! You can impersonate anyone you set your mind to. Think about it. It would be your ultimate acting role!"

Luella's excitement was as contagious as the flu and Horace felt it swarm over him.

Horace laid his cigar on the saucer they were using as an ashtray and looked toward the cloudless sky beyond the window. He had to let the idea digest in his brain for a moment. It was a crazy idea - so many questions. One part of him loved the idea, while the other side of him was terrified of getting caught. Killing someone didn't seem to bother him much, but the thought of going to prison or getting hung, was terrifying. He wondered if he was truly a good enough actor to pull off something of this magnitude?

"No, no, no," Horace said, taking another long pull from his wine glass.

"There are so many questions, like, how do we get the jobs in the first place? You just don't put an ad in the paper saying, 'Assassin For Hire, contact Horace Libersky and Luella Burnside at... And even if we somehow got an assassination job, how much would we charge? And how would we get paid? And the biggest question is - how would I get away without getting caught? Have you given these things any thought?" Horace asked. As intriguing as the idea was, this was getting way out of hand, even for Luella.

"Let me do some thinking," she said, filling his glass with more wine. "Your questions are good ones, but just minor details that need to be worked out." Her eyes were all aglow with excitement and her mind was racing at the speed of light.

"I can't believe we're even talking about something like this, let alone considering it," Horace said, his voice filled with frustration and his mind finally seeing the challenge he would be facing. He was an actor, not a paid assassin. He didn't even own a gun.

Luella could see Horace was about to balk, but she wasn't about to let that happen. The idea was already consuming her. Killers for hire – just the thought of it caused her more excitement than she could ever remember.

Before she went any farther, she had to have Horace on her side one hundred percent.

She stood up and undid the buttons of her dress and let it slide down her body to the floor, then reached out and took Horace by the hand and led him to the bedroom.

By morning, Horace was like putty in her hands. He would do anything she asked. And the first thing she needed to do was prove to him they could kill someone and get away with it. He had to know there would be no need to keep looking over their shoulders for the police to arrive and take them away.

She decided the first killing would be on the house – a practice run, if you will. During breakfast at a small restaurant down the street from their apartment, she sat reading the paper and a picture caught her eyes. Carson O'Brien was running for chief of police. He was running on the platform that he would not only clean up the city, but get rid of every lowlife criminal who tried to do business in Chicago.

That was it, she thought, as she thumbed through the pages, hoping to find someone to pin the killing on. Three pages back, she saw a small story about a man by the name of Antonio Giovanni – a man known to use force to get what he wanted, mainly protection money. He was one of the low-life criminal types O'Brien said he would get rid of – a man who extorted money from people so he wouldn't burn down their business or do worse.

When asked, Giovanni publicly scoffed at the idea of the police ridding Chicago of all the criminal types. "There are far too many cops on the take to even consider the idea," he'd told the reporter, laughing at the very thought of it.

Luella studied Giovanni's face and thought he would be perfect for the trial run.

It was easy to find out where Giovanni hung out and when he was normally there.

Dressed in plain clothes and wearing glasses, she sat at a table in the corner of the restaurant and waited for him to arrive.

Giovanni entered and stopped, looking around as though he was sizing everyone up. When his eyes locked onto Luella, he stared at her for a long time, as though he was trying to recall ever seeing her before. Finally, he shrugged and walked over to his usual table and sat down with several of his cronies, glancing in her direction from time to time.

She took notes on the way he walked, his personality, the type of clothes he wore, everything she could learn about him. He was not only arrogant, but also obnoxious and a bully, and had an opinion about everything. It didn't take Luella very long to get the information she needed and when she figured she had enough, she got up and left before he had a chance to approach her.

It would be easy for Horace to impersonate him; they were close to the same height and build. Now she just needed to convince Horace.

Back at the apartment, she set her idea into motion by having Horace walk around the apartment pretending to be Antonio Giovanni until he had the man down perfect.

To Horace, it was just another acting role; one that he would never play for real.

Later, that same evening, Luella dressed like a streetwalker, went out pretending to elicit her business along State Street, searching for a young man with a pistol, which didn't take her long to do. The lower east side of Chicago was full of young, would be thugs and criminals, all wanting to build themselves a reputation.

After enticing the young man into an alley, she pushed him up against the wall of a building, then clubbed him over the head with a piece of lead wrapped in a sock and took his thirty-eight-caliber pistol, his shells and the eighty-seven dollars he had in his pocket.

She walked away knowing he would not go to the police. It was part of the price of trying to be a tough guy; plus, he wouldn't want his friends to know he'd lost his gun and his money to a hooker. The pistol was more than likely stolen so he couldn't report it to the police.

She would dispose of it when the job was finished, so the pistol was no issue.

They dined out that night on the money she'd taken from the disillusioned criminal, who after what had happened might decide to go straight.

She didn't tell Horace where or how she got the pistol and ammunition and he didn't ask. He didn't want to know.

Finding a time to do the killing was the easy part. O'Brien was on a speech crusade to win votes and could be found on a street corner standing on a wooden crate, talking to anyone who would listen, almost every day.

There were a couple of problems to overcome. First, since O'Brien was running for chief of police, the man was always surrounded by policemen, which made it difficult to kill him and not be swarmed by half a dozen cops. Second, the killing would have to take place in front of a lot of witnesses so there would be no doubt as to the killers identity.

The third and most crucial problem she had to overcome was how to do the job and get away without anyone chasing them.

The perfect time presented itself a few days later, on a rainy Sunday morning as she sat reading the paper.

The police were burying a fellow police officer that had been shot in the line of duty. The officer had been killed during a skirmish with some bank robbers.

O'Brien was to make his appearance at the viewing, telling them this is exactly the kind of thing he would stop if he was chief of police. "I promise to make our city so strong that criminals will be afraid to step foot in Chicago, thereby saving many lives. I want Chicago to be known as the safest city in America," he'd shouted to the mourners.

Afterward, he stood outside in the rain and shook hands with each of the officers who approached him, telling each one how sorry he was.

If nothing else, O'Brien would get the vote of every police officer in Chicago.

He wouldn't be required to go to the cemetery, which left him free to talk to the people at a nearby church about the tragedy that had happened to the officer and hopefully get their sympathy and votes.

Several officers volunteered to go with him, but he convinced them he would be all right and would not need an escort.

Later, as O'Brien stood on the steps of the church, under a wide overhang, out of the rain, he assured the people of his sincerity about cleaning up the city and making it safe for decent folks like themselves. During his speech, a black horse drawn hearse, driven by Luella, dressed like an old man with long white hair and beard, pulled up to the edge of the street and stopped in front of the church.

Everyone turned and looked at the hearse, wondering why it had stopped here.

Horace, who looked remarkably like the gangster, Giovanni, stepped out of the hearse and walked up to O'Brien and shot him right between the eyes at close range. Horace turned and pointed the pistol at the churchgoers, who stepped back in fear and watched as he got back into the hearse and disappeared down the street.

An hour later, the horse and stolen hearse were found down near Lake Michigan.

There were seventy-five people who would swear they saw Giovanni get out of the hearse, walk up and shoot O'Brien, then get back in the hearse and leave.

Within a few hours, Giovanni was taken into custody under the protest of his attorney.

Giovanni swore he had witnesses who could prove he didn't shoot O'Brien.

He brought in twenty people, who would swear he wasn't within ten miles of the church at the time, but since his alibis all came from hoods like himself, no one believed them. !n less than a week, Giovanni was sentenced to hang by a judge who had been an O'Brien supporter.

-

"See, I told you it would work," Luella said, laughing so hard she spilled wine on her blouse.

Horace let out a sigh of relief. By now, he was convinced she was a genius. It had gone off just like she said it would and he was walking on air. When he'd stepped out of the hearse he hadn't been sure he could go through with it, but when he saw the fear in the people's eyes, something happened inside him and he became Antonio Giovanni.

Killing O'Brien and then walking away right through the crowd of people who stared at him with fear in their eyes was one of the best acting jobs he'd ever played. It gave him a bigger rush than he'd ever had before. It was a thousand times better than all the standing ovations he could ever hope for in the theater. He had killed someone in broad open daylight, in front of a large crowd of people and walked away without any fear of getting caught. And the best part was, the man he had impersonated had been blamed and was going to hang for it. It didn't get any better than that.

Luella could see the excitement in Horace's eyes and knew he was hooked. To make sure of his loyalty, Luella let her dress fall to the floor and reached out her hand. "You've earned a reward," she said, smiling at his eager face.

They were soon to find out, there were a lot of people in Chicago with enemies they wanted eliminated, and were willing to pay big bucks to have it done.

With a word here and there to the right bartenders, assignments began to come in. She had to pay a little something to the bartender, but she figured it was no more than the cost of doing business, which was becoming quite lucrative.

After doing several jobs and putting some money in their pockets, along with building a reputation, Luella decided they needed to move on. Based on the ideas O'Brien had left behind, the new chief of police was cracking down on crime, and along with a lot of other hoodlums, they left

Chicago. Instead of going east, they left on a train bound for Kansas City, Kansas.

Luella chose Kansas City because of an ad she'd read in the newspaper, which created another idea in her head.

-

In Kansas City, they bought the small theater Luella had seen in a for sale ad in the newspaper back in Chicago.

Horace, who changed his name to Massala Shakespeare, claiming to be a distant relative of the great playwright, William Shakespeare, went into the theater business, using the theatre as a front for the money they hoped to make from killing people. As the owner, he could choose the plays he wanted to star in, allowing him the freedom to do their killer for hire business at his leisure. Whatever money they made could go into the theater account, with no one the wiser. And the beauty of the whole thing was, no one knew his real identity.

As it turned out, neither of them had any regrets over what they were doing. As far as they were concerned, they were doing society a service by eliminating the country of scum, and for doing such a good deed, people were lining their pockets with money.

Luella was a shrewd businesswoman and a hint dropped here and there to bartenders about a service she'd heard about, the word spread far and wide like a wild fire. Hints about their success in Chicago, just added fuel to the fire, and soon the business began to grow.

There was never any face-to-face contact. She was too smart for that. Dressed as an older woman who walked with a cane, and a major limp, she rented a post office box under the name of, Vanquish The Sinners, a religious non-profit organization. People in need of their service could drop off an envelope with the cash money and information on the person to be eliminated. The cash would be placed in the theater account or a secret bank security box and within a short period of time; the job would be completed.

One morning, a large brown envelope was stuffed in the post office box, stating the victim was to be Senator Rodney P. Morgan, of Texas, along with ten thousand dollars in cold hard cash. It also had a time and place where the killing was to take place. It was the largest fee they'd ever had and they jumped on it like a catfish going after a worm.

-

Waco, Texas was a long way from Kansas City. They could go to Texas by train, do the job and be back in Kansas City in just a few days without anyone realizing they had been gone. The theatre was between plays so they were free of any commitments.

"Who will I be impersonating this time?" Horace asked, as they dined at an Italian bistro near where they lived.

Luella looked at him and said, "I've been giving that quite a bit of thought. It will have to be someone of importance. It will need to be someone everyone will instantly recognize and have no doubts about it when they identify him or testify against him in court."

Horace grinned as a thought entered his mind. "What about the Governor of Texas? Wouldn't most of the people in Texas recognize him? Seems I saw a picture of him in the newspaper recently and we're about the same size," Horace said with a grin.

Luella looked at Horace and smiled. "I think he would make an ideal shooter; that is if I can make you look like him. I'll do some research."

Luella was able to find a picture and story about Cramer Lovington in a newspaper at the library with enough information to allow her to transform Horace into the spitting image of the governor; right down to the way he walked and smiled. There wasn't enough time for them to investigate the governor's manner of speaking, so once again, they decided he would not talk, and if spoken to, he would point to his throat and mouth the word, laryngitis.

Since the time and location was already set by the person hiring them – all Luella needed to do was plan their entry and escape, which turned out to be quite easy.

"It will be a piece of cake," Horace said. "I'll walk in, nod my head, shoot the senator, and leave. Like always, with the element of surprise I'll be in and out before anyone can react."

Luella was pleased at the way Horace, or Massala, or whoever he wanted to call himself nowadays, was taking to this assassination business. It wouldn't be long before they could once again change identities and retire without having to look over their shoulders; living in luxury in Europe or anywhere they wanted to, like, Mexico or South America. Maybe they would just travel for a year or two as royalty from some small country no one had ever had heard of. She might even make up a country.

A few days before the senator was to be in Waco, they boarded the train in Kansas City in plain, ordinary clothes, looking like most of the other passengers. In Oklahoma, they boarded a different train; this time, looking like a rancher and his wife, and Horace even spoke with a Texas drawl.

When they arrived in Waco, Horace signed them into a small hotel not far from the train station as Mister and Mrs. J. Roundtree, from Hico, Texas - pretending to be a rancher and his wife. Other than eating in the dining room, they kept to themselves.

The following day, the senator arrived in Waco by train and they were nearby to make sure what he looked like so Horace wouldn't shoot the wrong man. In the end, it really didn't make much difference; the man standing on the stage with his mouth open, would be the senator. All politicians were alike; blowhards who talked a good game but rarely hit a home run.

In their room, Luella took her time and transformed Horace to look like the governor and when she finished, she looked at her work and smiled. As long as he didn't speak, the people would swear Horace was Cramer Lovington, Governor of Texas.

A little later, after the sun had gone down, they left by the back door and walked the block and a half to the town hall in the shadows along the backsides of the buildings.

Luella smiled. The place was packed. Horace waited in the dark, along the side of the building where he could see through a small window, yet not be seen, while Luella went off to take care of her part of the caper – making sure of their escape.

As an actor, Horace was a professional at timing his entry at just the right moment for the best effect, and when he saw the senator raising his hands, he knew it was time.

-

The job went off without a hitch, just as it had been planned. When Horace walked out of the side door of the town hall, he saw Luella waiting, dressed as a man, sitting on a stolen horse and holding the reins of a second stolen horse. Horace mounted and they raced away into the night.

When they were a mile out of town, at a place Luella had selected earlier, they turned the stolen horses loose, then buried the clothes worn during the job and transformed themselves back into Mister and Mrs. Roundtree from Hico, Texas; a man and his wife out taking their evening constitutional.

JARED MCVAY

Later that same evening, during all of the excitement, they boarded the northbound train as Hollister and Marsha Coons, a traveling minister and his wife. Both were dressed in black and carrying bibles.

The sheriff had all the roads out of town posted with deputies; checking anyone and everyone trying to leave town. He also put a hold on the train leaving town before he and his deputies could conduct a search.

Both Horace and Luella were sitting quietly, reading their bibles when the sheriff walked down the aisle looking closely at each and every passenger. When Billy Miles came to them, they looked up at him and smiled. "Is something wrong, Sheriff?" Horace asked with a hint of curiosity in his voice.

Billy gave them only a cursory glance and moved on down the aisle without answering.

A few miles north of town, Horace and Luella walked out and stood on the platform between the cars, laughing, smoking cigars and drinking whiskey from a flask he carried in the breast pocket of his suit jacket.

"You're the best," Horace said to Luella as he kissed her on the neck, indicating they would do more celebrating later in the confines of their sleeping bunk.

Luella pulled him into a passionate embrace. Just the thought of what they were doing and getting away with it got her excited. She would never forget the frustrated look on the sheriff's face.

As she watched the town of Waco, Texas disappear in the darkness, she thought about the bank accounts back in Kansas City. So far, she had opened accounts in four banks, along with her secret stash in three different safety deposit boxes. She had learned the hard way about keeping all her eggs in one basket and wouldn't be caught unawares, again.

Horace was content with letting Luella handle all the money. Money meant so little to him. It was the thrill of the game that got him excited. The adrenalin rush he got grew bigger with each killing and escape.

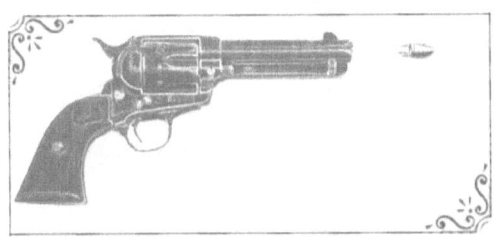

CHAPTER THREE

Billy Miles stood on the stage of the town hall and looked out over the large crowd of people who had come to hear what he was going to do about arresting the governor.

Everyone was in shock. How could the governor have done such a thing? And why hadn't Billy been there to protect the senator? There had been other killings in Waco, but nothing of this magnitude. Who would build the university now? And what would happen to the governor? Would he go to prison or would he be hanged like a common criminal? So many questions bounced around the room that it sounded like a pen full of chickens with a coyote trying to dig his way under the fence.

The only person to question what happened and who did it was the town's only barber, Howard Bellew. "It just don't make any sense. Why would the governor come into the town hall and shoot the senator right in front of all of us? If he wanted the senator dead, I think he would have hired somebody to do it. That would make more sense."

"But we all saw him," Wanda Clover said, getting nods from the other people standing nearby.

Howard looked at Wanda, and then let his eyes survey the others. "We saw someone who looked like the governor. But did anyone actually speak to him or hear him speak. He's got one of them voices everbody could recognize, you know. Speaks through his nose, kinda like."

There were murmurs among the people standing close to Howard and Wanda. He was right, the shooter had not uttered even one word; not a hello, how are you, nice to see you... nothing – but none could deny his looks. As far as the people who were there were concerned, it had definitely been the governor who shot the senator.

"Just because he didn't say anything, doesn't mean it wasn't him," Andrew Dawson, a teller from the bank said, raising his eyebrows.

More muttering was heard as Wanda chimed in to support Andrews's statement.

"Andrew is right. Just because he didn't say anything, doesn't mean it wasn't him. He wasn't here to give a speech; he was there to do the devil's work by killing poor Senator Morgan."

Once again, Howard spoke up. "Well tell me this, how did he get here and how did he leave? Whoever it was, he was here and then he was gone like a whiff of smoke. If the governor was brazen enough to walk in here and shoot the senator, don't you think he would have been brazen enough to come to town in his own train – not sneak in like some thief in the night?"

Everyone looked at each other, shaking their heads. No one had considered that part of it. Now there were new mutterings that no one had answers for.

Even with everyone talking at the same time, the town hall had good acoustics and Billy was able to hear several of the conversations, which made him wonder if Howard could be right, but immediately dismissed the idea. He'd heard everybody had a double out there somewhere, but the likelihood of a killer looking identical to the governor might be stretching it a bit. Still... it was hard to believe the governor could come into town, shoot the senator right in front of practically the whole town and then disappear like a snake slithering into a patch of weeds. No one had seen him arrive or leave.

Howard was right about one thing; none of it made any sense and that was partly why he was going to turn the case over to the rangers. He was just plain scared about trying to arrest the governor. If it turned out that it wasn't him that did the shooting, his days as the sheriff of Waco, Texas would be over and he would look like a fool. Plus, the fact he was too damn old to go looking for another job. On the other hand, if he was guilty and had shot and killed the senator, well that was something altogether different. The worry lines on his face were growing by the minute.

What if the governor could prove he was somewhere far away at the time of the shooting? That would throw a bind into the case. There was just too much to think about and he was beginning to get another headache.

Billy stepped to the front of the stage and raised his hands for everyone to get quiet and when they did, he said, "A terrible thing has happened right here in Waco. We were all taken by surprise. Like you, I was shocked and had no idea that anything like what took place would happen. If I'd had a clue, I would have had deputies stationed inside and out of this building. But the truth is, none of us had an inkling of what was going to happen."

The people seemed to sympathize with him and nodded their heads.

"I'm sure you will all agree, a senator getting killed in our town was bad enough, but to have the killer, who all of you identified as none other than our esteemed governor, gives the case a whole new meaning."

The silence in the room was nerve wracking as Billy stared out across the faces staring back at him. They were waiting for him to tell them what he planned to do about it.

"I know all of you want the governor arrested and prosecuted to the full extent of the law, and so do I, if, in fact, it can be proven it was him, but it isn't quite that easy. You don't just walk into the governor's office and put him under arrest; no sir, it's just not done that way."

Suddenly, there were mumblings all around the room and one lady sitting near the back stood up and asked, "Why not? He's a criminal, isn't he?"

Billy raised his hands once again for them to get quiet, and when they did, he took a deep breath and said, "Ma'am, Governor Lovington is the most powerful man in the state and he's got armed soldiers guarding him day and night. Now I'm not saying he shouldn't be arrested and tried for what he did, if he is guilty. I truly do think that's what needs to be done, but, whether he's a criminal or not, isn't for me ta say. I'm just a local sheriff and my jurisdiction only goes as far as the city limits. That's what you folks said when you hired me. And yes, I know the crime was committed right here, inside the city limits. But to be honest with you, even if I tried, I'm not sure I could get by those army guards, let alone, haul him back down here to Waco. And whether he's a criminal or not, isn't for me to say. That's up to a judge and jury."

Silence hung over the room like a heavy weight until Howard Bellew stood up and asked the question all of them wanted to ask. "I know you don't plan on hidin' in your office, thinkin' this might blow over because we all know it won't. And I know you want ta get this out in the open and done with; so... what do you plan on doin'? By this time tomorrow, it's gonna be in ever newspaper in the state. Somethin' like this can't be kept quiet very long," Howard stated.

Howard looked over at Clancy Harper, a small frail man with wire rimmed glasses, and asked, "Bein' the telegraph operator, Clancy, I'll bet ah dime to a donut you've already told somebody, haven't ya?"

Clancy stood up and cleared his throat, and adjusted his glasses before answering, and when he did, he spoke in a high-pitched voice, "I did. I wired a close friend of mine up at the state capital and told him what happened. I felt it was my duty. People need to know what kind of governor we elected. And yes, I am sorry to say, I voted for him, but how could any of us have known he is a killer?"

He let the statement hang in the air and watched as other heads nodded in agreement.

"And have you heard back from him?" Howard asked.

"I did," Clancy said, nodding his head, feeling the center of attention and liking it. "He said it was impossible because the governor was giving a dinner party in honor of his wife's birthday and there were over a hundred people in attendance who would swear he was there that night, and not in Waco."

Everyone in the room turned and looked at Billy, who was just as dumbfounded as they were. If the governor could prove he was at the capital at the time of the shooting, then who the hell killed the senator?

Billy was standing there, trying to think of something to say when the front door swung open and in walked Governor Lovington with an escort of six soldiers, each one carrying a rifle.

This time, the governor didn't smile or nod to anyone as he walked to the stage and climbed the steps.

When he got close to Billy, he stopped and said, loud enough for everyone to hear. "I didn't kill the senator, but I'm here to place myself in your custody. I want a trial as soon as possible so I can prove beyond a shadow of a doubt, that I was miles away when this tragedy happened. The senator and I didn't agree on much of anything, but I didn't dislike him enough to kill him, or have him killed. I'm sorry he is dead, but it wasn't me that killed him."

Out of the corner of his eye, Billy could see Adam Frazer, owner and editor of the Waco Free Voice newspaper. He was writing everything down on a piece of paper. Billy knew that between the newspaper and the telegraph, whatever he said or did would be all over the state come morning.

He also knew he couldn't put a man like Cramer Lovington in that rag-tag cell they called a jail and not get criticized for it. Hell, he was the governor - the most powerful man in the state. Pictures of the governor would be plastered across the front pages of every newspaper from here to hell and back; and maybe even Washington DC, of him sitting in the hellhole of a jail Waco was so proud of. He remembered someone saying when the jail was being built, "Criminals don't deserve anything nice. And so, it had been built with only the bare essentials."

Billy looked at the governor and swallowed. "Our jail ain't much, Governor. Maybe you'd be better off over at the hotel, under house arrest, so to speak. And the food is better, too," he said, hoping he was making the right decision and saying the right thing.

The governor smiled and said, "I appreciate that, Sheriff. Yes, the hotel would be better, but I want it known, I am turning myself in and I am in your custody. I'm hoping for a speedy trial so I can vindicate myself and get back to doing what I was hired to do; running this state."

Billy smiled. He'd made the correct choice. "If you'll follow me, Governor," he said.

As they walked toward the front door, the governor told him, "My attorney, Wendell Barnes will arrive by train tomorrow and my private train is still sitting in front of the station. I would appreciate it if you would have my engineer move it to the sidetrack until this business is finished. We certainly don't want the railroad yelling at me for blocking their tracks."

Billy nodded and looked at Clancy Harper, the telegraph operator, who nodded his head in return, and headed for the station. He had no objection to leaving because he was in a hurry to get back to his telegraph - he had messages to send.

Practically the whole town followed as Billy and the governor walked the short distance to the hotel, where the governor was given the best suite in the house. After signing the register he looked over at Billy and said, "I assume, since I'm under arrest and in your custody, you will be taking care of the hotel and food bill?"

Billy nodded his head and said, "Of course."

The governor turned and looked at the man behind the register desk and asked, "Is the restaurant open? I'm starving. I didn't have a chance to eat before I came down here."

"If it isn't, we'll open it," Riley Collins, the hotel clerk said with authority. "If you'll follow me, Governor," he said as he headed toward the opening to the restaurant.

The governor looked at Billy and said, "Please join me. We have several things to discuss."

A few minutes later, the dining room was filled to capacity, but not with diners. Over half the town stood nearby listening to what was going on. The other half was standing in the street, waiting to hear what had been said inside.

It was decided, since they were already there, the soldiers would act as his guards so he couldn't sneak away in the night, and also give him protection from any crazy person or persons who might try to take the law into their own hands and act as judge, jury and executioner.

Billy sipped his coffee, pleased with himself as he watched Adam Frazer write down every word. It was funny, Billy thought to himself, how things have a way of working themselves out. He wouldn't need to turn the case over to the rangers, after all.

Judge Harvey Michaels was in attendance at the town hall and had gone with them to the hotel, where he told the governor he would see to a speedy trial; hopefully within two days or less, if that would be alright with his attorney.

The governor agreed and said he wanted this to be over with as soon as possible. He had issues that needed taken care of back at the capital, and was sure his attorney would arrive tomorrow with enough proof of his innocence to satisfy the court.

-

The following morning, the governor's attorney, Wendell Barnes arrived on the train with a hundred witnesses, all well known, influential people, who would swear the governor had been no where near Waco on the night the senator had been killed, but in fact, was in his home, holding court over a birthday party for his wife.

After the jury had been chosen, which didn't take long, the trial began and Wendell Barnes marched all one hundred of his witnesses onto the stand and asked them all the same question, "Where were you and what were you doing on the night the senator was killed?"

Every one of them gave the same account. "I was at the governor's mansion, attending a birthday party for the governor's wife. The governor was there the entire time."

Several of the women testified they had danced with the governor, which made it impossible for him to be in two places at the same time.

The local prosecuting attorney, Samuel Tomlinson, a young man not long out of a law school from up in Dallas, sat in awe as the governor's attorney questioned each of the local witnesses. The man was relaxed and smooth and had an airtight case.

Without much trouble on his part, Wendell Barnes got each local witness to admit that he or she had not actually spoken to the governor. And with a bit more probing, they admitted, yes, because they were standing some distance away from him, it was within the realm of possibility that the killer could have been a man who looked remarkably like the governor, but not actually be him, which built doubt in the minds of the jury.

"Well, yeah, now that I think about it, I guess it coulda' been somebody who looked ah whole lot like the governor," Hank Embers, a local farmer admitted. "I was standin' ah good ways away, and it all happened kinda fast. The man just walked in the front door, sauntered down the aisle, shot the senator, then walked out the side door like he was on ah stroll and disappeared afore any of us could get over the shock, or do anythin'," he said, scratching his ear.

When the governor's friend, Conrad Bains, was called to the witness stand, the first thing Wendell did was establish that the bank president and the governor had been friends since childhood – knew each other like brothers.

Wendell Barnes placed his hands on the railing in front of where Conrad sat and said, "I want you to take a long, hard look at the man you say you've known for all these many years and tell me that without a shadow of doubt, he was the one who shot the senator."

Conrad studied his friend closely while the governor sat quietly looking back at him, and after a minute or so, the bank president shook his head and said, "At first, I would have sworn it was you, Cramer, but now, I'm not so sure. He looked an awful lot like you, but as I think about it, he didn't have that small scar near your left eyebrow. The one you got when we were kids and stealing a watermelon from old man Jespers melon field. Remember, you tripped and hit your head on a rock and broke the watermelon into a hundred pieces. I was standing close to the aisle, up close to the stage and would have been able to see it, but the man I saw, didn't have that scar."

The governor smiled and nodded, relief spilling from his eyes.

When the prosecuting attorney was asked if he had anything to add, he just lowered his head and said, "No, your Honor. I have nothing more to add. I no longer believe it was Cramer who shot the senator."

In truth, there was nothing more to add; even he believed the governor had been proven innocent.

It took the jury less than ten minutes to return with a verdict of not guilty.

The governor shook everyone's hands and thanked the judge for such a speedy trial and then hurried back to the capital.

Billy Miles went back to his office and sat down at his desk, staring through the window at the people walking up and down the sidewalk. If the governor was innocent, then who killed the senator?

He was beginning to get another headache and opened the desk drawer where a bottle of whiskey lay waiting to be put to use.

CHAPTER FOUR

-

Senator Shiloh Thompson leaned back in his chair, propped his feet on his desk and took a sip from his glass filled with some of the finest Tennessee sipping whiskey he'd ever had. The President of the United States, himself, had introduced him to it the last time he was in Washington DC. It was smooth and slid down his throat like honeydew rind water. It didn't have that burning sensation most of the local whiskey had.

Raising his glass, he proposed a toast. "Thank you, Mister President," he said with a smile.

He'd been in Washington DC to see the president about a problem they were still having with some of the Kiowa Indians, and the Indian affairs people the government had sent out to handle things. In his opinion, they knew nothing about Indian affairs and needed to be replaced before an uprising occurred.

After promising to look into the matter, the president offered Shiloh a drink.

"I think you'll like this, Senator," the president said. "It's made by a fella in Tennessee by the name of Jasper Daniel, but goes by Jack. He sent me a bottle and after sampling it, I bought a case.

And after having a glass in the president's office, he too, had purchased a case and had it shipped back to Texas.

He lowered his feet back to the floor and sat up straight. He reached across his desk and opened a cedar lined box and took out a long, thick cigar and lit it, then glanced at the newspaper laying in front of him.

In bold letters on the front page, it stated, Senator Rodney P. Morgan was shot and killed while making a speech down in Waco, Texas. At first, it was believed by witnesses who were present at the time, and had seen the killing, that it was governor Cramer Lovington who had done the shooting. But later it was proved that the governor was at home, giving a dinner party to celebrate his wife's birthday and the killer had been somebody who had an amazing resemblance to the governor, and fooling everyone there.

The article went on to say the killer, whoever he was, was still at large with no clues as to his identity, or his whereabouts.

Shiloh Thompson leaned back in his chair and took another sip of whiskey, then said, "Damn! They said you were the best and by god, I am now a believer. Not only did you do the job just as you promised, but you pinned it on somebody else – the governor of Texas, no less. Now that's genius, pure genius. Even if he did clear himself, you're still running loose, free, with no clues as to who you are."

Shiloh took a deep puff from his cigar and dumped the ash in an ashtray that had been given to him by one of his loyal voters. It was in the shape of the state of Texas. He blew out a smoke ring and glanced at the paper again, and chuckled. "You're worth ever dollar I paid you, whoever you are," he said. "You're ah damn chameleon, by god. Yes sir, that's what you are, ah damned chameleon. Even the people who hire you have no idea who you are; they just give you the money and the name of the person they want killed and in a few days the job gets done with somebody else taking the blame and you walk away, free as a bird. I'd give a pretty penny to know who you are."

After thinking about that for a moment, he reconsidered. If he knew who the assassin was, maybe whoever this person is, wouldn't like anybody knowing their identity and come after him. Shiloh shuddered at the thought and picked up his glass, then began to grin, his thoughts moving to his future victims. Their tickets to hell were about to be purchased and they had no clue the time they had left was limited.

Shiloh took another sip of whiskey and leaned back in his chair, thinking about the next person he wanted eliminated. It would cost him another ten thousand dollars, but it took money to gain the kind of power he was looking for. Besides, it wasn't like he would be spending his own money. His wife was rich and she would never even know the money was gone. She had never liked fussing with the banking side of her money and it had been easy for him to take control of it, especially when she never lacked for anything she wanted. The cattle ranch she'd inherited was big enough to keep her in style for as long as she lived and the money from the investments he'd made with her other money, along with what he made as a senator, allowed him the luxury of living like a senator should. It was a far cry from where he'd grown up as a sharecropper's son, living from hand to mouth, back in Arkansas, picking cotton until his back hurt and his fingers bled.

'As long as she lived,' he thought to himself. If something was to happen to her, it would all be his, the money, the cattle ranch, the investments, everything. Ever'body would sympathize with him for his loss and his position as senator from the great state of Texas would be all but guaranteed from now on. Shiloh grinned and took another sip of whiskey. As long as she lived... he thought again as the beginning of an idea was taking shape in his brain. As long as she lived...

CHAPTER FIVE

-

Since the assassination of Senator Morgan, jobs had seemed to come in nonstop. The first was a bank president in New York City, where they were still looking for the killer, but had no clues, and never would. No one had seen him do it.

Dressed as a milk man, Horace jumped off the stolen milk wagon, walked up, knocked on the front door of the house and when the bank president opened it, Horace, shot him in the forehead and left. When his wife came to see what the noise had been about, she found her husband laying in the front doorway, dead, with no one around.

Then, there had been the mayor of a small town down in Georgia. His rival opponent was still trying to prove his innocence. He claimed he was up at a nearby lake, fishing, but no one had seen him there. His wife said that's where he told her he was going, but she hadn't gone along, and he'd come home empty handed, saying the fish weren't biting that day. At the present, he was in a losing battle trying to prove his innocence.

There had been two jobs in Kansas City. The first one had been the head of a church, which caused Horace to shake his head in wonder. No one was safe, it seemed.

Luella had done some checking and found the minister was quite the ladies man, so it had been easy to set up one of the husbands, who was arrested within hours because several people had identified him as the shooter.

The second was a police officer found dead in the park with only one witness, a man who was too drunk to identify the shooter.

"With all the money we're making, it won't be long before we can retire," Luella said to herself as she sat sipping a glass of wine and looking at the night sky from the small terrace of their apartment. Horace was at the theater, doing what he liked to do best, getting applause and accolades for his performances.

Luella Burnside was smart enough to not put the money they made in the bank all at once or anything close to it, for that matter. Their theater in Kansas City was doing a thriving business, but not well enough for deposits of the size they were taking in. A few hundred; even a thousand was believable for a weeks worth of performances, but not ten thousand dollars or more.

Plus, unbeknownst to Horace, she always kept back some of the assassin money for herself as a nest egg in case anything should happen. She wanted a guarantee that she wouldn't be left stranded in case Horace should get himself in a spot he couldn't get out of. There was always a chance things wouldn't go as planned and Horace could end up getting himself arrested or killed and she would have to make a fast getaway. For that, she would need cash. At the last count, she had fourteen thousand dollars stashed away, which would get her far away quickly, if need be. But there could never be too much and as long as money kept coming in, she would keep building her nest egg, right along with the bank accounts she showed Horace.

Of course, her name was on everything, the bank accounts and the theater as well, but if she couldn't get to the bank funds for some reason or another - like being associated with Horace and a suspect by association, whatever money she carried with her at all times would be her salvation. Plus, she kept a bag with several disguises packed and ready. Luella was not a woman who liked leaving much of anything to chance.

She glanced up at the clock and saw that Horace would be getting home soon and would want to go out and eat. He was always wound up when he was doing a show, and this one was doing quite well. Melodramas seemed to be sweeping the country and the one he was doing now, was especially liked. The house was filled almost every night. The play was called, The Prisoner of Zenda, and Horace was playing several character roles, which put him in his glory. Of course, he was playing the lead – an Englishman on holiday in some country she'd never heard of, who gets drawn into impersonating the king and goes as far as getting crowned in a fake coronation. Horace said it was his favorite role so far.

Luella had trained a young woman to do his makeup so she didn't need to be there. She had more important things to do, like running their side business, which lately kept her hopping. Assassinations paid much more than the theater, but in between jobs, the theater kept Horace happy, and for once, he was behaving himself and the crowds seem to love him.

When Horace was happy, life was good.

Even though, technically, they lived in an upstairs apartment, Horace shouted as he walked in the door, "Woman of the house, I'm home. Are you ready to go?"

Horace was obviously in a good mood.

"Some big shot who liked my performance tonight is throwing a party for me at a new hotel over on the Missouri side of town. He even provided a carriage to take us there. It's waiting downstairs, so shake a leg, wench!"

Horace stopped suddenly and stared at Luella and the pile of money on the kitchen table. "A new job?" he asked.

"Yes. Another big one, down in Texas, again," she said. "I think it's the same client that wanted the senator taken out of the game. This time he wants two people taken care of, a Texas Ranger and get this, his own wife."

Horace whistled, eyeballing the money on the table. "Is the ranger and this man's wife having an affair?"

"No," Luella said, smiling. "It seems a Texas Ranger by the name of Clay Brentwood, has interfered with his plans on several occasions – went around arresting or shooting his business associates and he's angry about it. And from what I can find out, his wife is very rich and he wants her dead so he can have all her money.

"How much for each one?" he asked.

"That's what our benefactor wanted to know and I answered in our foundation ad, that when a loved one was involved, donations needed to be doubled."

"So you're saying," Horace said, eyeballing the pile of money on the table, "that money on the table amounts to thirty thousand dollars?"

Luella looked at him and smiled, lifting the money and letting it fall back down on the table like leaves falling from a tree in autumn.

Horace looked at the money and shook his head. He knew he would do it, whatever the price was. He had no interest in the money and allowed Luella to take care of that side of the business. For him, it was doing the job in front of people and getting away with it that always seemed to give him a rush like no other he'd ever had, until lately.

For the first time in his life, he was enjoying his work in the theater because everyone liked him, which was a huge change. Owning his own theater and deciding which shows to do and directing them himself, along with starring in them, was all Horace had ever wanted or needed; at least that's how it had been until he met Luella. The woman had ambitions and for the life of him, he couldn't say no to her.

"Be a sweet and get my coat," Luella said as she swept the money off the table and into a black bag like a physician would carry, then snapped the closure tight.

Horace hurried to do her bidding. He was anxious to get to the party where he would be the center of attention. Being a headliner and in the limelight was beginning to take the place of being a killer only he and Luella knew the identity of. Of course, he didn't want people to know he was a killer and wind up hanging from a rope until he was dead.

But, as the star of the show, he was admired and looked up to. People adored him, but as an assassin...? well, that was a completely different rush.

The carriage was a nice one and the driver delivered them in style to a grand restaurant over on the Missouri side of the river.

When they stepped out of the carriage, there was a large group of people waiting on the sidewalk outside.

Horace smiled and shook hands, and even signed playbills as they made their way inside where a gala affair awaited them. Luella smiled and stayed a few steps behind, allowing Horace to wallow in his limelight.

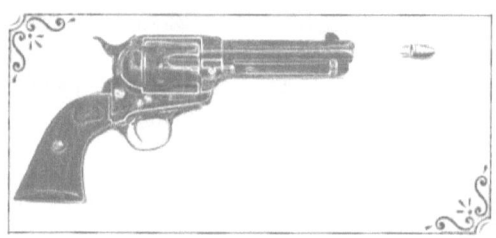

CHAPTER SIX

Having no idea there had been a hit placed on his life, along with an assassin already hired to do the job, Clay Brentwood closed the tally book and placed it in the center drawer of his desk, then stood up and rubbed his eyes. There was nothing he hated more than bookwork, but it needed to be done and it was his responsibility to do it. It had taken him almost all morning, checking cattle tallies, sales receipts, and making sure bank statement figures added up correctly. His attorney would need these records to keep his investments straight, so he did his due diligence.

For the time being, now that it was done, he would get a short reprieve, for a week or so, then he would have to do it all over again. He didn't envy lawyers and bankers, or merchants who spent all day inside, sitting at desks, piling over paperwork. He was a cowboy at heart and enjoyed being out in the open, along with the aches and pains that came from breaking wild horses or spending a long day in the saddle herding stubborn, mossy ole mule headed cattle.

Clay had seven men working for him who were all able cowhands, but when it came right down to it, there was some of the work he preferred to do himself, like training the horses.

As a widower for several years now, he needed to keep busy so he wouldn't think about how lonely it was without a woman to boss him around, although, Mrs. McIntyre, his housekeeper and cook, did her fair share of that. She had worked for him for close to a year, along with her daughter, Cindy, who was somewhere in the neighborhood of nineteen or twenty years old.

They did the housecleaning; mending and laundry, of which he paid them extra for, but that was as far as it went. They were both fetching women, but he had no interest in either of them in the romance department.

Besides, he was pretty sure Mrs. McIntyre had taken a fancy to Running Coyote, a Comanche Indian who was one of his two foremen. He was happy for them. Running Coyote was an educated man who spoke several languages, was a sub chief in his tribe and a top hand. In his opinion, she would have to look far and wide to do better.

And several times here lately, he'd seen Cindy taking walks in the evenings with his other foreman, Riley, a long drink of water, who was also a good man.

The only problem with seeing them together, smiling and laughing, was, it reminded him of his dead wife, Martha, who, after being murdered by the Beeler gang, had left an empty hole in his life.

He'd been blind with the lust for revenge and had gone after them relentlessly until he caught up with them and sent them to hell where they belonged. Even now, when he thought about it, it made his blood boil.

He'd always thought he might get married again, but, although he'd never experienced it, he'd been told that two women in the same house was asking for trouble since each one would want things done her own way. He wondered what Mrs. McIntyre would say if he brought home a wife - especially one who wanted to change things?

Shaking his head, Clay reached up and took his wide brimmed hat off the peg on the wall next to his office door and set it on his head.

What if his new wife didn't want Mrs. McIntyre here? Or, what if Mrs. McIntyre quit? If she did that, he was sure the men would riot. Not only was she a great cook, she made each one of them feel like he was special. Plus, she sewed on buttons, patched clothes and put medicine on their wounds.

No, a wife was not in the picture right now; although, it would be nice to have someone to sit on the front porch with in the evenings, discussing the ups and downs of ranch life, or to take into Seymour for the monthly dance the church put on. Martha always liked to go dancing and he'd enjoyed swinging her around the floor to a lively tune.

It would be nice having someone to buy presents for and watch her eyes light up as she tore open the packages. But most of all, he missed having someone next to him in bed at night – and maybe one day, have a son or daughter to leave this place to.

Before going outside, Clay stopped in the kitchen for a cup of coffee. Mrs. McIntyre and her daughter were elsewhere in the house, doing whatever they did during the day, but they made sure there was always a pot of coffee on the stove in case someone wanted a cup.

Clay sat down at the long kitchen table that had benches on each side and a chair at each end. Having his men eat in the kitchen made them feel more like family than ranch hands. He blew steam off his hot coffee while he thought.

There were at least two women he could think of who would be receptive to a marriage proposal, but he wasn't sure if he was ready yet.

Victoria Ontiveros was a young, vibrant widow who owned a large cattle ranch out in New Mexico. She was beautiful, sophisticated, and passionate. He knew that last part because of the one kiss they'd had in her kitchen, which she had initiated. But would she be willing to move to Texas and live here? Clay wondered if running two ranches so far apart would be difficult? The only other choice would be to sell, which he doubted she would want to do, and now that he thought about it, he wouldn't want to put her in that position.

Clay grinned at the next face that filled his mind; Loralie Benson, the wild, fiery redhead back in Tennessee. It seemed like every time she got herself in trouble, which was often because of her stubborn streak, Clay would just happen to be in the vicinity when she needed his help. It wasn't that she couldn't handle things on her own, she could, for the most part, but sometimes she bit off more than she could chew. He grinned; dreaming about what a handful she would be. He had to admit; it would be fun trying to keep a rein on her, knowing he would never be able to tame her completely, nor would he want to.

During the past year, he had received several correspondences from both women; each expressing hints about getting married, should he be of the same mind.

Clay emptied his coffee cup; stood up and walked over to the sink. There was an inside pump so they didn't have to carry water. He pumped the handle to get enough water to rinse out his cup, then set it on the sideboard.

As he headed for the front door, he sighed. Both women were far away, one to the east and the other to the west, and right now, his priority was ranch work, which left no time to go chasing a skirt; no matter how pretty or wild and exciting she might be.

Once again, he pushed the thought of marriage out of his mind as he stopped by the front door and took down one of the leather jackets hanging there. It was early fall, so it wasn't what you would call cold outside yet, but then on the other hand it wasn't hot, either. He could take the jacket off if he got too warm.

In another few weeks they would be making a cattle drive up to Abilene with five hundred head, where he was to meet with a buyer from Kansas City; a man by the name of JW Carlyle. The man had stopped by the ranch a while back and offered to buy five hundred head for top dollar. Mr. Carlyle said he had a buyer in Chicago who didn't mind paying top money for quality beef and from what he could see; Clay had some of the best he'd seen in a long time.

Clay had accepted the deal and since then, he'd been making preparations for the drive. Running Coyote and two of the other hands had brought in a small herd of wild horses that would need to be broken and turned into cow ponies before the drive. They looked to be a good bunch and he was looking forward to the rough and tumble it would take to get the job done.

Clay stepped out of the door and rubbed his sore back and was about to head for the corral when he saw a column of dust rising in the sky off to the south. He could see that it was moving toward the ranch, and coming fast.

"Somebody's ridin' hard to get here," Clay said, pulling the brim of his hat down a little closer to shade his eyes.

Clay studied the horse and rider. There was something familiar about them. From that distance, it looked like the rider was slumped forward down against his horse.

When he recognized the horse, the hair on the back of his neck stood on end and he ran out into the courtyard, where Riley and several other hands, who had also seen the dust, were coming to investigate.

The horse came to an abrupt halt right in front of them, and before anyone could get close, Bert, the youngest of their cowhands, fell off his horse, landing unceremoniously on the ground. His face, shirt and jacket were covered with blood. His face looked like a mule had kicked it. His nose was crooked and appeared to be broken and both eyes were black and swelled almost closed. His lips were puffed up and still bleeding. It didn't take a doctor to tell them Bert was in bad shape. The young cowboy's face was nearly unrecognizable.

Clay felt anger swelling up inside him but pulled it into check until he could find out what had happened.

At Clay's direction, they picked Bert up and took him into the main house and upstairs to the guest bedroom. Mrs. McIntyre and her daughter Cindy were only steps behind them, and when they laid Bert on the bed, Mrs. McIntyre stepped up next to the bed and said to her daughter, "hot water, bandages and that tin of salve I keep fer things like this – and be quick about it, lass, the poor lad's in bad shape."

Cindy looked at Riley who was standing near the door and nodded her head. When she left the room, reluctantly, he followed close behind her.

Mrs. McIntyre checked Bert's head and saw that it was only a flesh wound. Next, she checked the gunshot wound on the upper left hand side of his chest, close to his shoulder. Gently, she rolled him over just enough to see that the bullet had gone all the way through. She could tell this by the blood on the back of his shirt and the bullet hole in his shirt. She laid him back down, giving a sigh of relief. She wouldn't have to try and remove a bullet that might be near or embedded in a vital organ, but she would need to clean the wounds and stop the bleeding quickly. He looked as though he'd already lost a lot of blood. With practiced swiftness, she unbuttoned his shirt and looked at the hole in the upper left side of his chest. It was still oozing blood, but not gushing, which was a good sign.

Mrs. McIntyre looked at Clay and said, "Would ya be helpin' me ta remove the lad's shirt? And be easy about it. We don't want him hurtin' anymore than he already is."

Once Bert had been stripped to the waist, they could see not only the ugly hole where the bullet had entered his shoulder area, but also black and blue bruises to his body. It looked like he'd been kicked and stomped on by a stampeding herd of cattle, which caused Clay to grit his teeth. Anger was seething inside him and it was getting harder to control. Horses or cattle had not done this.

"Who the hell could' a done this?" Clay asked, looking at Mrs. McIntyre.

All she could do was shrug her shoulders and shake her head. "I'll not be known' the answer ta that, but whoever did this should be thankin' his maker I don't run inta him."

"Think you can patch him up?" Clay asked.

THE CHAMELEON

Mrs. McIntyre sighed. "I can only try. He's lost a lot of blood, but he's young and strong and if the good Lord's willin' he'll pull through," she said. Being the good catholic she was, she crossed her chest with her hand, making the sign of the cross.

After a moment, she straightened up and shooed everyone from the room, saying, "I don't think the bullet hit anything vital. He's still breathin' and that's somethin', at least. Now go on with ya, I won't be needin' ya standin' around in me way while I do what needs ta be done. I'll let ya know as soon as he wakes up. Now go have some coffee or somethin' and tell Cindy ta hurry up with them bandages, I ain't got all day."

At the door, Clay stopped and looked at his housekeeper, "I need ta talk to him as soon as he wakes up. If I'm gonna be able ta go after whoever did this, I need ta know what happened, and where."

"Sure, sure," she said. "'Tis ah wee bit of doctorin' he'll be needin' first, I'm thinkin', but I'll send Cindy fer ya as soon as he's able ta speak."

Clay went down to the kitchen where the others were already gathered at the long table, trying to figure out what had happened.

"I don't reckon it was Injuns," Louis L'Croix, one of Clay's ranch hands said, looking over at the four Comanche braves who were standing at the far side of the room. "If it had been Injuns, they would' a killed him an took his hair wouldn't they?"

He Who Bites, looked at them and shook his head from side to side. "In case you haven't noticed," he said with perfect English, "The Comanche are not only friends with us, but their chief, Walks Tall and Mister Brentwood, or White Warrior as he is called by them, are half-brothers. No, it was not Indians who did this."

Clay poured himself a cup of coffee, then went to the cupboard and took down a bottle of whiskey and laced each of their cups with a good dollop. The four Comanche braves stayed standing at the far side of the room. None of them drank coffee or whiskey.

"His face looks more like he got into an argument with a buffalo or an ornery ole bull," Sleeps a Lot, said.

"Last I heard, buffers, err bulls don't shoot their victims," Louis L'Croix said, looking over at Clay.

Normally, Louis was the silent one of the group, but what happened to Bert rankled his skin and he wanted revenge. The young cowboy rode for the brand and they took care of their own.

The only thing Clay knew about Louis was he came from Louisiana where he'd killed a man in a knife fight over a woman's honor, and had gone to prison for it.

Louis told Clay he'd done his time and was looking for a chance to start over. Clay had liked his honesty and gave him a job. So far, Clay had no reason to regret his decision.

"No, I don't reckon animals do much shootin'," Clay said, "but..."

Before he could say more, Cindy called from the top of the stairs, "Mister Brentwood, he's awake and wants to talk to you."

Clay set his coffee cup on the kitchen table and bounded up the stairs, taking them two at a time.

Other than asking to talk to Clay, Bert had watched without making a sound as Mrs. McIntyre put bandages over the bullet holes and bandaged them, and he lay still as she cleaned and put salve on his bruises, gritting his teeth so he wouldn't pass out again from the pain. He needed to talk to the boss and let him know what happened.

Mrs. McIntyre had just eased Bert down onto his back when Clay entered the room.

She looked at Clay and said, "Tis just ah crease in that thick skull of his and the other bullet went all the way through. I don't think it hit anything vital because I was able ta get the bleedin' stopped. So... ta my way of thinkin', with some of my beef soup and ah wee bit of rest, he'll be back on his feet soon enough."

Bert was laying on the bed, looking pale through all the bruises. He was conscious and breathing in ragged gasps. Clay could barely see his eyes because of the swelling.

Mrs. McIntyre had done a good job of cleaning and bandaging Bert's wounds, but there wasn't much she could do about the bruises, although, she had wrapped a bandage around his ribs to help him breathe easier.

According to her, back in Ireland, with five brothers and a roughhouse father who would almost rather fight than drink, she and her mother had had their hands full with wounds of all kinds, so tending these cowboys wasn't much different than being back in Ireland.

Without a word, Cindy picked up the pan filled with bloody water, the salve and the material used for bandages and left quietly, leaving Riley standing just outside the door, trying to get a peek at Bert. He was worried about Bert and his face showed it.

Clay looked down at Bert and felt his blood begin to boil, again. Bert was barely twenty-one and had worked on the ranch for a year now and was a good hand. Clay had hired him up in Wichita to help bring a herd of white face cattle down to his ranch, here in Texas. He was a good-natured young man who pulled his own weight and along with a couple of the other wranglers he'd hired, he kept Bert on at the end of the drive. Seeing him this way brought tears to Clay's eyes and anger to his chest. Whoever did this was going to pay.

Through tiny slits that were turning purple, Bert looked up at Clay and said in a hushed voice so quiet Clay had to lean in close to hear. His words came in ragged gasps.

"Rus... Rustlers... Close ta... twenty... or more. Headed..."

That's all he'd been able to say before drifting back into unconsciousness, but it was enough for Clay. He turned to Mrs. McIntyre and said, "Take good care of him. We'll be goin' ta find the men who did this and take our retribution. How many do I need to leave here to help protect the place in case there's trouble?"

Without mentioning the tears she saw in Clay's eyes, which broke her heart, she said, "Two. With Cindy and me here ta help, we can close the gates and the four of us can stand off an army, I'm thinkin' - should it come ta that."

After the death of his wife, Clay had rebuilt the place like a fort with a ten-foot wall all the way around and hung a heavy gate at both the front and back. Inside, on the lower part of the wall, he built a railing where a person could stand just below the top of the wall and shoot through the square holes that were every few feet apart. With only a few well-armed shooters, they could defend the house and barns against intruders. It looked and was patterned very much like the Mexican hacienda of Victoria's place.

Clay nodded and walked out of the room and headed down the stairs with Riley trailing close behind.

Mrs. McIntyre watched him go, then turned and pulled a sheet over Bert, saying, "He's ah good man and he'll see ta the men who did this to ya, ya don't need ta be ah worrin' about that. Now get some rest and I'll be ah seein' about some soup fer ya. It'll help ya get yer strength back."

As she walked out of the room, she was crying and hoped he would wake up long enough to take some nourishment.

When Clay got downstairs, the men were waiting for him. "He's gonna pull through, but he'll be laid up for awhile. He was able ta tell me it was rustlers that did this to him. I'm not sure which, whether there are close ta twenty rustlers who are stealin' some of our cattle, or they're takin' twenty head or so. He passed out before he could say, but he did say when he broached them, they did this to him."

Clay used the word *our* because every time he sold any of the cattle, he gave a portion of the money to the men, which made them feel like they were part owners of the ranch. Clay didn't miss what he gave them and it made them feel more like family, so to speak, and they worked that much harder to see the ranch was run as good as it could be. He knew each one of them rode for the brand, but a little extra incentive didn't hurt.

Clay talked each of them into taking a portion or all of their bonus money and saving it or investing it. If they were like most cowboys, they wouldn't be able to cowboy all their lives. By the time they were too old to wrangle any more, most cowboys were dead broke, and without any other kind of job to go to. Clay didn't want that to happen to his men and they all seemed to appreciate what he was doing for them and were glad for the chance to put some money by.

Being the youngest of them, Bert was treated like he was their younger brother and he loved it. To the man, each one swore vengeance on the men who did this to him.

Mrs. McIntyre came down the stairs and was about to head for the kitchen to clean up, when Clay stopped her.

"I'm gonna leave Running Coyote and He Who Sleeps A Lot here to help you watch the place. The rest will come with me."

He knew Running Coyote would be worried if she was left alone and not be at his best if he was with them. Plus, both Running Coyote and He Who Sleeps A Lot, were good with a rifle and would make any would-be attackers have second thoughts.

Turning back to the men, he said, "Go pack your gear and each of ya get an extra horse so we can switch mounts in case we need ta do some hard ridin'."

Mrs. McIntyre smiled and said, "You'll be needin' ah bit of food ta take with ya, I'm thinkin'. We'll put some tagather."

Clay turned back and said, "Nothin' we can't carry in our saddle bags. We'll be travelin' hard and fast."

Like her mother, Cindy was always eager and willing to help. She loved living here and said, "Come by the back door and we'll give each of you something you can share with the others. That way you can have enough to have a real meal when you find the time.

After gathering two horses apiece, packing an extra shirt and a cold weather coat, their ground sheet for sleeping and as much ammunition as they could carry, each man went to the back door of the kitchen where Cindy doled out coffee, beans, bacon, biscuit makings, dried meat, canned peaches, and other things they could share.

To Brave Eagle, Mrs. McIntyre gave a small quantity of medicine and bandage material he might need in case of gunshot wounds or other injuries to the men or horses.

Other than Mrs. McIntyre, Brave Eagle knew more about medicine than any of the rest of them. In fact, he had introduced Mrs. McIntyre to some medicinal herbs she'd never heard of, like wild lettuce, which was the best pain medicine she'd ever seen, even better than laudanum.

Too eager to find the men who had beaten and shot Bert and taken their cattle, they bypassed the noon meal and rode out at a high lope, riding southeast, toward where the main herd was pastured.

The sound of horse's hooves on the hard ground filled the air, while the trail of dust rising into the sky gave evidence to the direction the men were headed. Mrs. McIntyre and Running Coyote stood in the open gateway of the hacienda and watched until they were out of sight.

Mrs. McIntyre was a peaceful woman, but right now she wished she was going with them. Life here was a far cry from what her home in Ireland had been, but these men, these, rough and tumble cowboys were her family now. Bert was almost like a son to her and she'd be damned if she'd tolerate anyone hurting him. If only she was a man and could go with them, she thought to herself as Running Coyote put his arm around her shoulder and pulled her close.

She looked up at him and marveled that she could be enamored with an Indian. What would the people back in Ireland think if they knew she had fallen in love with what they considered to be a heathen redskin; which he definitely was not.

In Texas, a horse or cattle thief was no better than a rattlesnake. In fact, a rattlesnake might rate a bit higher than a horse or cattle thief. A rattlesnake would at least give you some warning before he struck, but a horse or cattle thief would sneak in like cowards and hopefully steal your stock without anyone knowing it until they were long gone.

They knew if they were unlucky enough to be caught, they would be hung from the nearest tree and the men who did it would feel they had given the rustlers exactly what they deserved and the law would agree with them.

Like bank robbers and other thieves of that time, most of them thought they could get away with whatever crime they were committing, so they gave little thought to getting caught. They were men who led a rough life, living outside the law. They had no qualms about shooting anyone who got in their way, which is what happened to Bert. He'd come along at the wrong time and interfered, and it had nearly cost him his life.

Clay and the men rode in silence, each one of them hoping to get his hands on at least one of the men who had ganged up on Bert and left him for dead.

Images of Bert's battered face was embedded into each man's brain and to the man, they wanted to see the rustlers battered and beaten like Bert had been. They wanted to see them begging for mercy before they slipped a rope around their necks and hung them from the nearest tree, or trees.

If there were twenty of them, then twenty men would be left hanging from the trees as a notice to anyone else who came around looking to steal their cattle.

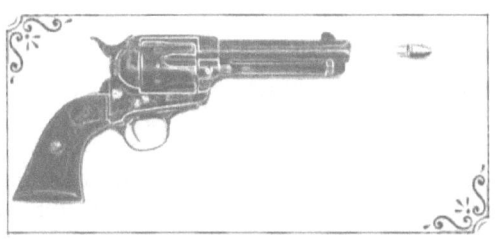

CHAPTER SEVEN

-

There were twenty of them - twenty of the meanest hombres JW Carlyle could find to do his dirty work. To the man, they were all wanted by the authorities for horse and cattle rustling, murder, bank robbing and a long list of other crimes.

No one could accuse them of being loyal to Carlyle, or anyone else for that matter, but the jobs were relatively easy and the money was decent, so when he sent word, they rode in, stole some cattle, delivered them, then disappeared.

As long as the money kept coming in, and the work remained the same, they did as they were told and asked no questions. If anyone got in their way, well, that was their bad luck.

JW Carlyle, which was not his real name, but a name he'd chosen to use when doing his illegal business - had a good thing going and was getting rich. He would go into a town and in general conversation, usually in a saloon, ask about the local ranchers. Who had the biggest ranch, the best cattle and such?

Bartenders were a great source of information and knew who had the best beef cattle.

Carlyle would rent a horse and ride out to what was considered the best ranch in the area and introduce himself as a cattle buyer. When he would ask to see the stock, most ranchers were proud of their herds and rode out with him to inspect them.

If he was satisfied with what he saw, he would offer to buy five hundred head, offering top dollar – which so far had always been accepted. He always gave them a note, promising payment upon delivery to whatever nearby town he selected, and also to be delivered on a specified date.

He did it this way so there would be plenty of time for his men to steal the cattle a week or more in advance of the delivery date without much trouble.

His men would steal the cattle and drive them to a section of railroad he would set up - load them into railroad boxcars he owned, and haul the cattle away before the ranchers realized they were even gone. So far, Carlyle had over two hundred and fifty thousand dollars sitting in a bank in Chicago, under his real name, Sydney Meier, investment broker.

People could go looking for JW Carlyle all they wanted but would find no trace of such a man.

The good part for him was when it came time for the rancher to deliver the cattle and most of the time they couldn't because he'd already stolen a large portion of their stock, he would tell them how sorry he was and move on, leaving them high and dry. If by some chance they had enough cattle to still bring a herd of five hundred to whatever site he'd selected, most of the time he would already be gone and the rancher was still left high and dry.

If by some chance he was still there, he told the unfortunate rancher that he'd already purchased another herd from a ranch closer to Kansas City, at a lower price, but if they wanted to sell at the lower price he'd be happy to take them off their hands.

This way, if they did sell their cattle to him, and they usually did because by now they were desperate, he wound up getting a thousand head of cattle for very little money; and far below the going market price.

Any way he looked at it, he won. At the worst he would wind up with five hundred head of virtually free cattle to sell to the slaughterhouses in Kansas City with forged bills of sale. He paid the rustlers just enough to keep them in whiskey money and broke by the time the next time he needed them.

Clay's ranch had some of the finest beef he'd seen in this part of Texas, or anywhere else for that matter, and J.W. Carlyle figured he could make some easy money. The ranch was large and from what he could tell, the cattle grazed a good distance from the ranch house, which made them easy pickings for his gang of cutthroats.

A few weeks before the cattle were to be delivered to him up in Abilene, Kansas, Carlyle sent his thugs to rustle the cattle and drive them to a nearby railhead spur where he would have his private cattle cars waiting to take them away to Kansas City or Chicago.

Everything had been going as planned. They had moved Clay's cattle close to five miles when a young cowboy came riding up to them and asked what they thought they were doing?

Trying to bluff their way through, one of them told him they'd bought the cattle and was driving them to a ranch in New Mexico.

The young cowboy, who turned out to be Bert, shook his head and said, "Then you'd best turn'em around and head'em in the opposite direction, cause you're headed east, and in case you're interested, New Mexico is west of here."

When Bert looked down and saw the brand on the cows, he became suspicious and said, "I work for the BR brand that's on them cows, there, Mister. Now I'm not doubtin' yer word, but I'd take it kindly if you'd show me ah bill of sale."

With that, one of them rode up next to Bert and knocked him to the ground, and then jumped down from his horse and began to kick Bert in the ribs, chest, stomach and head. Three other outlaws decided to join in the fun and climbed down from their horses and began to kick Bert, too. Being the kind of low life men they were, they laughed as they kicked him from his head to his knees.

Before they left, one of them, a greasy looking man of about fifty that had a pock marked face and long hair that had turned mostly gray, said, as he pulled his pistol, "Don't reckon there's any point in leavin' him here ta tell anybody about us, is there?"

No one argued with him. In fact, they all turned back toward the herd and began moving the stolen cattle in the direction they had been told to go.

With a coldness that comes from living too long on the owl hoot trail, the rustler shot Bert twice - first, in the head and next, in the chest. "Ah dead man cain't testify ta nothin'," the rustler said as he dropped his pistol back in his holster, before riding off, laughing.

One of the younger rustlers tried to catch Bert's horse but it ran away and after awhile, he decided not to spend any more time trying to catch a horse that didn't want to be caught; they had cattle to deliver to a spur line east of here and they'd wasted enough time, already.

Later that same afternoon, they spotted another good looking herd and decided to steal a second bunch, hoping Carlyle would pay them something extra. If not, they would drive them down into Mexico and sell them there.

Before the sun went down, they were driving a thousand head of top stock toward the east. This many cattle would slow them down a little, but they figured they'd still make the spur line in plenty of time. Since killing the young cowboy, they weren't concerned that anyone would be coming after them.

Even so, as always, they took no chances and took turns keeping an eye on their back trail.

The following morning, Bert, hanging on to life by sheer tenacity, tried to open his eyes, but had a hard time seeing through the slits because his face was swollen so bad. He hurt from his head to his hips and it was hard to breathe. Turning his head, he thought he could see his horse standing nearby, eating grass. Through swollen lips, he called his horse over close enough to where he could reach a stirrup, and with the sheer willpower of a determined man, Bert hauled himself to his feet and leaned his head against the saddle, breathing hard from his broken ribs, and wincing in pain for his effort.

After resting for a minute or so, trying to catch his breath, with almost his last bit of strength and willpower, Bert pulled himself onto his saddle and turned the horse toward the ranch.

"Take me home, boy, take me home," he said, then leaned forward and hung on for dear life.

The next thing he remembered was waking up to the smiling face of Mrs. McIntyre and the first words he uttered were, "Is my horse all right?"

She had nodded her head, yes, giving a big sigh of relief, then reached down and kissed him on the forehead before sending her daughter to let Mister Brentwood know Bert was awake.

"Beat to within an inch of his life and he's worried about his horse," she mumbled to her- self.

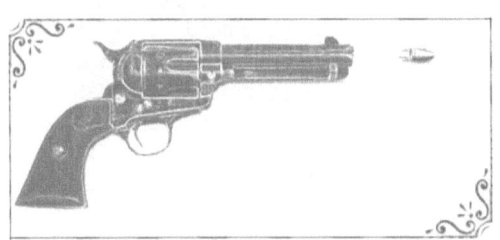

CHAPTER EIGHT

-

Clay and his men topped over a rise close to a mile from the ranch and saw his cattle milling around, cropping grass. The herd was large and without a count, it would be hard to tell at a glance how many had been stolen, if any.

Off to his right, Clay saw a rider headed in their direction and sat waiting for him to get close enough to recognize, his hand not far from his pistol.

Riley reached into his saddlebag and pulled out a long glass and put it to his eye, and after a moment, he said, "Mister Sooner."

Marion Sooner was Clay's neighbor and a good friend. Clay wondered what he was doing over here? Could he have lost some cattle, too? If there were rustlers around, it made sense that they would steal some from each herd, making it hard for each rancher to notice until they were long gone.

Marion Sooner rode up and asked, "You lose some cattle, too?"

Clay looked at him and said, "Accordin' ta Bert, we've got us some rustlers who were in the process of stealing some of our cattle when he rode up to'm and asked what they was doin'? They beat him half ta death, then shot him twice and left him for dead, but somehow, he made it back ta the ranch house. How many did you lose?"

"I'm guessin' close ta five hundred or so," Marion said. "How's Bert doing?"

"Mrs. McIntyre says with some of her tender lovin' care and ah few bowls of her soup, he'll pull through."

Marion Sooner chuckled and asked, "You goin' after'em?"

"That's why we're out here," Clay said with a grin. "You wantin' ta tag along? We can use an extra gun hand."

Marion nodded his head, yes. "I saw where they joined our cows together and headed east," he said, pointing in the direction where he'd seen the sign. "I'll need ta go home and tell Rebecca and get ah couple of fresh horses and a couple of my men." He looked at the mount Clay was riding and said, "I see you and that black stallion are still runnin' together."

Clay nodded his head and grinned, "Don't think he'd like it if I went on ah trip like this without him. We'll start trailin'em while you go home and get a couple of fresh horses and your men. My best ta Rebecca, and tell her not ta worry, we'll get the cattle back."

Before leaving, Marion said, "There's ah new spur line east of here, between Seymour and Dallas. If that's where they're headed you'd best not waste any time. We'll catch up before you get there, hopefully, but it's gonna be ah close race. If they push'em, they could get'em loaded and be gone by the time you get there. If that happens there'll be no way ta track'em. They'll be sold in Wichita or Kansas City with bogus bills of sale, and be long gone before any of us can catch up to'em."

Clay nodded his head and said, "Movin' that many head of cattle will take a good bit of time; plus, loadin' that many will add some time, also. We'll follow the tracks for a bit and if that's for sure the direction they're headed, we'll pick up the pace."

Clay grinned and said, "You'd best get ah move on if you plan on catch'n us before we catch up to them. Wouldn't want you ta miss out on the party."

Marion pointed again, toward the far side of the herd, indicating that's where they would find the tracks of the stolen cattle, then put two fingers to the brim of his hat, and without a word turned his horse and rode off toward his place at a gallop.

Clay and his men circled around the herd and had no trouble finding the tracks of the stolen cattle. They turned their mounts east and lit out at a gallop, knowing time was of the essence. At first, it was just the tracks of their cattle, then a few miles later, the size of the stolen herd doubled, and they knew Marion Sooner had been correct in his assumption and it looked to Clay, like they were headed for the new spur line with cattle from both herds.

Following a thousand head of cattle across this part of Texas was easy and they made good time, but the rustlers had better than a day's head start, and were pushing hard.

He and his men had gotten a late start due to the time of day Bert had arrived and then waiting for him to tell them what had happened.

The sun was lowering itself below the horizon to the back of them when Clay called a halt. They no longer needed to see the trail because they had a good idea where the rustlers were headed, but cattle or no cattle, the horses needed to rest and so did the men. It had been a long, tedious day with no food in their stomachs since breakfast.

Even the black stallion Clay rode was showing signs of fatigue. He was a far cry from being old, but he was no longer a young stallion, either.

They were just finishing their evening meal of beans, bacon and biscuits when Marion Sooner and two of his riders rode up close to the camp and hailed, "Hello the camp."

Clay recognized Marion's voice and called for them to come in, but it wouldn't have mattered whether they hailed the camp or not because Brave Eagle startled them when he stood up just a few feet from where they'd stopped.

"You bout gave me ah heart attack," Marion Sooner said with a grin.

The men riding with Marion Sooner were new hands and looked around to see if there were any more Indians but saw none, but still eyed Brave Eagle suspiciously.

Brave Eagle grinned and motioned them on towards the camp. As they nudged their horses forward, one of Marion's men turned to take a second look at Brave Eagle and saw nothing but grass and cactus. Brave Eagle had already melted into the landscape.

"How do they do that, boss?" the young cowboy asked Marion.

"Do what?" Marion replied.

"Disappear like that. One second he was standin' there, and the next, he just up and disappeared like ah snake vanishin' inta ah hole."

Marion grinned and rode on, only shrugging his shoulders. He'd wondered the same thing more than once and was definitely glad they were on the same side.

Marion was riding a speckled gelding and leading a gray mustang mix of some kind. Each of his two riders were also leading a second mount.

In this part of the country there were a lot of wild horses and both Clay and Marion would from time to time, ride out together and catch a few. It didn't always work, but they tried to catch an even amount so the split wouldn't be uneven.

"I see you're ridin' a couple of the horses we caught a few weeks back. Didn't take ya long ta get'em busted and trained."

Marion grinned a lopsided grin as he helped himself to some supper. "Funniest thing. As you know, neither of'em was wearin' a brand when we roped them."

Clay nodded his agreement.

"But as it turned out, both of'em were already saddle broke," Marion said. "There ain't no other ranches close to ours, so I'm still wonderin' where they came from? Probably never find out, but I sure am glad I didn't have to do much to turn'em into cow ponies."

"Why don't you have that kind of luck, boss?" Riley said as he walked up and handed Marion a cup of coffee to go with his supper.

Clay was trying to think of something to say to that, when a rifle shot filled the night air.

In no more than the blink of an eye, the men were laying flat on their stomachs with a gun in their hand, searching the darkness; trying to find the shooter, but seeing anyone outside the light of the campfire was almost impossible. One of Marion Sooner's men, called Roscoe Barnes, yelled, "I'm hit!"

They looked in Roscoe's direction and saw that he was laying on the ground with his pistol in his hand, but there was a red spot on his jeans down around the calf area of his leg that was getting bigger.

"Hello the camp," a voice called out, and immediately, pistols began to roar.

"Hold your fire!" Clay yelled, knowing the man had already moved and they would just be wasting their ammunition.

"Speak your piece, mister. What do you want?" Clay yelled into the darkness.

Clouds had covered the moon and most of the stars. The brightness of the campfire made night vision impossible. The man would be just outside the perimeter of the light and they wouldn't be able to see him.

A graveled voice came from approximately ten feet to the left of where the shot had come from.

"Turn around and go home. There's more of us than there is of you. We ain't amin' ta kill ya, but we will if ya don't leave. We'll give ya til sunup. If yer still here then..."

And then there was silence.

After a few moments, Clay stood up and walked over to where Roscoe lay holding his bandanna over the gunshot wound.

Marion was there almost as soon as Clay was, and squatted down next to Roscoe. "I'm real sorry about this Roscoe," Marion said, laying his hand on the cowboy's shoulder.

Roscoe was a man in his late forties who had been over the trail many times, and like most cowboys, he rode for the brand, so the possibility of getting shot or even killed, came with the job.

"Look what I found," Brave Eagle called out as he pushed a man in front of him into the light of the campfire.

They all turned and watched as Brave Eagle brought in the man who had ambushed them and shot Roscoe.

The man stopped next to the fire and glared at them. He was in his late thirties, with long greasy hair and what appeared to be several knife scars on his face. His clothes were dirty and he had a rank smell about him that caused Clay to shake his head.

"Well, looks like you'll be outnumberin' us by one less if we don't like the answers to our questions," Clay said, matter of factly.

"Got nothin' ta say, mister, cept'in if I don't show up, they'll come lookin' fer me and they won't take it none too kindly if somethin' was ta happen ta me."

Clay walked over and slapped the man alongside his head and watched as he lost his balance and fell to the ground. "Haven't asked you any questions yet, but if I had, that wouldn't have been a good answer."

The man got slowly to his feet and rubbed the side of his face. "You won't get away with this," he said, glaring at Clay. "My friends will ride in and cut ya down like mowin' hay."

Quicker than the man could react or duck, Clay slapped him along the other side of his head and knocked him down, again.

Doing ranch work toughened a man's hands and getting slapped felt like being hit with a leather strap.

"You must like gettin' slapped," Clay said, shaking his head. "Runnin' off at the mouth like that before I've even asked you the first question ain't real bright, but you do what you think best."

When the man regained his feet, Clay looked at his men and asked, "What'ya think, should I waste my time interrogatin' this hombre or should I just turn him over ta Brave Eagle and Sleeps A Lot?"

The man turned and saw two Comanche Indians standing just behind him and his eyes went wide. "What'er they doin' here?"

"They work for me and as I'm sure ya know, or at least have heard, Indians have ways of torturin' ah man for days before they let him die – and even then, it's a slow, painful way ta die that I wouldn't want ta go through. I've heard men beg the Indians ta kill'em just ta get out of their misery. Now, bein' the kind-hearted man I am," Clay said, holding his hands out in front of him, "I'm gonna give ya a choice, either answer my questions straight up, and no lie'n, or I'm gonna turn ya over to these two Comanche Indians. One way or another, the easy way or the hard way, I'll get the information I want. The choice is yours."

The man licked his lips and looked again at the two Indians standing behind him and swallowed. The tall one had taken a mean looking knife from its sheath and was turning it in his hand. The other one had an evil grin on his face and his eyes were dancing with anticipation of what they would do to him, and the images in the rustler's mind weren't pretty ones.

"Hell, I ain't no hero. What do you want ta know?"

Clay grinned and said, "That's probably the smartest thing you could have said."

Clay indicated for the man to sit next to the fire, while Brave Eagle went to tend to Roscoe's gunshot wound.

When they were seated, Clay poured two cups of coffee and handed one to the rustler.

"How far ahead of us are they?"

The rustler took the cup of coffee and began to sip on it. He'd been on guard duty and had missed supper. Grateful, he took a swallow, then said, "Twenty-five, thirty miles."

"Is someone comin' ta relieve ya? And if there is, when?"

The man took a long pull of the coffee and felt new energy flow through his body. He thought about conjuring up a story, but decided against it after thinking about the two Comanche Indians here in the camp. "Nobody's comin' ta relieve me. If'n there ain't nobody followin' us, I'm ta catch up as soon as I can. And if there are, I was ta warn'm off, then hightail it back ta the herd and tell the boss."

"How many of you are there, and where are you takin' the cattle?" Clay asked.

The man finished the coffee and held out his cup.

"Answer my question first," Clay said and took a sip from his cup.

The man sighed and said, "Countin' me, there's twenty of us. We're ta tak'em to a spur track south of Seymour. Ah train with cattle cars will be wait'n there ta haul'em away."

"Just ah couple more questions," Clay said, indicating more coffee for the both of them. "How do you get paid, and will the man who hired ya, be there?"

The man took the fresh cup of coffee and blew on it before he spoke. It wouldn't do to try and convince him they were innocent of any wrong doing by telling him they thought the man who hired them said they were his cattle, bought an paid for. Especially when they'd decided to steal cattle from a second herd. He knew these men wouldn't buy it.

"Personally, I ain't never seen the man who hires us, only Zeb has. He's our ramrod. In the past, he's always been wherever we deliver'em, usually on ah side track like where we're tak'in this herd. Zeb will collect our money from him and then he pays us."

Clay nodded his head. "I see. Would you happen ta know the man's name?"

The rustler looked into his cup and studied for a moment. If he told them the man's name, he was as good as dead, but if he didn't, he'd be turned over to a couple of blood thirsty Comanche Indians and tortured to death.

"Carlyle. Don't know his first name, and like I said, I ain't never met him face ta face, just heard him called that."

Clay felt the numbness go through his body. That was the name of the man he'd agreed to sell his cattle to. Suddenly, he felt like a damn fool. It was all of a sudden as clear as a picture on a wall. He'd been so eager to sell at a price far above what he ever expected to get, he'd allowed himself to be duped like a schoolboy.

The rustler noticed the change in Clay's face and saw the anger growing in his eyes and didn't like what he saw. He knew what they did to rustlers out here, and right now he wished he'd chosen a different occupation. Dropping his gun hand to his side, it brushed the handle on his pistol and he realized they hadn't taken his handgun, only his rifle.

JARED MCVAY

Letting out a sigh, he made a decision. If he was gonna die, he was gonna die with a gun in his hand and maybe take somebody with him.

Out of the corner of his eye, Clay saw the rustler lean to his left and let his right hand drop for the pistol at his side. He saw the outlaw's pistol coming out of his holster and then heard the boom of his own pistol.

Clay had not thought about it, only reacted, and when the smoke cleared, the outlaw was laying on his back with a bullet hole dead center in his chest; his pistol not quite all the way out of its resting place. He hadn't wanted to kill the man, but he'd been given no choice. Thinking about it, he couldn't blame him; it was better than hanging.

Without a word, He Who Sleeps A Lot dragged the dead carcass out away from the camp and began to strip him of his gun and holster, along what little money he had – six dollars. The man had nothing else of value and He Who Sleeps A Lot walked away and left him to the will of nature. Bad men were not to be buried. Their souls would walk the earth forever and never go to the great beyond. The beasts of the plains would devour their flesh as Mother Nature intended, and their bones would be left as a sign to other would be outlaws; this was not a country that abided cattle rustlers.

Brave Eagle checked Roscoe's leg and declared him fit to ride.

With the whiskey they'd poured into him and on his wound, Roscoe was in no pain and readily agreed he was fit to ride and ready when the others were.

Clay told them to get some rest. They would leave at first light. He said he hoped to catch them loading the cattle into the boxcars; figuring the cattle would be bunched with some of them in the pens associated with spur lines. If so, there would be less of a chance the herd would stampede, or at least the majority of them.

He was also hoping to catch the rustlers busy and off guard, because, never in his wildest dreams did he believe they would just give up. They were wanted men and knew the penalty for what they'd done. He had no doubt they, like the one they'd left on guard duty, would rather take a bullet than hang.

Clay stood for a moment before he said, "With them in the majority, there's a good chance some of us could get killed or wounded. So... if any man wants ta stay behind when I leave, I'll understand and not judge ya."

Marion Sooner took the toe of his boot and dragged a line in the dirt and then stepped across it and stood next to Clay.

"The same goes for my men as well," he said, looking directly at Roscoe.

Without another word being spoken, every man stepped across the line and stood with Clay and Marion. They rode for the brand and there was nothing more to be said.

"So be it," Clay said. "Now, let's turn in and get a few hours rest. We've got a big day ahead of us tomorrow."

As Clay was laying out his bedroll, Brave Eagle walked up to him and asked, "If you'd have turned that outlaw over to us, what did you expect us to do? I've never scalped a man in my life. And I sure as hell ain't never tortured anybody."

Clay laughed and said, "Never figured ya had. Truth is, never reckoned I'd need ta turn him over ta the two of ya. The fear of what was done by your ancestors was enough. Now let me get some rest."

Brave Eagle walked away, chuckling and muttering to himself about the devious mind Clay had. He would have a story to tell.

Before closing his eyes, Clay looked around the camp. These were good men and he hoped there would be no casualties tomorrow – at least none on their part.

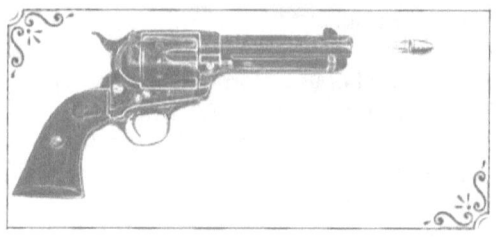

CHAPTER NINE

-

After a quick breakfast of biscuits, bacon and coffee, Clay saddled the black stallion and loaded his saddlebag and other gear behind the cantle. He'd thought about riding the buckskin and giving Midnight a rest, but the big horse seemed to know what was going on and wanted to be there when the fighting began.

The buckskin was a good horse and had plenty of sand, but there had never been a horse to compare with the black stallion. He seemed to have a second sense about him and knew Clay's every move; sometimes before he did. When the chips were down, he wanted the black stallion between his legs.

Looking around, Clay noticed He Who Sleeps A Lot was already gone and knew he would be scouting ahead so they wouldn't run into a trap.

They were riding at a brisk pace when the sun came over the horizon. It was staring them in the eyes when He Who Sleeps A Lot came riding toward them. Clay saw the serious look on Sleeps A Lot's face and felt a jolt in his stomach. Were they too late?

As He Who Sleeps A Lot rode up, Clay, Marion and the others pulled up, waiting for the bad news that seemed apparent on the Indian's face.

For a long moment, Sleeps A Lot sat his horse and stared at them.

"What's wrong?" Marion Sooner asked. "Have they already loaded the cattle and gone?"

He Who Sleeps A Lot looked at the ground for a moment, then looked up at Marion and said, "No sir, Mister Sooner, they're just over that hill over there," he said, pointing to a hill in the far distance.

"Then, why the serious face?" Clay asked, wondering why he was being so evasive.

After a long, pregnant pause, Sleeps A Lot said, "I think it would be best if you ride to the top of the rise and see for yourself."

By now, everyone's curiosity was piqued to the utmost.

Clay touched his feet to the black stallion's side and rode out toward the hill Sleeps A Lot had indicated, wondering what was going on?

As they topped over the hill, they came to a halt and stared. The cattle were grazing in a lazy fashion and none of the cattle cars had been loaded. Instead, the outlaws and a man dressed in a suit, stood trussed to the sides of the boxcars.

Off to the side, they saw a Comanche Indian camp with maybe a dozen braves, and it looked like they were cooking a side of beef.

As he sat there, grinning, Clay saw his half-brother, Walks Tall, look in their direction. He waved, then ran and leaped onto a pony and headed in their direction. Clay touched the sides of the black stallion and went to meet him half way.

When they hauled up next to each other, Walks Tall said, "White Warrior is too late. We have saved your cattle and those of your neighbor, Mister Sooner. And as a courtesy to the two of you, we captured the ones who stole them from you."

Clay reached across and clasped hands with Walks Tall. "I don't know what to say, except, thank you. How did you know they'd taken my cattle and how did you capture them? Was there a fight?" Clay's head was filled with questions.

Walks Tall grinned and said, "Slow down, my brother. You ask too many questions all at one time. Come, we will go eat and then I will tell you all about it."

"About that," Clay said. "Whose cows are you cookin'?"

"So far, one from each of you," Walks Tall said as he kicked his horse in the sides and went racing toward the camp, whooping and yelling.

Clay and the rest followed, knowing they wouldn't get any answers until they'd eaten.

When they'd had their fill, Walks Tall looked at his half-brother and grinned. "I know you want to know how we did this miraculous feat when there are twenty of them and only twelve of us?

Clay knew Indians loved storytelling and his half-brother was no different, so he waited patiently, nodding his head.

Walks Tall stood and walked around, looking at his waiting crowd and smiled to himself, getting the story straight in his mind.

Finally, he stopped and looked around. Every eye, cowboy and Indian, was waiting for him to begin.

"It was a sad time for us," he said shaking his head and looking at the ground. "Our people are hungry for the juicy taste of buffalo meat, but there are no buffalo to be found. The white man, in his greed for hides, has killed nearly all of them, leaving the poor Indians to die a slow, painful death from starvation."

Clay wiped his mouth so the others wouldn't see the grin spreading across his face.

While Clay knew what Walks Tall was saying was true - and he felt pain for his red skinned brothers, Walks Tall would take a simple explanation and turn it into a story to be told for years to come about how they saved the cattle of his half-brother and his neighbor.

In the end, it would cost him some cattle, but it would be worth it to get the cattle back without a fight.

Walks Tall could see he had their attention and continued, raising his arms to make his point.

"We had been riding across the barren prairie for three days, searching for the buffalo that no longer roams this part of the world. Our stomachs were growling. Our bodies were growing weak. Prairie dog meat does not satisfy like the juicy taste of buffalo."

Walks Tall took a short pause to let the picture of starving Indians sink into their brains, then took a big sigh and continued.

"We had almost given up hope of finding buffalo to save our women and children from starvation. We were headed home to tell our wives and children that they must make due with rabbit and prairie dog meat. In shame, we would have to tell them there would be no buffalo meat to eat or hides to warm them on the cold winter nights."

Clay looked around and saw the eyes of every man there were focused on Walks Tall as he pranced around, telling his story like one of those traveling preachers that sold bibles on the side.

Walks Tall glanced at Clay and Clay saw an ever so slight grin on his half-brother's mouth.

"I was ready to tell my people that I was no longer fit to be their chief. I would have to tell them they should look for a new leader - one who could provide for them." Sorrow was written all over his face. "Then, like a great miracle, the gods must have heard the growling in my stomach and seen the sadness in my soul, for one of my scouts came riding over to me and told me he'd seen a large herd of cattle just to the north of us. He said they were waiting to be loaded onto the cars of the iron horse and taken away."

Clay wondered how long Walks Tall would stretch this story out without getting to the point, but however long it took, he would wait. They had their cattle back without a fight and the outlaws were tied up, waiting to be taken to jail. Besides, the steak he'd just eaten filled his stomach and the coffee he was drinking was hot and strong, and he was feeling content.

Walks Tall was coming to the part where he and his braves would become the heroes of his story and he wanted to make sure to get the point across with as much flare as he could conjure up.

"The moon was high in the sky and with the stealth of the wolf or the cougar, we crept close to the white man's camp and looked upon them, sitting around their campfire as white men do, thinking they own the land, laughing and drinking. All but one was dirty and we could smell them long before we got close. These were not my white brothers. These were cattle rustlers and then, like a vision, a question burst into my head. Whose cattle have they stolen? Were these the cattle of my brother, White Warrior and maybe his friend?

"So... with the swiftness of the wind, I circled close to the cattle and saw with my own eyes, the brands of my half-brother, White Warrior, and those of his neighbor, Mister Sooner."

Walks Tall shoved his hands forward, pointing at Clay and Marion, and said, "My half-brother and Mister Sooner have been good to the Comanche and given them beef and blankets during the cold time when we could find no game. We do not forget these men of honor."

Turning his head slowly, Walks Tall stared into each man's eyes. "I could not allow this to happen to the only white people I respect. No. I had to save their cattle from being hauled away by these bad men, these cattle thieves and they're iron horse. So... while they slept, we came into their camp like shadows drifting across the land, disturbing not even a leaf, and carried away all their weapons.

Of course, Walks Tall neglected to mention one small fact. They were all drunk and passed out, and snoring so loudly an earthquake wouldn't have awakened them. But it was his story and he could tell it however he wanted to.

"Then, after leading their horses away, we woke them up and tied them to the sides of the train cars, knowing my white brothers would come looking for their cattle and be happy when they found the Comanche had saved them and captured the men who had taken their cattle."

Again, Walks Tall neglected to mention another minor detail. They had awakened the rustlers, one at a time, and tied and gagged them, so as not to wake up the others and have a fight on their hands. It was the end result that counted, as far as Walks Tall was concerned and he felt no need to lessen his story with small, insignificant information.

Walks Tall turned and looked at Clay and Marion Sooner and said, "For our efforts, we took only one cow from each of you to fill our empty bellies," he said pointing to the cows roasting over the fire. Opening his arms wide, he continued on with his great oratory.

Raising his arms into the air for effect and a sad look on his face, he said, "It is with great humility that I ask, not as your half-brother, White Warrior, nor you, Mister Sooner, but as your good friend - a man seeking only meat for his people, the poor, starving women and children of our tribe who will surely parish without the life giving meat they so badly need. I ask you, good men of honor, may we take but a few more head so we can fill their empty bellies and save their lives? Is that too much to ask for risking our lives to save your cattle from those bloodthirsty cattle rustlers?"

The look on Walks Tall's face was so sad and forlorn that Clay had to turn his head.

The white man, who had lived among them many years ago, had taught them to speak English. He was also the father to both Clay and Walks Tall, with different mothers of course, which made them half-brothers by blood, giving them a strong bond.

Thinking of his father and the things he'd learned from him while he was growing up and all the wisdom he must have brought to the Indians as well, made his father a strong teacher in Clay's eyes. If Walks Tall was a white man, he would have made a great evangelistic preacher, or a terrific con man, but no matter how much education he had, he would still be just an Indian – a heathen in the eyes of many of the whites.

Clay looked at Marion Sooner and grinned. Marion looked at Walks Tall and said, "Hell, you can have twenty head of mine and I count myself lucky to have you as a friend. Thank you for what you've done."

"And the same from my herd," Clay said, standing up, offering his hand to Walks Tall.

Walks Tall took Clay, then Marion in a bear hug, saying, "If only all of the whites could be the honorable men the two of you are, there would be no wars between us."

The truth was, both Clay and Marion felt angry about the way the government treated the Indians. The Comanche were an honorable people and would have welcomed the white man; but the sad truth was, most of the white people who came here and stole the land from them and killed off the buffalo had no respect for the people who had lived here for hundreds of years before the, greedy, bible thumping whites showed up.

As they stood, looking at each other, Clay hoped someday things would get better for them but had little faith that it would. "What about the prisoners? Have you fed them?" Clay asked, knowing the answer, but thought he should ask, anyway.

Walks Tall looked at Clay and Clay saw the wrinkles form on Walks Tall's forehead.

"Why would we do that?" Walks Tall asked. "Why should we waste food on men who are going to die for what they have done? That would be wasting good meat, " he said as if that said it all.

"Come, let us fill our stomachs again before we will leave," he said to Clay and Marion. "You have much to do, taking your cattle back to your ranches and seeing to the men who tried to steal them from you. I thank you, again. My people will know your names and will speak of you with honor."

Clay and Marion looked at each other, then followed Walks Tall to where the side of beef was roasting over the fire; neither of them worrying too much about the rustlers starving before getting into a jail cell in Seymour. Besides, when they thought about it, what Walks Tall had said made a good deal of sense.

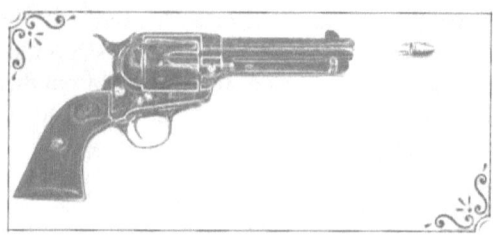

CHAPTER TEN

-

The white men made coffee, a pot of beans and a large pan of biscuits to go with the beef the Indians were roasting over a large fire, and shared it with them.

While they were enjoying their meal, the voice of one of the outlaws came from the area where they were tied to the train cars.

"Hey, we're hungry too. How about feedin' us instead of them stinkin' redskins? What kind of ah white men are you putin' them red scum above ah white man?"

Clay looked at the others and saw their contempt, then stood up. Carrying his tin plate with him, he walked down to where the outlaws were tied to the sides of the cattle cars.

What he saw disgusted and saddened him. It was hard to believe that men, no matter what their skin color was, would allow themselves to sink this low. Except for the man standing at the far end, not far behind the engine, they were all far overdue for a bath and a shave and had no right to call the Indians stinking. He could easily smell them long before he got close to them. Their clothes were filthy to the point they needed to be burned instead of washed.

He'd been out on the trail for days at a time where there was no chance of getting a bath, but tried his best to stay clean, even if it was nothing more than a sponge bath taken from water seeping from a crack in a rock, or a small pool somewhere; but these men, for whatever reason, had obviously chosen not to do so. Maybe they were so used to their own filth, their smell didn't bother them.

As he stood in front of them, eating slowly, they eyed him with hungry eyes, staring at him like a tied up animal who would not only eat his food, but him as well.

"So, you boys are hungry, are ya?" Clay asked, taking a bite of meat, and letting the juice run down his chin.

"You know we are, you Indian lovin' bastard," a heavyset man who could stand to lose a pound or two, said. He had a full beard, beady eyes, and brown, tobacco stained teeth that showed when he spit in Clay's direction.

Clay wiped his chin, then shook his head. "Let me get this straight. As I recollect, you stole my cattle, then sent a man ta shoot me if I came lookin' for'em."

"So what's yer point?" the heavyset outlaw asked before Clay could go farther. "Don't change the fact that we're white men an they's filthy Injuns, an you're feed'in them an lett'in us go hungry!"

Clay looked at him and shook his head. He was like so many of the white people who thought of the Indian as uneducated heathens who should be eliminated from the face of the earth. He stared at the heavyset man with contempt, wondering how he could think he was better than them? Truth be told, probably not one of these men knew much about the red man, nor had they spent any time with them. If they had, and were honest about it, they would sing a different tune. In Clay's mind, not a one of them was worthy to stand alongside the worst Indian he'd ever met.

After swallowing a mouthful of food, Clay looked at the heavyset man and said, "Those filthy Injuns, as you called them, have more integrity in their little fingers than any of you do in your entire body."

"And yes, they were gonna steal a few head ta feed their women and children because white men like you killed all the buffalo, which they prefer to cattle, but when they saw the brands, they knew the cattle were mine and my friends, and instead of stealing any of them, which they could' a done easy enough, they took the cattle away from you and held them here, along with you, until we could get here to reclaim our cattle and take charge of you. Now, think about it, who should I worry about feedin', the white trash that stole my cattle and shot one of our men, or the Indians who got our cattle back for us?"

Carlyle spoke for the first time. "You have no grounds to hold me, Mister Brentwood. I came here in good faith, expecting to buy cattle with a clean bill of sale. I did not know they were stolen; nor did I know they belonged to you and your friend."

"Like hell you did," Zeb, the leader of the rustlers, yelled.

"Shut up!" Carlyle yelled back.

Zeb looked at Clay and said, "Don't matter no how, rancher. It's just yer word against ours that we stole yer cattle. Who's ta say we weren't told they was bought and paid for cattle and we was just deliverin'm ta that man down there," he said nodding his head toward Carlyle. "He's the one that needs ah bill of sale. He's the one what tole us ta cull out five hundred of the best ones and bring'm here."

Clay looked down toward JW Carlyle, who was staring at Zeb with hatred in his eyes.

"So's it looks like you'd best be turnin' us lose, mister rancher man, or we're liable ta sue ya fer wrongful doin', an holdin' us again our will," Zeb said, triumphantly.

"Now that ain't what that fella you left guardin' your back trail, said. Accordin' ta him you and Carlyle down there were in cahoots in the cattle rustlin' business," Clay said.

"An where is that fella now?" Zeb asked. "I don't see him struttin' round yer camp."

Clay sighed and said, "He decided a bullet was a better way ta die than a rope."

Zeb grinned and looked at his men, then back to Clay. "Well ain't that just Jim-dandy. I reckon even ah dumb rancher like you is smart enough ta know that dead men cain't do no testifin'."

"That's true enough, but the judge will have my word on it," Clay said casually.

"And who are you, mister Injun lover – high an mighty rancher man?"

Clay took his time and retrieved his Ranger badge from his vest pocket and held it up.

Technically, he'd served his time as a ranger, but had been told by Bill McDaniel to keep his badge in case he might be needed again. Clay looked at the cattle thieves and figured this might count as one of those times.

"Clay Brentwood, Texas Ranger," Clay said with a grin.

Clay watched as their expressions sunk at the sight of the Ranger badge.

Again, Clay looked at them and said with a casual voice, "As a Texas Ranger I have the authority to arrest ya and do as I see fit. And as the rancher you stole cattle from, I can hang ya right here and be acquitted by the judge in Seymour for savin' the state the time and money it will cost for them ta do the same thing."

Clay watched as what he'd just said sunk in. They were doomed no matter which way it went.

About then, Walks Tall and Marion Sooner walked up and stood next to Clay.

"I'm thinking, instead of hanging them, how about turning them over to us?" Walks Tall asked, seeing their eyes go wide at the thought of being turned over to the Indians.

"You ain't gonna do that, are ya, Ranger? You got ah responsibility ta take us inta Seymour and turn us over ta the law," one of the rustlers said.

"Shut up," Zeb said. "He ain't gonna hang us or turn us over ta them redskins. He's a Texas Ranger and he's got one of them codes of ethics they go by. Ain't that right, Mister Texas Ranger man?"

Clay turned and looked at Walks Tall. "I guess if I was out checkin' my cattle and they was ta up and disappear without me knowin' where they went, I'd have my cattle back and that would be the end of it. Wouldn't be no need ta go lookin' for'em would there? I could tell the judge in Seymour they escaped while I was seein' to my property."

Zeb had a panicked look on his face. "Ya can't do that! You gotta take us inta Seymour and turn us over ta the law, there. You promise ta do that and I'll tell ya anything ya want ta know."

"Talk," Clay said, staring at Zeb with a look that broached no lies.

Zeb licked his lips, took a breath and then said, "Carlyle and me's been doin' business fer several years now. He tells us where and how many ta take and where ta deliver'm. He's the boss - the one that sets everthin' up. We just do what we're tole, and if I gotta hang, he's gonna hang right along side of us."

All the while, Carlyle stood silently, watching and waiting. He had known all along, when the chips were down, Zeb would turn on him and he was prepared.

Looking toward Clay, Carlyle called out, "Mister Brentwood, if you would be so kind as to look in the breast pocket of my coat, you'll find a bill of sale given to me by Zeb and signed by him stating he bought five hundred head of cattle from you. You'll notice it also has your signature and since I've never seen your handwriting, I would have no idea whether or not it had been forged by Zeb or one of his men."

Clay walked down and retrieved the bill of sale from Carlyle's coat pocket and examined it. It looked real enough, except that wasn't his signature on it. Someone had forged his name.

He then walked back and showed it to Zeb. "That your signature?"

Zeb was about to blow a cork, he was so angry. "I didn't know what I was signin'. I thought it was a receipt for the money he was ta pay us. I cain't read. It was Carlyle what taught me ta sign my name."

Clay nodded his head and walked back to Carlyle. "What about the five hundred head they stole from Mister Sooner? You have a receipt for them too?"

JW Carlyle looked Clay in the face and said, "I don't know anything about them. I only contracted for five hundred head of cattle. Maybe he thought he could sell them to me as well, I don't know. Possibly, if the price was right and he had a bill of sale signed by Mister Sooner, I might have bought them.

By now, Clay and Marion's men, along with several of the Indians had come down and stood watching in silence.

Clay walked back and stood in front of Marion Sooner and asked, "What'ya think, should I give'm to the Indians or take'm inta Seymour and turn'em over to the law?"

Marion scratched his ear and said, "That's ah hard call - too close for me to say."

Marion reached into his pants pocket and pulled out a coin. "Maybe we'd best leave it to chance."

Marion flipped the coin into the air and said, "Heads, the Indians get'm, tails, they go to Seymour."

Every man there watched as the coin turned over and over as it flew through the air and finally landed in the palm of Marion Sooner's left hand, which he immediately covered up with his right hand.

"Well, what's the verdict?" Clay asked with a slight snicker in his voice.

Taking his time, Marion bent his head close to his hands and opened them just enough so he could peek at the coin.

After looking at the coin, he dropped it back into his pants pocket and grinned, which drew a groan from the outlaws, thinking they knew the answer.

"Are you gonna tell us or not?" Clay asked.

With a big sigh, Marion said, "Looks like they're going to Seymour," which received an audible sigh from the rustlers.

After some discussion, it was decided Marion, along with his men and Walks Tall and his braves would drive the cattle back to the respective ranches, while Clay and his men took the cattle rustlers into Seymour by way of Carlyle's train.

"You tell the sheriff and the judge, if they need me to, I'll come into Seymour and file charges as well," Marion told Clay just before Clay boarded the engine.

Clay nodded and said, "Don't think it will be necessary, but I'll tell'm."

"Take us into Seymour," Clay told the engineer, who had been cleared of any charges. Neither the engineer nor the tender knew Carlyle. They had only met him two days ago when the engineer agreed to drive Carlyle's train to pick up some local cattle and deliver them to Chicago.

"He told me he'd been having a hard time finding an engineer with enough free time to make that kind of a trip," the engineer had told Clay. "I was let go about three months back because they said I was gettin' too old. Since I have nothing but time on my hands now, and the money he quoted was good. I agreed to drive his train for him. I was to get paid in Chicago, but now I guess that's not gonna happen."

Clay laid his hand on the man's shoulder and said, "Don't worry old timer, I'll see that you get your money, even if I have to pay you, myself."

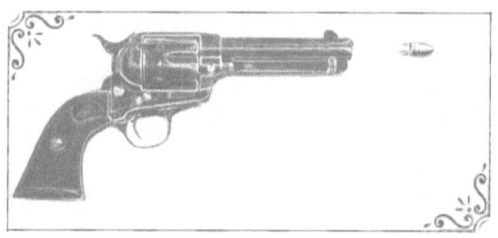

CHAPTER ELEVEN

The people of Seymour, Texas watched as the train pulled into the station and were curious as to why there were dirty, greasy looking men in one of the boxcars instead of cattle, while the private car had cowboys from the BR ranch, and another car held their horses.

Clay swung down from the engine and walked along the cars to the station where the sheriff was standing, looking at the train and scratching his head as he watched Clay coming toward him.

Sticking out his hand toward his friend, the sheriff, Clay asked, "You meet every train that comes in, Hank?"

"Purtnere, the sheriff said, reaching for Clay's outstretched hand. "I kinda like knowin' who's comin' and goin'. Makes for ah more peaceful town."

Hank Singleton was a powerfully built man, a head taller than Clay and had him by a good twenty pounds. He was only thirty-nine, but his hair had already started turning gray because he was a worrier. Clay knew he ran a quiet town and could back up his play when the occasion arose. He might not be the fastest gun around, but he rarely missed what he shot at. And if it came to a rough and tumble, Hank's size and reputation as a man who could stand with the best of them came in handy.

"Those hombres in the boxcars belong to you?" the sheriff asked with a grin.

"Only til I turn'em over ta you," Clay said with a smile, as they watched his men unload their horses, along with the rustlers mounts, leaving the rustlers in the cars until Clay or the sheriff gave them the okay to unload them.

Clay didn't know what else to do with the outlaw's horses, so he brought them along in case any of the rustlers had relatives or some such who could come and get them.

Otherwise, they would be sold at auction, with the money going to the town to help pay their expenses.

"It's only ah wild guess, but I'm guessin', cattle rustlers?" the sheriff asked, looking at the men staring at him from the cattle cars, knowing Clay had a large spread to the west of Seymour.

"That would be ah good guess," Clay replied. "They stole ah thousand head. Five hundred of mine and five hundred of Marion Sooners."

"How many of them are there?"

"Used ta be twenty one. Now it's twenty. Had ah run-in with one of'm and he pulled iron on me and I had ta kill him."

The sheriff nodded his head.

"Nineteen of'em are rustlers hired by the man in the suit, who also owns this train. Goes by JW Carlyle. Don't know if that's his real name or not. He came by my place a few weeks ago wantin' ta look at my spread, and after he'd looked at'm, he told me he wanted to buy five hundred head – offered top dollar. I agreed and promised ta deliver'm ta Abilene a few weeks from now.

"One of the rustlers who goes by, Zeb, told me that's how he operated. He'd pretend ta be ah cattle buyer, and if he liked what he saw, offer ta buy five hundred head, then send his men ta steal the cattle, leavin' most ranchers with nothin' ta sell and he'd wind up with five hundred head of prime beef, for almost nothin'."

Hank Singleton looked toward the boxcars and saw the man dressed in a suit, staring back at him.

"Heard that name before. A small rancher up north claimed ah man by the name of Carlyle promised ta buy five hundred head from him and his cattle disappeared before he could deliver them. Said Abilene was where he was ta take'm too. Said he didn't have but three hundred left ta take, and took'em up there, hopin' this Carlyle fella would take them, but when he got up there, this Carlyle fella was no where ta be found. Told me he had ta turn around and drive his cows back and start over."

"Sounds like the same man ta me," Clay said.

"Twenty, ya say. That's ah site ta hang all at one time," the sheriff said, nodding his head up and down.

"Reckon that'll be up ta the judge," Clay offered.

"Well, let's get'em down ta the jail where you can sign the papers again'm and then we can go have somethin' ta eat. I didn't get a chance ta eat breakfast and I'm hungry."

Clay looked at the sky and saw it was directly overhead. He directed his men to unload the prisoners and take them down to the jailhouse. He told Riley that after he'd signed charges against Carlyle and his bunch, he and the sheriff would meet them at the cafe.

As Riley and the others were unloading the prisoners, one of them broke loose and ran toward Clay. The man was holding a hideout pistol he'd hidden in his boot. Clay looked up in time to see the man raise the pistol and put pressure on the trigger.

One second, Clay was standing, empty handed, talking with the sheriff and the next, he stood holding a smoking forty-four pointed toward the outlaw with the hideout gun. The outlaw was laying flat on his back with a bullet dead center in his chest, the small pistol still clutched in his hand. In his death throw, the outlaw had squeezed the trigger of the small derringer, but the bullet had gone harmlessly into the dirt near his feet.

"Make that, nineteen," the sheriff said, shaking his head. "Sure glad you're on our side."

As they marched the rest of the cattle rustlers toward the jail, a small crowd of people were staring and making comments. It had happened so fast that none of them had seen Clay draw and fire. It would be a story to be told many times and embellished by each teller, as time went by.

An elderly man and his wife, who had witnessed the shooting, took particular interest in the badge pinned on Clay's vest.

Clay passed within a few feet of the couple and as Clay presented his back to them, the old man turned and spoke to the tall, skinny man standing next to him, "That was some shooting. Would you happen to know the man's name?"

The tall, skinny man grinned and said, "Yes, it was. But I'm not surprised. Reckon most folks around here know who he is, but I guess I probably know him better than most. I'm his barber. Name's Rance Tilford and his name is Clay Brentwood. He's not only a big rancher in these parts, but also a Texas Ranger and the best one they have, if I do say so myself."

Horace Libersky nodded his head and said, "A Texas Ranger, you say. I'm impressed. Thank you neighbor. And you say he's one of the best?"

"The best, in my books," the barber said with assurance. "Did you see how fast he drew and fired and hit the man dead center in the chest? Nope, they don't come any better than Mister Brentwood."

Horace and Luella eased away from the crowd and made their way to the hotel without speaking, but once they were back in their room, Luella said, "Looks like this one won't be quite as easy as we thought. Did you see how fast he drew and fired? And he did it without a warning of any kind! I saw the man coming with that small gun in his hand and thought maybe he would do our job for us. The ranger wasn't even facing him. The man must have a very wide range of vision and seen him out of the corner of his eye."

Horace pulled his gray wig off and laid it on the dresser, then loosened the top button on his shirt. The weather was turning cool, but even so, Horace was sweating. "I saw, but I didn't see. I've never seen a man who could draw and shoot that fast. And for sure, not be able to shoot that accurate," Horace said with a tremble in his voice. His hand was shaking as he reached for the whiskey bottle sitting on the stand next to the bed.

Horace didn't bother with a glass. He put the bottle to his lips and chug-a-lugged a long swallow, hoping the liquor would help calm his nerves. This was a new wrinkle he hadn't had to face before and he wasn't sure how he felt about it.

"Oh don't be so nervous," Luella said. "Maybe this once we'll have to change our tactics, but we'll still get the job done."

"That's easy for you to say," Horace said, "but you're not the one that has to face him."

Horace took another pull from the bottle of whiskey and wiped his lips on his shirtsleeve.

"No, I'm not, but I'm in this up to my neck just like you are," she said, taking the whiskey bottle from Horace and pouring a drink for herself in one of the glasses sitting on the small table next to the bed. After taking a sip and feeling the raw whiskey begin to calm her insides, she asked, "Don't I always find a way?"

Horace looked at the floor and nodded his head up and down.

As she sat down on the bed and took another sip of her whiskey, an idea began to formulate in her head.

"Maybe this time, I will do the shooting, or maybe both of us at the same time. I may not be as good as you are Horace, but if the conditions were right?"

Horace's head came up and he stared at Luella with a confused look on his face like he couldn't believe what he'd just heard. She had never mentioned wanting to actually take part in the killings before.

The more Luella turned the idea over in her mind, the better she liked it and she began to get excited as her thoughts began to grow.

Horace took another swallow of the rotgut whiskey and felt it burn its way down his throat. He wasn't sure how to approach this new idea of her or both of them doing the shooting. What could she be thinking about?

"Yes, my dear, you always find a way – and as always we pass the blame onto some poor slob who doesn't know a thing about it until he's arrested. But what you'll come up with this time, I have no clue. You've always stayed in the background before. And for the life of me, I can't think of anyone in their sane mind who would broach this ranger unless they had a death wish."

Luella tipped her glass and emptied it, then set the empty glass on the side table and reclined on the bed and raised her arms. She wasn't quite ready to reveal her thoughts, and needed time to cultivate them – and Horace needed to be relaxed when she finally revealed her new plan.

Horace stared down at her and felt his nervousness evaporating. He sat down on the side of the bed and pulled off his shoes, anticipating what her raised arms meant.

It wasn't long before Horace forgot all about killing the ranger.

With no clue that his death was being planned, Clay signed papers charging Carlyle and his bunch with the rustling of both his and Marion Sooner's cattle, along with attempted murder, stating dates, times and places.

While Clay was doing this, the sheriff had a thought and went to have a talk with Carlyle.

Clay had just signed his name as the sheriff walked back into the room. Clay grinned and held up the paperwork.

"While you were busy tryin' ta figure out how ta sign your name, I had a thought and went back to ask Carlyle and his men about it," the sheriff said with a smile.

"What thought was that?" Clay asked, sidestepping the sheriff's attempt at humor.

"Well, I got ta wondering what I was gonna do with their possessions? You know, guns, horses, money and whatever else they might have. So, I went back and asked if any of them had a relative I should contact - but not a one of'em does."

"Looks like the sheriff's office is about ta inherit ah few more firearms and maybe some money," Clay said with a grin.

"Looks like," the sheriff said with a grin, the seed of an idea building in his mind, but not wanting to mention it yet. He wanted to wait and talk to the judge about it. If he could pull it off, it would make for a nice surprise.

With Clay, his men and the sheriff, along with the regular customers, the small cafe was crowded. No one seemed to mind having to wait a little longer for their food. In fact, they were more interested in hearing about how Clay and his men had captured the outlaws than they were about eating. It wasn't every day a gang of outlaws the size of this one was captured and brought into town. As far as the people of Seymour were concerned, Clay Brentwood, Texas Ranger just went up another notch on their tote board.

The sheriff ordered food to be taken to the jail for the prisoners. "But wait til one of my deputies is there ta oversee things," he told the waitress. "They're ah mean bunch and I don't want nobody gettin' hurt."

Once the sheriff had taken his seat at the table, everyone looked at Clay, waiting to hear the story.

Clay was wise enough to pass the telling over to somebody who enjoyed doing this sort of thing - Riley.

With arms waving and his voice going from low to high and back down again, Riley was having a heyday. If Clay or the other hands made notice of the slight embellishments Riley added from time to time, none of them said anything. If anything, they were more focused on trying to hide the chuckles they felt. Walks Tall couldn't have done any better.

After their meal, Clay instructed Riley and the men to take the horses down to the livery barn and see they were rubbed down and given a good bait of oats, while he and the sheriff went to see the judge.

They had just left the cafe when they saw the judge coming down the sidewalk and approached him.

"That was some piece of shooting you did down at the station, I was told," the judge said, shaking Clay's hand.

Judge Limon Hoffmeyer was in his sixties, but looked younger. He was about the same size and build as Clay, but was turning gray around his temples. And instead of using a buggy to get around, he rode a fine Appaloosa stallion he'd acquired from Clay two years back. For several years, he'd been the town's only lawyer, but as the town grew, two more attorneys moved in, and Hoffmeyer was elected judge.

The town was pleased they had done so because he was considered to be a fair and honest man that could and did wield out justice with an iron fist.

"How's Lawyer?" Clay asked - chuckling to himself over the name the judge had given his horse because of his feistiness and always wanting his own way.

"I'm guessing he can still keep up with that black stallion of yours," the judge said with a grin.

Wanting to expedite their business, the sheriff interjected, "Are you available to go to your office, Judge? I'd like to get this business over and done with as soon as I can. Twenty men will eat us out of house and home real quick like, and I don't want the town council on my back for lollygaggin'."

"Yes. As a matter of fact, this would be the perfect time. I assume the papers are signed and the witnesses are available?" he asked.

"Yes sir. Everything is in order and ready," the sheriff said.

"What about court convening at two o'clock? Can you have twelve jurors rounded up by then?" the judge asked.

"Two o'clock will be just fine, Judge. And I can't imagine finding a jury of twelve honest men in this town to be a problem," the sheriff said, shaking the judge's hand.

The town had not yet built an official courthouse so the church was deemed to be an ideal place to use until they could get one built.

While the sheriff was out passing the word and collecting twelve men to serve on the jury, Clay and the judge went to the judge's office and talked.

In his official capacity as a Texas Ranger, Clay related the story to the judge about what had happened, including his ideas about what had happened to other ranchers.

The judge nodded, recalling a similar incident a month or so back.

"I'm sure, with all the evidence against them, it won't take long for the jury to come to a decision," the judge said, ushering Clay to the door. "I'll see you at two, and not a word about our talk to anyone."

Clay nodded his head as he walked down the stairs. Sometimes justice had a way of getting what it wanted with only a little help here and there.

Down on the sidewalk, Clay headed for the livery stable. He wanted to head off his men before they made it to the saloon bent on celebrating.

Clay wanted them sober when they went on the witness stand. They could celebrate later, when the trial was over, and not before.

CHAPTER TWELVE

It was the fastest turnaround time from arrest to trial in the history of Seymour, Texas.

The church was set up; volunteers for jury duty acquired, and the prisoners marched through the center of town to the church under six quickly deputized townsmen.

The judge was in the back room, about to dawn his robe when the sheriff entered and asked to speak with him.

After hearing what the sheriff had to say, Judge Hoffmeyer smiled and said, "I will take that into consideration after hearing the verdict from the jury."

"That's all I can ask for, Limon," the sheriff said as he turned and left the room.

The judge was about to make his way into the makeshift courtroom when the sheriff entered the room again, and said Carlyle was demanding to speak with him before the trial began.

The judge thought for a moment, then said, "Tell him if he has something to say, he will get his chance in the courtroom."

When the judge entered the courtroom, he saw the hatred in Carlyle's eyes. One look told him the man was used to getting his way and he was seething with anger.

The judge could tell by the way Carlyle was dressed; he didn't like being treated like the men he was sitting with. He had a smug look and sat apart from them.

"Well Mister Carlyle, you should have given that some consideration before starting this whole mess," the judge said to himself.

"All rise," the bailiff called out as the judge walked over and sat down at the table that had been set up for his use.

The judge went through the preliminaries of opening a trial, then looked at the men sitting on the front pew bench and asked, "Do any of you have anything to say before this trial begins?"

Carlyle was on his feet almost by the time the judge finished his question. "I do, your Honor," he said, adjusting his suit coat.

"And you are?" the judge asked.

"JW Carlyle, your Honor. I am an innocent victim here, and demand to have my lawyer present so I may refute the charges against me."

"You speak very well for an accused cattle thief," the judge stated, then asked, "And on what grounds do you believe yourself to be innocent?"

"May I approach the bench, your Honor?" Carlyle asked respectfully.

Judge Hoffmeyer considered Carlyle's request for a moment, knowing the man had the right to request an attorney. He motioned for Carlyle to come forward - his interest and curiosity piqued.

Carlyle approached the desk where the judge sat and laid some papers on the desk in front of the judge.

"This is a bill of sale given to me by a man named Zeb, whose last name I don't know, who I understand is the ramrod of the men he works with. I was given to understand he had purchased the said cattle from Mister Brentwood and was selling them to me. I am a victim here and was apparently duped by these men."

Judge Hoffmeyer looked at the man standing in front of him and had to admire his audacity.

"I will grant your request for an attorney to represent you, but to expedite matters, he must be one from here in town."

Looking out over the crowd, the judge noticed Clarence Bowden, Seymour's newest attorney and motioned him forward. He liked the young man and decided to give him some business, and follow the letter of the law at the same time by providing Carlyle with representation. In the judge's mind, Carlyle didn't have a leg to stand on, but the man had requested an attorney and by god he'd have one.

When the young attorney approached the bench, the judge said, "I am assigning you to represent this man in this case."

The judge looked at Carlyle who was about to protest and said, "It's him or no one. His fee is one hundred dollars. Pay the man, or go back to your seat and shut up."

Young Bowden's eyes went wide. A hundred dollars was more money than he'd seen in the four months he'd been here.

The judge rapped his wooden hammer on the table and said, "We will take a fifteen minute recess while Mister Carlyle confers with his attorney."

Wanting to be fair, he looked at the other outlaws and asked, "Do any of you want to be represented by council?"

Zeb was the first one to raise his hand, then following Zeb's lead, the others raised their hands, also.

The judge nodded his head and continued. "The attorney's fee is one hundred dollars apiece – payable in advance."

Every hand was lowered and the judge nodded. "So be it. Let the record show the defendants were offered council and all but Mister Carlyle, declined it."

Clay watched the procedure with a slight grin gracing his face.

"What about my signed papers and the things I told you?" Carlyle asked the judge.

"You have fifteen minutes to bring your attorney up to date. I advise you to use that time wisely. When Mister Bowden presents your case during the course of the trial, I will take the information under advisement. After all the testimony has been heard, along with the decision of the jury, I will render my findings. You may go back and take your seat and consult with Mister Bowden," he told Carlyle, who glared at him.

As the judge watched Carlyle walk back and sit down, he muttered to himself, "This man has just enough learning to make him dangerous. I'll need to be careful."

Back in his chambers, the judge studied one of his law books, searching for information, and when the fifteen minutes was up, he returned to the courtroom, such as it was.

One by one, the witnesses, mostly Clay's riders, all came to the stand and said about the same thing, which didn't surprise the judge. It was simple and straightforward.

When Clay was finally sworn in and took the stand, the judge took special notice. This was not only a man he held in high regard, but also a Texas Ranger. He'd already heard the story once, but as duty dictated, he listened again, making notes in case he had missed something or needed to clear up any small points.

As far as the judge was concerned, Clay's information pretty well sealed the rustler's fates, but it was the notice of a surprise witness that did it for him.

When he'd asked the sheriff if there were anymore witnesses, the sheriff said, "Yes, your Honor. I have one more witness. He was not a part of this case but I believe his testimony is relevant to this trial."

Carlyle looked over and saw the rancher he'd duped a few months before and felt his heart begin to pound.

"I object!" Carlyle shouted, standing up and looking at the judge.

"On what grounds, Mister Carlyle?" the judge asked.

"On the grounds that he's not part of this case. That's what the sheriff said, didn't he? He's not part of this case," Carlyle pleaded, panic in his voice.

"The sheriff also said he thought this man's testimony would shed light on the case," the judge said. "I'm going to allow it for now. If it turns out not to be relevant, I will dismiss him, and instruct the jury to disregard anything he may have said.

Clarence Bowden stood up, knowing he had not a chance in the world of winning the case, but had been, by the judge's order, retained to represent the defendant, JW Carlyle, and doing his duty, he said, "In due respect, your Honor, since this new witness has no part in this case, I would like to make a motion disallowing any and all testimony he might present, before he influences the jury falsely."

The judge looked down at the new, young lawyer and thought for a moment, then said, "Overruled, I'm going to allow him to testify. I'm interested to hear what the man has to say."

Clarence Bowden didn't like the idea of losing, but the judge had dropped the case in his lap. Carlyle reminded him of a cunning weasel caught in a trap of his own doing and looking for a way out, leaving those dirty miscreants who said they worked for him to take all the blame. Bowden smiled as he sat back down, win, lose, or draw, he had one hundred dollars resting comfortably in his pocket.

The judge recognized the surprise witness as soon as he stood up and headed for the witness stand, and thought to himself, 'Well played, sheriff, well played.

Elmer Osgood was the small rancher whose place was north of town and had come to see him a few months ago about losing five hundred head of cattle that he said a man named Carlyle had promised to buy, but this Carlyle had disappeared by then.

Judge Hoffmeyer glanced over at Carlyle. The man was visibly shaken and his face had taken on the color of burnt wood ashes.

During Osgood's testimony, he pointed out Carlyle as the man who had promised to buy his cattle, but was not in Abilene when he went to see him after his cattle had been stolen.

"Purely coincidence!" Carlyle jumped up and shouted. "I purchased other cattle for a lesser price and had to deliver them."

"Sit down and be quiet, Mister Carlyle. You'll get your say in due course," the judge admonished.

Carlyle slumped back down on his seat. Clarence Bowden turned to him and said, "If you have anything to say, do it through me, Mister Carlyle. Whether you like it or not, I am your attorney!"

JW Carlyle was the first to take the stand and in a very convincing voice told the jury how he'd been misled and how this whole thing was a big mistake and if Zeb and the others were cattle rustlers, he'd known nothing about it.

Zeb started to protest, but the judge waved him down, telling him he, too, would get his turn.

The judge watched the men of the jury closely. The sheriff had chosen wisely. All of them were either ranchers or farmers and wouldn't be easily fooled by Carlyle's slick talk.

When Zeb took the stand, he told a completely different tale about how Carlyle had contacted him and how they'd struck a bargain. Carlyle was to set up the cattle to be stolen, along with instructions where to get them and where to deliver them.

The rest of the rustlers said they took orders from Zeb, but had never actually talked to Carlyle. They'd only heard his name mentioned by Zeb.

The jury was out for only ten minutes and brought in a verdict of guilty for all of them.

Carlyle jumped up and demanded a retrial for himself with his own lawyer present. He had property and bank accounts that needed seen to and if he allowed himself to be railroaded in this kangaroo court, it would all be lost.

The judge had heard enough and looked at Carlyle and said, "Mister Carlyle you're an intelligent man and as far as I'm concerned, a flim-flam man to boot. I'm sure you knew, here in Texas, the penalty for horse or cattle thieving is hanging; which you should have thought of before plying your trade in this state. You have legally been found guilty by a jury of your peers, so your request is denied."

"But what of my assets?" Carlyle cried.

The judge thought for a moment then said, "You'll be escorted to my office where you can give me all the information pertaining to your properties and I will see that it goes to help the people you've stolen from and if there are any funds left, they will go to help build schools, or hospitals."

"But, but..." Carlyle started to say, but the judge slammed his gavel down against the desk several times, bringing quiet to the courtroom.

Looking at the accused men staring back at him, the judge said, "You have been found guilty of cattle rustling on more than one account by a jury of your peers. As dictated by the laws of the state of Texas, I sentence each of you to be hanged by the neck until dead, three days from today." He knew they would need some time to build the scaffold.

Again, he slammed his gavel down on the desk and turned to the men of the jury. "The court thanks you for your time and commitment to justice. You are excused. Dinner at the hotel restaurant will be served at six o'clock for each of you, paid for by the town of Seymour. Thank you again for your service."

He rapped his hammer down on the desk a third time and said, "Case closed."

As he stood up, he looked at the sheriff and said, "I would appreciate it if you would bring Mister Carlyle to my office."

The sheriff nodded and watched as the judge left.

Two hours later, Clay was summoned to the judge's office by the sheriff. Clay looked at the sheriff and asked, "What does he want from me, now?"

"Reckon you'll have ta ask him," the sheriff said with a broad grin.

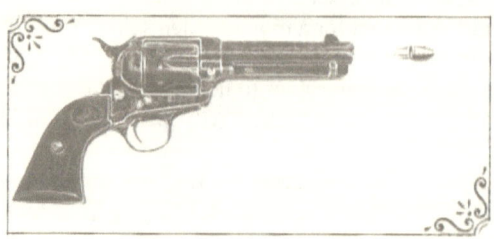

CHAPTER THIRTEEN

Over drinks, the judge told them they had found papers in Carlyle's private train car that had given his real name and his bank account information, along with other information.

"The man has enough money to repay every rancher we can find that was a victim, and enough left over to be of some real help to the school and hospital systems here in Texas."

"Well, that's real nice ta hear, judge, but what's that got ta do with me?"

The judge grinned and poured each of them another drink. "Actually, spreading the money around to the ranchers and schools and hospitals was the sheriff's idea, along with one other idea that I agreed with."

Clay glanced over toward the sheriff who was grinning from ear to ear. He lifted his glass as though he was making a toast and nodded his head.

"What's goin' on here?" Clay asked. "What have you two been cookin' up?"

The judge took a long pull from his drink, smacked his lips and set the glass on his desk. "Mister Brentwood, you've gone out of your way to help make the state of Texas a safer place to live and there are those of us who appreciate what you've done... and continue to do. So... with that in mind, we'd like you to have something as a reward for what you've done."

The sheriff was grinning like he just done something very mischievous.

Clay raised his hands. "Whoa. I'm not lookin' for any reward. Besides, I don't need the money. I was railroaded inta becomin' ah ranger in the first place, so, if you don't mind... just keep the money, and..."

The judge raised his hand for Clay to stop talking. When he did, the judge said, "You've got it all wrong. We're not offering you a financial reward and we know all about how you came to be a Texas Ranger. It's what you've done since then that we're talking about."

"I don't understand." Clay said, totally confused by now.

The sheriff spoke up. "Clay, what do you do when you want to take some cattle up to Abilene or Wichita?"

Clay looked at him and said, "I do like any other rancher, I reckon - I round up however many cows I want ta take, and then I contact my friend, Marion Sooner ta see if he wants ta take some, too, and if he does, we make a drive. Otherwise, I go by myself."

"Wouldn't it be easier if there was another way?" the sheriff asked, casually.

"What'er you talkin' about, Hank?" Clay asked, eyeing his friend with suspicion."

"What I'm talking about is taking them by train," the sheriff answered.

"Huh?" Clay said, scratching his neck.

"What the sheriff is saying, Mister Brentwood, is that you are now the proud owner of your own train and can ship your cattle by rail anytime you want to."

"My own train? What the dickens are you talkin' about?" Clay asked.

"You heard me correctly," the judge said. "Mister Carlyle owned that train, and we have to do something with it. The sheriff thought it might be a good idea if we gave it to you in appreciation for what you've done to help clean up this state."

Clay was speechless. He was having a hard time digesting what the judge had just said. He now owned a train? But how was he going to get it home? There were no tracks going to his ranch or Marion's. He would have to leave it here or on that spur line Carlyle had used."

"Let me get this straight. You're tellin' me you're givin' me Carlyle's train free and clear?"

"By Jove, I think you've got it," the judge said, chuckling. "Along with the engine and cars comes several spur lines where mister Carlyle kept it when it wasn't in use."

Clay downed his drink to calm his nerves. He'd thought about how much easier it would be to ship horses and cattle by rail if he owned his own train, but had left it at that. Now, out of the blue, he owned a train and some railroad track. Then a thought hit him. What about coal and water and an engineer to run the damn thing? Why didn't they sell it to somebody? The town would make a nice profit. Where was the catch?"

When he posed these concerns to the judge, the judge chuckled and said, "Mister Brentwood, you're a smart man and I'm sure you'll figure things out. But there is one thing. There are no catches." And with that he slid the ownership papers for the train and spur lines across his desk. "They've been signed and witnessed by me."

The sheriff grinned. "If you recall, the judge mentioned Carlyle left ah ton of money in ah bank up north under his real name, Sydney Meier. We found the papers in that private train car of his." He shook his head. "Oh yeah, there's one other thing, you've also got your own private train car ta ride in when you make your deliveries. How about them apples?"

Clay sat there, speechless. What would his men think? He now owned a train with his own private car. They would whoo-raw him to no end.

The judge smiled as he escorted Clay to the door, slapping him on the back. "I think this calls for a celebration – drinks and dinner on you... Mister Railroad Tycoon."

Clay left the judge's chamber, muttering to himself something about this all being Bill McDaniel's fault for forcing him into the Rangers in the first place.

As he walked toward the hotel, he thought, 'If Martha was only here ta see this.' He would bet she would like the idea of having a private train car to ride in, and he hoped she would be proud of him.

He heard music coming from the saloon and changed directions. This called for a small celebration - just one drink with his men. It wasn't everyday ah man became ah railroad tycoon.

CHAPTER FOURTEEN

Still posing as an elderly couple, Luella and Horace sat in the far corner of the hotel dining room eating their supper and quietly discussing their problem.

"We could blame this one on the judge. I could make you look like him but we would have to make sure the judge was someplace out of the way – preferably where he wouldn't have anyone to collaborate his whereabouts."

"I can't just walk up and shoot him!" Horace whispered, trying to control his fear. "You saw how fast he is with a gun. He would kill me before I could get my gun out."

Luella looked across the table at Horace and shook her head. "No one's asking you to walk up face to face and shoot him when he has a chance to shoot back. No, sweetie," she said, her eyes staring out of the window as though transfixed.

After a moment, she smiled and said, "I have something else in mind. Something new. Something we've never done before."

Horace cut off a piece of steak and stuck it in his mouth and began to chew. She'd always come through in the past, so he had no reason to believe she wouldn't come up with the perfect plan this time. Still, it would need to be something where there would be no risk of him getting caught, or killed.

Suddenly, she stood up. "I have an errand to run, so be a dear, pay the bill when you're finished, then go up to our room and pack our bags," Luella said, dropping her napkin on the table.

"Are we leaving town?" Horace asked, wondering what was going through that mind of hers.

"No dear, but we may be changing residence," Luella said as she turned and left, leaving Horace in total confusion.

Like an obedient child, Horace finished his supper, then did as he was asked.

Horace was sitting on the chair next to the window of their room when he saw Luella coming down the sidewalk, looking very much like the old woman she was pretending to be. Her gait was slow, and she walked like she had stiffness in her joints. She was very believable and Horace thought for the hundredth time, she should join him on the stage. She would be sensational.

When she entered the room, she pulled off her wig and picked up the half full bottle of whiskey and poured herself half a glass, then sat down in the other chair, which was on the opposite side of the window where she couldn't be seen from the street.

Horace waited patiently for her to tell him what she'd been up to.

After her second sip of the brown liquid that burned all the way down into her stomach, she looked across at Horace and said, "When it gets dark, we'll check out of the hotel and move to that little white house at the edge of town. I rented it for a month, so when this is over, we can take our time about leaving and watch the action."

"What? I don't understand. Does this mean you've come up with a plan?" Horace asked.

She smiled and downed the rest of the whiskey before answering.

"I have," she said. "And it's foolproof."

Shortly after the sun had gone down and the stores had closed for the day, Horace and Luella moved their luggage into the small white house at the edge of town.

As he carried their bags to the bedroom, Horace noticed the inside. It was small, but very clean and nicely furnished. The house was at the south end of town, just far enough away to allow them privacy.

After renting the house, Luella stopped by the general store and purchased food, coffee, and another bottle of whiskey, which she took to the house before returning to the hotel room.

Horace was surprised when he smelled coffee brewing and hurried into the kitchen.

Luella had set the table with a small plate of muffins and was about to pour coffee for both of them when Horace came in and sat down.

"How did you know I was hungry for some muffins?" Horace asked as he took a bite of the muffin and a sip of the steaming hot coffee. "With walnuts. My favorite."

"You always want a muffin with walnuts," Luella said, shaking her head. He was so predictable, she thought to herself.

Luella sat down and took her time enjoying her coffee and muffin. Horace eyed her and saw a twinkle in her eyes.

"You said you would tell me about your plan when we got to the house," Horace said. "Well, here we are."

Luella stood up and walked over to the stove; set the coffee pot off to the side of the heat and then came back and sat down across from Horace and took a sip from her cup.

During his anxious, nervousness, while waiting for her to disclose her plan, Horace had eaten two muffins and was about to reach for another when Luella held up her hand to stop him.

Luella could see he was about to pop a blood vessel and finally explained her plan.

When she finished, Horace sat there as if in a stupor and stared at her. She could almost see the little wheels in his head spinning round and round, trying to digest what she'd just told him.

"It's a perfectly doable plan," Luella said with confidence, hoping he would agree. "There are just a couple of small details to work out and when we clear those up, we'll be ready to take action."

Horace took another sip of his coffee, and nodded his head. "You're right, it is a good plan. I mean it - it's brilliant. I'm always amazed at how you can come up with ideas as easily as you seem to. I do, however, have a couple of suggestions I'd like to offer."

Being the prime player in their little assassin game, Horace had begun to take more interest in the plans Luella came up with, and a couple of times, he'd made some useful suggestions.

"Sure, go ahead. What do you have in mind?" Luella asked, knowing in the end, they would do it the way she wanted.

CHAPTER FIFTEEN

Since Clay was a Texas Ranger and the one who'd brought the rustlers in, he'd been asked to stay for the hanging as a witness, and had promised to do so since it would be the largest hanging Seymour had ever had, and probably the largest one the state of Texas had ever had. The hanging was to be in three days, which gave Clay time to take care of some business.

Since his men were needed on the ranch, he sent them back with instructions to take over for Walks Tall and his braves, who had returned their cattle for them. He also told Riley to see to it that Mrs. McIntyre sent plenty of fresh vegetables with Walks Tall to take to his people for the children; along with the cattle he'd given them.

Since they had grained their horses, along with a night's rest, they all agreed it would be an easy trip back.

"You give Walks Tall a hand in picking out twenty good beef cows," Clay told Riley before seeing them on their way.

They had all been excited about Clay becoming the owner of his own train and Riley grinned and said, "Too bad we cain't take our new train back to the ranch. Sure would be easier than sittin' ah saddle."

"And we'd arrive in grand style," one of the others said.

Clay laughed and said, "And I reckon you'd want ah hot meal and plenty of beer so's you could enjoy your ride better."

"Well, now that you mention it..." Riley said with a big grin.

"Get outta here," Clay said, slapping Riley on the back, "before I send you packin' and hire me some real cowboys."

It was all in good fun and they left still talking about the boss now having a train of his own and how much easier it was going to be come roundup time.

After they'd gone, Clay walked over to the livery and saw to Midnight, his black stallion. Not figuring he would need it, he sent the buckskin back with the men. It was only a little over fifteen miles to the edge of his land, then another nine miles to the ranch house – an easy trip for the black stallion and they didn't need to be in any hurry, so he wouldn't need the second mount.

After seeing to his horse, Clay walked down to the rail yard and had a confab with the engineer, who said, he would take care of the engine and cars on a regular basis, and make himself available to run Clay's train if given a few days notice each time, which Clay agreed to. The old engineer said he would need a tender to help, and said he knew of one; a retired fella like himself. They struck a financial agreement and Clay paid him in advance.

Next, Clay went to see the stationmaster and made arrangements for the train to be stored on the sidetrack next to the depot, for a small sum, paid up front.

By now, it was getting close to suppertime. He was supposed to meet the sheriff and the judge at the hotel near the sheriff's office and headed in that direction.

While all of this was going on, Luella had been busy. Dressed in traveling clothes and made up to look like an affluent Mexican of upper middle class, she'd gone to the local gunsmith and purchased a thirty caliber rifle, stating she was on her way back to Nuevo Laredo and was buying the rifle for her husband as a birthday present.

"Gracias, Senor. My husband, he very much likes to hunt the deer," she said with a Mexican accent. "He will be very pleased with me."

The gunsmith assured her it was a fine rifle, and very accurate.

He watched as she walked out of his shop, thinking, how lucky her husband was to have such a woman as her, then frowned at the thought of his bible thumping wife who hated guns and his business, which, in his opinion, kept her quite nicely. He sighed and then sat down and went back to work on a pistol he'd taken in trade that needed a new firing pin.

-

The hotel restaurant was about half filled up by the time Clay walked in and spied the sheriff sitting at a table in the far corner. It was set for three, but the sheriff was the only one sitting there.

"Guess I beat the judge," Clay said as he pulled out his chair and sat down.

"Got ah message from the judge. Said he'd be a little late."

They waited a respectful time, but when the judge still hadn't shown up, they went ahead and ordered.

"I'll drop by his office when I finish," Clay said, scooping up a mouthful of beans and fried potatoes that went with the steak he'd ordered.

"That'll be fine with me," the sheriff said. I have ta ride out ta one of the ranches. Got ah note sayin' some of his cattle are missin'."

"Need me ta go with ya?" Clay asked.

"Naw, they just probably wandered off," the sheriff replied. "Lots of gullies and ravines out that way, and he's just a small rancher – works the place by himself except during roundup and brandin' time."

The sheriff finished first and left.

A few minutes later, Clay saw him ride past the restaurant, heading out of town.

Clay stood up and patted his stomach. "Shouldn't have had that piece of pie," he said to the man and woman sitting at the table next to him.

They smiled and nodded to Clay, rolling their eyes and smiling.

Before going to the judge's office, which was on the top floor above the mercantile store, he stopped by the livery again. This time he went to the hostler's office and paid his bill.

As he was leaving, he heard a noise and turned to see the judge's appaloosa raising a fuss and walked down to speak to him. For some reason, the horse seemed agitated. Clay looked around the inside the stall but couldn't see anything that would make the horse nervous. He tried to pat his nose, while speaking gently to him, but the horse wouldn't stand still long enough. He even tried to nip Clay's shoulder.

Finally, Clay gave up and left, heading toward the judge's office. He would mention it to the judge and let him take care of it. After all, it was his horse.

As he left the livery barn, a young boy ran up to Clay and gave him a note. Clay gave the boy a dime and watched as he ran down the street in the direction of the confection shop.

The note was simple and to the point. Come by my office. Something important has come up. It was signed by the judge.

Since he was headed there to begin with, he'd find out soon enough what the note was all about.

The judge was just leaving to go meet the sheriff and Clay for supper when the front door opened and two men with small bags over their heads came in. The bags had slits for the eyes to see through, and that was all. In one of the men's hand was a forty-four pistol. The other one was carrying a rifle.

The man with the pistol ordered the judge to turn around and face the wall, and when he did, the second man tied his hands behind his back and put a gag in his mouth; then put a blindfold over his eyes.

He was made to sit down in the corner of the room and told in a rough voice to make no noise or he would die.

The judge nodded his head.

Luella, dressed as one of the two men, left by the back door and climbed onto the roof with the thirty-caliber rifle and took a position where she had a view of the steps leading up to the judge's office. She was both nervous and excited at the same time. This was to be her first killing and her heart was beating rapidly.

She cocked the rifle so she wouldn't take a chance on him hearing it and shooting her.

From where she crouched on the roof, she watched the boy hand Clay the note she'd written, and smiled when he headed in her direction.

Horace - dressed to look like judge Limon Hoffmeyer, stood near the front door of the office and waited, wiping his sweaty hands on his pants legs. He hoped and prayed Luella would not miss. The hand holding the big forty-four caliber pistol was shaking.

Clay headed up the stairs, wondering what information the judge had that was so all fired important?

He was about three-fourths the way up the stairs when he saw the glint of light off a rifle barrel above him and reached for his pistol. He drew and fired toward the roof. At the same time, he turned to leap over the side of the railing and hopefully out of sight of the shooter.

Before Clay could leap over the rail, a thirty-caliber rifle bullet smashed him in the back, driving him forward, down the steps.

At the same time the rifle bullet struck Clay high on the right shoulder, the door to the judge's office opened and Horace, looking like the judge, stepped out and fired two bullets directly into Clay's back.

At least a dozen people were standing on the sidewalk and watched as the whole thing unfolded. They were stunned and just stood there, looking up as the judge turned and went back inside his office. It all happened so fast no one had seen the shooter on the roof - their eyes were locked on Clay, laying face down on the sidewalk.

Inside the office, Horace wasted no time hitting the judge over the head, rendering him unconscious, then stretched him out on the floor and untied him and took the gag out of his mouth. Next, he pulled the blindfold from his eyes, then stuck the pistol barrel against the judge's temple and pulled the trigger. After placing the pistol in the judge's hand to make it look like the judge had taken his own life, Horace hurried out the back door, where he found Luella waiting. They made their way quickly down the back steps and like two ghosts, disappeared into the shadows of the nearby buildings. The people of Seymour stood out front, stunned and immobile, waiting for the sheriff to arrive, but since he'd been sent out of town on a wild goose chase, they would have to wait until he got back giving Horace and Luella plenty of time to make their getaway.

Once they were inside the rented house, Horace bandaged the ridge in Luella's left shoulder made by Clay's bullet. "You were lucky," he said as he tied the bandage tight.

"I suppose so," Luella said, wincing in pain. "I guess I was fortunate he was turning away from me as he drew and fired. Lord that man is fast and has eyes like a hawk."

Reaching out with her good hand, she picked up a glass and motioned toward the bottle of whiskey sitting on the table. "I need a little pain medicine, along with a celebration drink. Would you do the honors?"

After a couple of drinks, they changed clothes and became the old man and woman, again. They wanted to confirm the ranger's death and went back into town to check on his situation. On the sidewalk, they were shocked to learn he was still alive.

"I don't understand," Luella said. "We shot him three times, didn't we?"

"Yes, we did," Horace said, "and that should have been enough."

Luella sighed and asked, "So, what do we do now?"

"All we can do is wait, and hope he dies," Horace said, shaking his head.

"No," Luella said, we need to come up with another plan in case he somehow lives.

Over supper at the restaurant, they went over several plans, but Horace vetoed each one, saying there were too many chances of them not working.

Back at the rented house, and deep into the night, they plotted and schemed but failed to come up with a concrete plan.

CHAPTER SIXTEEN

For five days, Clay was in and out of consciousness, his fever raging as his body tried to combat having three bullets torn into it. From time to time, Clay would come to just long enough to take a little broth or soup, then slip back into that place pain takes you when you want to escape and feel relief.

Several of the townswomen came and sat with Clay while the doctor was off taking care of his regular patients.

They would later recount Clay's thrashing around and yelling at the demons he must have been fighting in his dreams, and having to try and hold him still so he wouldn't

injure himself more than he already was - while at other times he would only groan and mumble unintelligently.

"But he continues to hang on," they would later say. "The poor, poor, dear man."

On the sixth day after the shooting, Bill McDaniel, head of the Texas Rangers, stood next to Clay's bed and took a deep breath. It had been almost a week since he'd received word that his best ranger was on deaths door. He'd tried to get away sooner, but duty had kept him in Austin.

Bill told the woman sitting with Clay that he would relieve her until the doctor got back and she had thanked him and left after saying, "You don't need to do much, just sit here and watch him. We all feel terrible. The whole town is praying for him."

Less than an hour later, Bill turned his head and watched as the doctor entered the room and set his bag on the bureau sitting against the wall.

Clarence Overholster was of medium height and a bit overweight. He had watery eyes and a gentleness about him that belied the gruffness he pretended to have. Even with his gruff exterior, the man was well liked and considered to be a first-rate doctor. He looked at the strange face and noticed the ranger badge on the man's shirt.

After introductions were made, Bill asked, "What's your best guess, Doc?"

Clay was laying on his stomach on a narrow examination table that could also be used as a bed when need be. The three bullet wounds on his back were covered with white, cloth bandages: all three stained with blood. Clay was unconscious and his breathing was ragged, at best.

Before answering, the doctor reached down and took Clay's pulse and listened to his breathing.

When, at last, he turned to Bill McDaniel, the doctor said, "As far as I can tell, the only thing keeping him alive is pure stubbornness and a constitution as strong as a horse."

Bill McDaniel made a slight grin and said, "That describes Clay alright, for sure. What's your professional opinion, Doc, is he gonna pull through?"

The doctor reached into his coat pocket and pulled out a well-used briar pipe with an ancient looking face carved on the front of it. He filled the bowl with tobacco from a leather pouch he'd retrieved from his other coat pocket, and then lit it. After taking a few puffs to get his pipe going, he looked at Bill McDaniel and said, "That's hard to say. By all rights, the man should be dead, but as you can see, he's not."

Bill McDaniel stepped closer and looked down at the side of Clay's face and watched as his back moved up and down with its labored breathing.

"To be honest with you, I think it could go either way. Right now, it's the man's strong constitution that's keeping him alive," the doctor said. "I've done all I can do - it's no longer up to me."

The doctor took another puff on his pipe, blew the smoke into the air. "When I removed the bullets, I found something interesting," he said, looking directly at McDaniel. "Two of the bullets were from a forty-four-hand gun, but the third bullet was from a thirty-caliber rifle. You can check them for yourself, they're in the small dish sitting on the bureau over there," he said, motioning toward the bureau. "And from the angle the rifle bullet entered Mister Brentwood's back, I'd say the shooter was on the roof."

Bill McDaniel walked over and examined the slugs, then lifted Clay's pistol, checking the cylinders. He turned back toward the doctor and said, "Looks like he got off one shot. Anybody else come by with a gunshot wound, besides Clay?" McDaniel asked.

When the doctor shook his head, no, McDaniel continued. "And I assume the sheriff has all this same information and has checked Clay's pistol? Knows he got off a shot, does he? More than likely, we've got somebody else out there with a gunshot wound. Clay rarely missed anything he shot at."

"The sheriff checked Mister Brentwood's pistol and came to the same conclusion you did, and, yes, I told him about the two types of bullets, and he told me to keep that information quiet, at least for now. But seeing how you're a lawman and the head of the Texas Rangers, along with being Mister Brentwood's boss, I'm guessing you'll keep this information to yourself."

Bill McDaniel stared at the doctor for a moment, then nodded his head, yes, and said, "I can see where he would think that to be the best idea, especially if he doesn't think the judge did it and the shooter or shooters, are still out there."

Bill McDaniel looked down at his hands as though he was studying them, then raised his head and said, "On the way over here from the train station, I heard people saying it was the judge here in town who did it, then committed suicide, but that's not what you or the sheriff believe, is it?"

"Yes, the general consensus is that Judge Hoffmeyer shot Mister Brentwood, but no, I don't believe it for even a minute and I'm sure neither does the sheriff. The judge didn't shoot Mister Brentwood," the doctor said with confidence, taking a handkerchief from his pocket and wiping his watery eyes.

Bill McDaniel stared at the doctor, trying to digest what the man had just said. "And what makes you think the judge didn't shoot Clay? There seems ta be ah whole passel of witnesses who will state otherwise, isn't there?"

The doctor, still holding the pipe in his hand, reached up and scratched behind his ear while shaking his head as though he was trying to get things right in his mind, then reached up and rubbed his jaw.

"I've known Judge Hoffmeyer for a good many years, and in all that time, I've never known him to even own a gun. He hated them. He said he'd had too many men in front of him for shooting somebody in a fit of anger, or by accident, and he said he couldn't count the number of men, women and children that had been killed from a gunshot wound, accidental or on purpose."

The doctor took another puff from his pipe and shook his head, again. "Besides, he thought highly of Mister Brentwood – thought he was an upright citizen – an honest man. No, in my book, the judge had no reason to shoot Mister Brentwood. I think the shooter, or shooters wanted to make it look like the judge had done it, and it appears they did a good job."

Bill McDaniel stared out the window for a moment, thinking; then reached inside his coat and pulled out a newspaper clipping and held it out toward the doctor.

"Interesting you should say that," Bill said. "The man who runs the newspaper back in Austin has a theory about some killings that have been taking place recently - politicians and men in influential positions who have, each, been killed by what appears ta be a leading citizen most folks know. But when charged, each one has proven they were miles away at the time of the shooting."

"Hum," the doctor said. So, what's his theory?"

"Well sir, the fella that runs the newspaper believes," McDaniel said, "and this takes a wee bit of thinkin' ta grasp the meanin'. He believes there's ah paid assassin runnin' loose out there who disguises hisself as somebody everbody will recognize. He kills his victims in plain sight, lookin' like whoever he wants folks ta believe he is, then while the witnesses are standin' there, dumbfounded and confused, he walks or rides away and nobody tries ta stop him. The newspaper editor is callin' him, The Chameleon. You know, like one of them lizards that can change colors, only this man changes faces and appearances."

Bill watched as the doctor digested this new bit of information.

"That's an interesting theory," the doctor said, shaking his head back and forth. "And you say he's done this before?"

"As far east and north as Chicago – several in the Kansas City area, and other places I'm not sure about, but he does seem ta move around ah lot. Ah senator down in Waco was shot and killed by ah man everbody swore was the governor, but the governor proved he was up in Austin at the time. And before the sheriff down there even heard about the senator bein' shot, the shooter had disappeared, leavin' everbody swearin' it was the governor that had done the shootin'.

"And you think this assassin fella might be here in Seymour?" the doctor asked.

"I don't know, but it has all the same earmarks, except for one," McDaniel said.

"What would that be?" the doctor asked.

"There's never been two shooters before, at least that I know of," McDaniel said.

"That you know of," the doctor answered, raising his eyebrows.

At that moment, Clay groaned and opened his eyes and tried to turn over.

"Hold on there, Mister Brentwood. You were shot in the back, three times, and you need to stay face down for awhile longer," the doctor said, laying his hand on Clay's shoulder and forcing him back down onto his stomach.

"Did they... get the... shooters?" Clay asked in a raspy voice that came in short spurts and with difficulty.

"Shooters?" the doctor asked, glancing over at Bill McDaniel. "A whole lot of folks saw the judge do it and then before he could be arrested, he committed suicide," the doctor said, gently.

"Wasn't... the judge. He didn't... shoot me... Some... somebody... else. Two of'm," Clay said right before he slipped back into unconsciousness.

Bill McDaniel's eyes lit up with this information and would have loved to learn more but Clay was in no condition to talk.

The doctor immediately checked Clay's vital signs and sighed. "He's still with us, but he's in bad shape. All we can do is wait and hope his will to live and strong constitution pulls him through."

Bill McDaniel looked down at the newspaper clipping in his hand and said, "Maybe the newspaper editor back in Austin wasn't so far off the track after all."

"What newspaper editor?" a voice asked that caused both McDaniel and the doctor to turn around.

Bill McDaniel had a gun in his hand when he did, but slid it back into his holster when he saw who it was.

The sheriff had come into the room and heard the tail end of McDaniel's statement.

Bill McDaniel saw the badge on the sheriff's shirt and stuck out his hand. "Bill McDaniel, head of the Texas Rangers. Clay Brentwood works for me and I've come to check on his condition."

The sheriff reached out and took McDaniel's hand. "I know who you are, Mister McDaniel. Clay has mentioned you on several occasions."

"All good, I hope," McDaniel said, trying to make light of the statement.

"You can relax. You're ah good man in his eyes," the sheriff said.

Turning toward the doctor, the sheriff asked, "How's he doin'?"

The doctor directed them out of the room and into his private office where he set three glasses on his desk and poured brandy into each one. "Medicinal purposes," he said with a serious look on his face, as he downed the contents and poured a bit more into his glass.

When they'd all settled into chairs, the doctor brought the sheriff up to date, telling him everything, including Clay's last statement.

The sheriff looked relieved and said, "That's real interesting. I never believed the judge did it in the first place. The judge was ah good man and as far as I knew, he liked Clay, and like the doc here said, the judge didn't own a gun – hated them. So, why would ah man who hated guns, shoot somebody in front of practically the whole town? Hell, he could haul him in on trumped up charges and have him hung, if he'd been that kind of a man, which he wasn't. None of this makes any sense. This assassin idea seems more likely ta me, but who hated him bad enough ta hire an assassin?"

The doctor took a sip of brandy and said, "Maybe while Mister Brentwood was doin' his ranger work, he might have made somebody mad enough to want him killed and hired this assassin fella to do it."

Both McDaniel and the sheriff nodded their heads in agreement.

"Have there been any new faces in town that you've noticed?" Bill McDaniel asked, knowing it was a stupid question. There were always new people coming and going.

The sheriff thought for a moment and said, "There's always fresh faces, most ever day, but there is one couple that comes ta mind – an old man and woman, but it don't seem likely it was one of them. They arrived ah few days ago and was stayin' at the hotel, but then they up and rented a small house just at the edge of town, for ah month."

McDaniel's eyes perked up. "Are you sure they're an old man and woman. The killer is believed ta use disguises," Bill said.

The doctor looked at McDaniel and asked, "If I was here to kill someone, why would I rent a house for a month? Wouldn't I ease into town, stay out of sight, do my business, then leave before anyone could connect me to the killing, like this chameleon fella you talked about does? After all, if it was this assassin fella, he sure made a lot of people believe it was the judge."

"But what if I wasn't worried about being connected to the shootin', and wanted to make sure I had completed my mission? The whole town is talkin' about Clay still survivin' after bein' shot three times in the back. If it was me, I'd be lookin' ta find ah way ta get another try at him," McDaniel said, nodding his head. "Then, once I knew for sure he was dead, I could slip away with nobody takin' notice.

"Of course, he'd have to come up with a new disguise," the sheriff ventured.

Both the doctor and Bill McDaniel turned and looked at the sheriff.

Bill McDaniel was about to say something when a groan came from the other room and all three men rushed in to see Clay up on his elbow, awake, but pale faced and staring at them.

"I'm hungry. Any chance I could get ah steak with fried taters and maybe some cooked vegetables, Doc? And some coffee ta go with it sure would taste good."

The doctor shook his head as he checked Clay's pulse and wounds. Clay's head felt normal and his heart rate was beating nicely. He was still a bit pale, but that was to be expected. He turned to Bill McDaniel and the sheriff and said, "By Gawd, I think he just may pull through. Maybe some food will help him. All he's had for five days is soup and water."

The sheriff grinned and said, "Glad ta see you awake, my friend. I'm goin' passed the cafe on my way back to the office. I'll stop in and have'm send over some food.

As the sheriff turned to go, Clay took a deep breath and called out, "Hank."

The sheriff turned back. "Yes?"

"What about the hangin's?" Clay asked, his voice becoming weak.

The sheriff looked at Clay for a long moment, then said, "What with the judge's funeral, and you bein' all shot up... well I didn't get around to it yet, but startin' tomorrow I'll be back on schedule and the first round of hangin's will start at noon. I figure it's gonna take two full days. Never hung that many men at one time before."

Clay turned his head and asked the doctor, "Is there any way I can be there? I was ta be ah witness in an official capacity – as ah law man, and the one who brought'm in."

The doctor blew out a long breath of air, then said, "We'll see how you feel tomorrow. I've got a wheelchair in the back room. Maybe we can use that... but only if you're able to sit up that long. I'm not sure you'll be strong enough, yet."

Clay nodded his head. "Was I hurt that bad? My back feels real tender in several places and it's kinda hard ta breathe because of the wounds, but other than that..."

"You took three bullets in the back; two forty-fours and one thirty caliber. You were lucky nothing vital was hit. If you hadn't have been wearing that heavy leather jacket, you'd more'n likely be dead. It was just thick enough to slow the bullets down some - that and your stubbornness to stay alive is why you're still with us. But you're a long way from being able to get up and go traipsing around town. You still need lots of rest – at least two or three weeks of it," the doctor explained.

"Is it possible I could rest at home, back on my ranch?" Clay asked with a slight grin.

Bill McDaniel had come back into the room with the doctor and the sheriff, but was standing to one side where Clay hadn't been able to see him.

McDaniel stepped forward and looked down at Clay. "You get some rest, ranger. If they need a witness to the hangin's, I'll go down in your place, and if the doctor says it's all right, I'll see you get home safe and sound."

Clay's eyes went wide. "McDaniel, what are you doin' here?"

The sheriff spoke up. "I sent a telegram – figured he needed ta know."

"One more thing, Hank," Clay said. "It wasn't the judge that shot me. Looked ah lot like him, but it wasn't him. There wasn't much time for me ta get a real close look but I'm sure it wasn't him and I'd swear to it. And somethin' else, there were two shooters. One of'em was on the roof. I took a shot at him but don't know if I hit him. And I'm sorry ta say I didn't get a shot at the one who looked like the judge."

"That's kinda what I've been figurin'," the sheriff said. Did you see anything else?"

"I don't know. My head's still a little foggy. If I remember anything else you'll be the first ta know."

The sheriff nodded his head.

Clay eased himself back down on his stomach. "But right now, I feel like layin' back down and gettin' a bit more rest until my steak gets here."

"Later then," the sheriff said with a grin as he slapped his hat on his head and headed for the front door.

"Let me help you lay back down," the doctor said, taking hold of Clay's shoulder. "You need to stay still until your wounds heal better before you do much moving around. If you feel up to it, you can sit up while you eat, but then you need to get some rest."

Clay didn't resist and closed his eyes. His breathing was becoming labored again. Just leaning up on his elbow for that short period of time had taken a lot out of him.

CHAPTER SEVENTEEN

Horace and Luella were in the cafe having coffee, trying to pick up information about Clay's condition from the people who seemed to have nothing else to talk about except the shooting. Not a one of them could understand why the judge had shot the Texas Ranger, but each and every one of them was convinced the judge had done it, and then committed suicide so he wouldn't have to stand trial or face the hangman.

Horace smiled. Stupid people; their ruse was still working. People were so easy to fool, Horace thought to himself. Making people believe someone they knew did the killing had been easier than he'd believed it would be when Luella had first proposed the idea, but as she'd said, "People are so gullible. They would even turn on their friends if they thought they saw them do something with their own eyes."

Taking a sip of his coffee, Horace sat patiently waiting for news of the ranger's death. The man couldn't live much longer with three bullets in him.

It had been awhile since they'd heard any word as to whether Clay was alive or dead and Horace was getting nervous. He was beginning to think this would never be over when the sheriff came walking into the cafe, grinning from ear to ear.

"Looks like he's gonna live," the sheriff told the people in the cafe.

There was a great deal of cheering and clapping.

One man was overheard saying to his wife, "Well then, the judge committed suicide for nothing, didn't he. If only he'd known."

His wife shook her head. "But he would still have been arrested for attempted murder, wouldn't he? And he was such a nice man, too," she said, dabbing her eyes with her handkerchief.

There were mumblings among the people and a man sitting near where the sheriff was standing, asked, "You really think he's gonna make it, do ya?"

"Come to, bright eyed and bushy tailed, and hungry as ah bear," the sheriff said. "Asked for ah steak, fried taters, cooked vegetables and some coffee. Doc says that's ah good sign."

Again, the talk was passing back forth about Clay and the judge with a great many of questions on why the judge had shot the ranger in the first place.

Luella saw Horace's face go pale and reached over and squeezed his hand, hoping he wouldn't over react and say or do something he shouldn't.

They waited until the sheriff had given the waitress Clay's order, to which she said she would add a piece of apple pie, on the house. The sheriff nodded his appreciation, then left to go back to his office.

Shortly thereafter, Horace and Luella made their way out of the small cafe and headed for the rented house.

"What are we going to do now?" Horace asked as they walked down the sidewalk.

"I need to think," Luella said as she hurried on down the sidewalk with Horace trailing a few steps behind.

As they stepped onto the front porch of their rental house, Luella turned and looked back toward town and in the far distance, she saw a woman walking in the direction of the doctor's office, carrying a tray. She gritted her teeth. She couldn't understand their bad luck. Why couldn't he just die? They still had the senator's wife to dispose of.

Inside, Horace headed straight for the bottle of whiskey sitting on the kitchen table, pouring himself and Luella stiff drinks.

Luella sipped hers slowly, while Horace gulped his down and poured a second.

"Slow down, Horace," she said, laying her hand on his arm. "Now is not the time to panic, we need to keep our minds clear."

Horace looked at her and set the glass on the table. "You're right," he said. "It's just that I'm stunned the man is still alive. We shot him three times. How could he live through that?"

"You don't suppose they're just saying that to fool us in case we're still hanging around? Maybe they hope we'll make another try at killing him so they can draw us into a trap."

That thought had occurred to Luella, also, and it disturbed her. She needed to know for sure. They had taken money from the person who wanted him dead and she wasn't about to give it back, which left them only one option, and that was to make sure the Texas Ranger was dead and six feet under the ground.

She wanted to be shed of this little one horse town. She wanted to be back in Kansas City where she would feel safe. As one of the shooters, she was in just as deep as Horace was and she'd heard in Texas, they hung women right along with the men. From now on, she would let Horace do all the killing.

-

After his meal, which he couldn't eat all of, and a short talk with McDaniel, Clay was worn out and happy to go back to sleep.

Bill McDaniel decided Clay was on the mend and wouldn't need constant watching, so he elected to slip out and get some things done while he could.

Outside, he headed straight for the barbershop. He needed a bath and a shave, and then something to eat. He could finally relax some now that Clay seemed to be doing better. Maybe both of them could get a decent night's sleep.

-

When night came, black clouds rolled in, blocking the stars and only once in a while could a sliver of moon be seen, making it perfect for what Luella had in mind.

Dressed as a Mexican peon, Horace staggered down the alleyway behind the doctor's office, pretending to be drunk. When he got close, he could see there was a lamp on inside the room and eased up next to the window, glancing around to make sure he was alone. The lamp had a shade in front of it so as not to shine its light directly on the bed.

When Horace peeked through the window he could see Clay laying on the bed and heard his ragged breathing and snoring.

Before leaving the doctor's office, the sheriff suggested to the doctor that he keep the window closed and locked and the blinds pulled shut, just in case the killer was still in town and might decide to make another attempt on Clay's life. The good doctor had agreed with him and went back to his bookwork. An hour or so later, John McPherson came rushing in, saying his wife was having her baby and dragged the doctor out the door before he had a chance to do any of the things he'd promised to do. McDaniel, in his haste, had also forgotten to close the window and the shade, leaving Clay exposed to anyone passing by.

With the window being left open just a little so fresh air could come in, the shade still wide open and the lamp burning brightly, even a kid with a slingshot could have hit Clay, easily.

Horace couldn't believe his luck. He looked around to make sure he was still alone, then eased up next to the window and studied the room more closely. Except for Clay, the room was empty. Horace felt an adrenaline rush and had to take several deep breaths to calm himself, then reached over and put his fingers under the bottom of the window and lifted upward, all the while, keeping a close eye on Clay for any movement. He didn't think the ranger had a gun, but he wasn't about to take any chances.

The window had gone up about six inches when it made a scraping noise, causing Horace to stop lifting. The last thing he wanted to do right now was to wake the ranger up. Even in his weakened condition, Horace was afraid of him. He had no trouble killing someone as long as they didn't shoot back.

His heart was pounding against his chest and his hands felt clammy as he reached down and pulled the forty-four pistol from his waistband and stuck the barrel in between the bottom of the window and the window sill.

He tried several different angles, but couldn't get a decent shot. He had no choice but to open the window a little bit more.

After putting the pistol back in his waistband, he lifted the window a little at a time so it made no noise. Finally, the space was wide enough so he could get a decent shot.

Horace took several deep breaths to calm the excitement he was feeling. He was going to shoot the ranger and disappear down the alley. It would finally be done and over with for sure this time and it was him who was making the decision, not Luella. He was reaching for his pistol when a hand came down on his shoulder.

Horace yanked the pistol out of his waistband and spun around, ready to shoot, and almost did before he realized it was Luella, also dressed like a Mexican peon.

"Don't do that!" he whispered. "I almost shot you!"

"You were back here a long time and I came to see if you were alright?" she said, visibly shaken at the thought of Horace shooting her.

"What have you been doing? You were going to try and see whether he was still alive, or not, then come right back.

"The stupid doctor not only left a light on and the shades open, he left the window open, too. I was able to get my fingers under the window and lift it up enough so I can get a shot. That's what I was about to do when you showed up and nearly gave me a heart attack," Horace said, matter of factly.

Luella stepped over and looked through the window and smiled. "Stupid doctor. Lucky us. Let's do this and get out of here," she said, her voice filled with excitement.

Horace eased up to the window again and had just stuck the barrel of his pistol through the opening when a voice from the far end of the alley called out, "Hey! Hey! You there! What'er you greezers doin' down there?"

Horace jumped like he'd been stuck with a hot branding iron and squeezed off a shot that went into the wall behind where Clay was laying. Horace jerked the pistol out of the opening and swung it in the direction of the voice and fired three fast shots. The man at the end of the alley dove to the side and returned fire, but too late - Horace and Luella had already sprinted down the alley in the opposite direction, running into the darkness between the other buildings and out of sight.

The man dusted himself off, then made his way, cautiously, down the alley to where the two Mexican men had disappeared. "What the hell was those Mexicans lookin' for, and why was one of'm pointin' ah pistol in the window?" he asked himself as he holstered his own pistol and turned back in the direction he'd come from.

He stopped long enough to look in the window and saw Clay with his head up, looking around, wondering if he'd dreamed about hearing gunshots?

After Clay put his head back down and closed his eyes, the man eased the window back down, so as not to disturb the ranger, then went to the sheriff's office and was glad when he saw light streaming through the window.

-

The sheriff was reaching over to blow out the lamp and call it a day when the man came in and told him what had happened.

"You're sure they was Mexicans?" the sheriff asked. There weren't that many Mexicans in Seymour and he thought he knew all of them and couldn't think of even one of them that would be prowling around outside the window late at night, let alone trying to shoot a Texas Ranger.

"Well, it was dark, but I could see'm plain enough in the light comin' from the window. Looked like two Mexican men, ta me. They was dressed like peons – you know, dirty white pants and shirts and big straw hats. And it looked like one of'm was about ta take ah shot at somebody through the window. After they run off, I took a look inside and saw it was the ranger everbody's talkin' about. He was awake and lookin' around, so I reckon he wasn't hit."

"Did you get a look at their faces? Would you recognize'm if you saw'm again?" the sheriff asked.

"Doubt it. Greezers all look purty much the same ta me. I just happened ta see'em as I walked by the alley. I heard ah noise and looked down that direction. One of'm was stickin' ah pistol barrel through the open window of Doc's place. I yelled att'em, and that's when he shot at me and then run off. I closed the window afore I come over here, but the shade is still open," the cowboy said for a second time.

None of this made any sense. Even when they were drinking, the Mexicans stayed down in their part of town and had never caused any trouble. "And you're sure one of'em was stickin' ah gun barrel through the window?"

"I hope ta shout. When I yelled att'm, he fired the pistol inside the room. Then he jerked the pistol out of the window and fired shots at me. Course, I shot back but don't think I hit anybody, it was too dark," the man said. "But the point is, if they weren't up ta no good, why did they shoot at me? And if they was just curious, why did one of'm take ah shot at that ranger inside the room?"

The sheriff had no answer to that and locked up his office, then walked over to the doctor's office with the cowboy trailing a few steps behind.

Except for music coming from the saloon, most of the town had gone to bed.

The sheriff opened the door to the doctor's office, and called out, several times, "Doc? You here?" but got no answer.

After checking every room, he decided the doctor had left for some reason or another, but hadn't taken time to lock the front door, which seemed strange. They'd talked about that very thing just before he'd gone back to his office.

The sheriff walked to the front door and looked out in both directions, hoping to see the doctor, but the street was empty.

"Hello... Doc?" Clay called from the other room.

The sheriff went into the room where Clay was laying on the small bed and saw the window still had the shades drawn back.

"The doc's not here. You wouldn't happen ta know where he went, would ya?" the sheriff asked.

"No. I was hopin' you was him," Clay said, making a small grimace.

"I could use ah little somethin' for the pain in my back. I was dreamin' about somebody shootin' at me and the shots seemed so real, it woke me up. I tried ta go back ta sleep, but ain't been able to."

Clay shook his head. "Sure was ah realistic dream."

The sheriff didn't say anything about the Mexican men outside the window, or the shooting that had taken place; nor the bullet hole in the wall just behind where Clay was laying - he didn't want to upset him.

"Well, the doctor's got ta be someplace nearby," the sheriff said, "and I reckon he'll be along directly." The sheriff stared at the window, hoping he was right.

The man who scared off Horace and Luella in the alley, had followed the sheriff into Clay's room and said, "Ah little afore I come ta see you, I saw John McPherson come ridin' inta town hell bent for election on that plow horse of his. I hear his wife's near her berthin' time. Maybe that's where the doc went."

The sheriff nodded his head, then walked over and locked the window. When this was done, he pulled the curtains closed, then asked the man for some help and moved Clay and his bed to a different spot, where he couldn't be seen through the window.

"What'er you doin' this for?" Clay asked.

"Call it ah precaution," the sheriff said with a grin.

The sheriff found several curtains on frames and placed them in front of the window, making it hard to see inside the room. If the shooter came back for another try, he was going to make it as difficult as he could for him.

When this was done, the sheriff went over and retrieved a bottle of whiskey from the cupboard against the far wall and turned back toward Clay.

"I'm not licensed ta give ya any pain medicine, Clay, but there's nothin' that says we can't have ah drink or two together, you know, ta celebrate your recovery."

Clay gave a weak grin and with some help from the cowboy, he pulled himself up into a sitting position, then reached for the bottle and took a long pull.

-

Horace and Luella were breathing hard when they let themselves in the back door of the rented house and collapsed on the bench next to the kitchen table.

Horace took a long pull straight from the bottle of whiskey and said, "That was too close."

"I agree," Luella said, not understanding their bad luck. "Maybe we should get out of here while we can. We can always come back after things have calmed down."

Relieved at Luella's suggestion, Horace stood up and said, "I'll start packing. I think there's a train leaving for Dallas in about an hour and we need to be on it."

In record time, they had their bags packed, and were headed for the train depot, staying shy of the main street, hoping they wouldn't be noticed. Their luck held and when they walked up onto the platform in front of the train station, it was empty.

The ticket taker was surprised when he looked up and saw an elderly couple enter the station at this time of night.

"Two tickets to Dallas," the old man said, offering no explanation.

The ticket taker looked at the man and got the impression he was in a hurry. As he glanced out of the corner of his eye, he could see the old man glancing toward the window and the door. He seemed a mite nervous.

"That'll be three dollars," the clerk said, sliding the tickets across the counter.

Horace reached into his pocket and pulled out three dollars and laid the money on the counter. "How long until the train gets here?" he asked.

The clerk looked up at the clock and said, "Oh, maybe... twenty minutes or so when it's on time, which is most of the time. But if something has happened, it's anybody's guess. I haven't heard of anything, but..." he said, pointing toward the telegraph.

Horace nodded his head and said, "Thank you."

The clerk watched as the old couple walked out onto the porch and sat down on the bench to wait for the train.

They were the only ones waiting, which wasn't unusual. Most folks left during the early morning hours, but not many folks left at night, which made the clerk wonder why they were so anxious leave town. At the sound of the telegraph, he turned and walked over and sat down at the desk and picked up a pencil. It was just a telegram to the saloon owner, confirming his load of whiskey was on its way.

CHAPTER EIGHTEEN

The sheriff asked the cowboy if he would mind staying with Clay while he went to check on the Mexicans.

The cowboy grinned and said, "I reckon I can, I got no place else in particular ta be right now."

When the sheriff had gone, the cowboy found a newspaper and settled down in a chair, laying the paper on his lap, prepared to talk some before looking at the help wanted ads but Clay had closed his eyes again and the cowboy could hear light snoring.

He grinned and settled back, turning to the page that offered work. As a drifting cowboy, he seemed to be on a constant hunt for work. He liked the Seymour area and had spent some time here. He'd worked at several jobs besides cowboying during the past three years, so he scanned the paper for anything that might catch his eye.

As the sheriff walked by the saloon, he heard loud yelling and went in to investigate.

Two young cowboys were in a heated dispute over who was going to take the young woman standing nearby, upstairs. The bartender was trying unsuccessfully to break them up.

She was no more than eighteen - blonde, with a turned up nose and bright blue eyes that sparkled when she looked at a man. She was petite and loved the thought of two men fighting over her, which seemed to happen all too often as far as the sheriff was concerned.

The bartender had hired her two months back and there had been trouble ever since.

The other patrons of the saloon weren't helping the matter by cheering for one or the other of the two cowboys.

Normally, it turned out to just be a slugfest, but not this time.

As the sheriff walked up behind them, the one closest to him reached for the pistol hanging at his side and was about to draw on the other cowboy, but before he could pull his gun out of the holster, the sheriff grabbed him by the arm and said, "Hold on, young man."

The young cowboy had been drinking heavily and in his drunken stupor, turned and swung at the sheriff, hitting him in the jaw.

While the blow wasn't hard enough to knock the sheriff down, it was hard enough to make him mad.

The cowboy was so drunk he didn't realize who he'd just hit and once again reached for his pistol.

The sheriff, having enough of this nonsense, drew his own pistol and smashed the barrel down over the young cowboy's head.

The young cowboy's legs buckled and he landed on the floor in a heap.

A hush went over the onlookers, and the bartender backed off a few steps.

Pointing his pistol at the other cowboy, the sheriff ordered him to pick the young man up from the floor and carry him over to the jail.

When the other cowboy, who had also been drinking heavily, fell down twice in his attempt to pick up the young man on the floor, the bartender stepped up and helped him by picking up the unconscious young man by the shoulders, while the other cowboy picked up his feet.

Once they got them over to the jail, the sheriff put the two cowboys in separate cells for the night so they could sleep it off.

As he hung their gun belts on pegs in his office, the bartender, a small man with dark spots on his face, said, "Thank you, Sheriff. You saved a possible killing in my place tonight."

The sheriff gave him a stern look and said, "You tell that little blonde over there, if she causes any more trouble I'll see the last of her. She'll be on the first train out of here."

The bartender backed up a couple of steps and said, "But... but she's..."

The sheriff raised his hand. "No buts about it. Either you rein her in or she leaves town and that's final. Now go on back over ta your place and see that things remain quiet or I'll be hangin' ah closed sign on your front door. Do I make myself clear?"

The bartender glared at the sheriff but said, "Yes sir."

The sheriff watched him leave, knowing no matter how much he threatened there would be more trouble over at the Blue Bird saloon. He also knew the town council would not let him close the place down, the place brought in a considerable amount of money - but he could run the little tart out of town if she didn't behave herself, and he would, too.

-

The sheriff walked down to where a small group of Mexican laborers had thrown some tents together and were sitting around a large fire, drinking and talking. One of them was strumming on a guitar.

When they saw him walk up, they all turned and looked at him with curiosity in their eyes. They had had no trouble with him so they were only mildly curious at his visit.

A tall Mexican man who the sheriff knew only as, Mendoza, stood up and stuck out his hand. "Buenos noche, Senor Sheriff. What brings you down to our camp? Do you need us to catch some robbers for you?" he asked, grinning broadly.

The sheriff grinned at Mendoza's joke. "Maybe," the sheriff said.

Looking closely at them for a reaction, the sheriff continued. "I just came down here ta have ah talk with the two men who were window peekin' in the alley behind the doctor's office."

The reaction was about what he expected it to be, looks of confusion, but none of guilt.

Mendoza looked around at his friends, then back at the sheriff. "Senor Sheriff, you make the joke, si?"

"No, it ain't no joke," the sheriff said. "A man saw two Mexican men peekin' in the window behind the doctor's office about an hour or so ago and I'm wonderin' what they were doin' there? If all they wanted ta do is get ah peek at the wounded ranger, I could understand that, but when they were yelled at by a man down on the street, one of'em took several shots at him and that makes me suspicious as ta why they were there in the first place."

Mendoza listened carefully to every word the sheriff said and then scratched his right eyebrow before saying, "I'm sorry, Senor Sheriff, but it could not have been one of us. We have all been right here all evening."

This was about what the sheriff expected. He'd had no trouble from them before and saw no reason why they should start now, but had to ask, "You seen any other of your people in town today?"

Mendoza looked at the other men sitting around the fire and watched as each one of them shook his head, 'no.'

Mendoza looked back at the sheriff and shrugged his shoulders.

"No, Senor Sheriff. There are only us, and I tell you, again - none of us have been in the alley behind the doctor's office, or anywhere else but right here.

The sheriff nodded his head and shook Mendoza's hand. "I believe you, but I had ta ask."

"Si, I understand. I will keep a lookout and if I see anyone or hear anything, I will come see you," Mendoza promised.

As he walked back toward his office, thoughts began to drift through his head. What was it McDaniel said about the assassin? That he used disguises? Well, what if it was this assassin who had pretended to be the judge and now a Mexican peon, trying to get another shot at Clay?

Maybe he wanted to check and see whether Clay was alive or dead, and if he was still alive, the alley would be a perfect place to finish the job.

His mind was in a whirl as he walked back toward town and suddenly the old man and woman jumped to the forefront of his mind and he headed in the direction of the house they'd rented.

As he approached, he noticed the house was dark. He stopped and studied the place. It looked as though they had already gone to bed, which was not unusual for old people.

He decided he should wait until morning, and turned back toward town. He had only gone a short distance when he heard a train pulling into town and felt the hair on the back of his neck stand on end.

Turning, he hurried back to the house and knocked on the door and waited for a minute or so. When no one answered, he knocked again, louder this time.

When there was still no answer, he tried the door and found it unlocked. He stepped inside, found a lamp and lit it, calling out, "Hello the house. This is the sheriff and I need to talk to you."

It didn't take long to search the small house and find it empty. The furniture was still there but no personal items such as clothes or other items. There was a small amount of food in the kitchen cabinet, but that was it.

Hank Singleton had been a sheriff for a good many years and thought of himself as a good lawman, but right now he felt like a fool.

At the railroad station, he queried the station master who said, "Why yes, sheriff, an old man and woman did leave on the train just a few minutes ago. The man bought tickets for Dallas."

The sheriff went out and stood on the platform and looked down the tracks. Even on horseback, he wouldn't be able to catch the train.

Turning, he went back inside and told the stationmaster, who was also the telegrapher; he wanted to send a telegram to the sheriff in Dallas.

CHAPTER NINETEEN

Horace and Luella had taken a Pullman berth on the train so they could get some rest. It was an eight to nine-hour trip to Dallas, depending on the stops along the way and after a late supper, they turned in and went immediately to sleep.

They had been asleep for seven hours when the train began to slow down and Luella heard the conductor walking through the car, calling out. "Fort Worth coming up. Now coming into Fort Worth, Texas."

Luella's eyes flew open and she punched Horace in the ribs with her elbow. "Get up, we're getting off the train."

"Huh? What?" he said groggily.

"Hurry up. Grab our bags. We have to get off this train, now!"

Horace wasn't sure why they had to get off the train in Fort Worth, but if Luella said they had to, he wasn't about to argue with her. He would find out soon enough, once they were off the train.

He grabbed his wig and hat and crawled out of the berth, dragging their bags behind him. Luella was already heading down the aisle with her old woman's limp.

Once off the train, Luella headed for the train schedule hanging on the outside of the station and saw that a train was leaving for Austin in three hours.

With Horace tagging along behind, carrying their bags, Luella checked into a hotel just a block from the station and paid for one night.

In the room, they cleaned up and changed their disguises again – this time they wore their Texas rancher disguises and then went down to breakfast.

In the dining room, Horace broached the subject he'd been wondering about. "Honey," he said with a grin, "Why did we have to get off here in Fort Worth? We had tickets for Dallas which isn't much farther on down the line."

Luella sighed and looked at the ceiling, then back down at Horace. "Call it what you will, woman's intuition, a sixth sense, a premonition, I don't know. I just know that if we went on into Dallas, we would find ourselves face to face with the sheriff. The feeling was so strong that I was shaking until we were off that train."

Horace just nodded. He'd seen these intuitions before and so far, she'd always been right.

"So, what do we do now?" he asked, taking a sip of his strong, black coffee.

"There's a train leaving for Austin in just over an hour and we'll be on it. That's where we were headed when we left Seymour. We'll just be going by a different route, that's all."

Just before they entered the station to purchase their tickets to Austin, Luella gave Horace some money.

Using his best Texas accent, Horace stepped up to the teller's window and bought two tickets to Austin. "How long ah ride is it?" he asked.

The teller looked up at him and said, "Nine to ten hours, depending on how many stops the train has to make or if the Indians have torn up any of the tracks. Haven't had one in a while, but there's still always a chance of train robbers, which can make for a long delay, also."

Horace was feeling good and lit a cheroot and blew smoke in the direction of the teller. "We keep our Indians in line out where we're from," Horace said, ignoring the part about train robbers.

"Where might that be, mister...?"

"Swain. Rodney Swain. Me and the little missus hail from out west of here – the Bar Slash S ranch," Horace said with bluster. "Mayhap you've heard of us?"

"No sir, can't say as I have," the teller said, wishing the train would hurry and show up. He was from Cincinnati and was ready to go back. As far as he was concerned, Texas had more blowhards than any place he'd ever seen.

"Actually, our ranch is in two places – the northeast corner of the New Mexico territory, and the west end of the panhandle in Texas," Horace bragged, blowing cigar smoke toward the ticket taker, again.

-

Over breakfast, the sheriff told McDaniel about what had happened the night before and McDaniel stopped eating and asked, "Why didn't you come get me?"

The sheriff looked at him curiously and asked, "What could you have done that I didn't do?"

McDaniel grinned and said, "Good point. Probably nuthin'. Besides, it's kinda late ta speculate on what could'a happened, ain't it?"

The sheriff nodded his head and went back to enjoying his breakfast; and when he'd finished he ordered more coffee.

Hank Singleton liked McDaniel and said, "Maybe we'll hear somethin' from the sheriff in Dallas. I wired him their description as best I could. Got a wire back that said he would meet the train."

"We can only hope," McDaniel said, finishing off his own breakfast. "Whoever this killer is, he's smart and seems ta have ah sixth sense when it comes ta escapin' from the law."

-

When the train pulled into Dallas, a deputy climbed into the engine compartment and told the engineer he would let him know when he could go on, but for now, the train would sit here while the sheriff and several other deputies boarded the train and did a thorough search.

The train was filled mainly with cowboys, drummers and regular folks.

An hour later, after talking to three older couples and searching their bags, they came up empty and had to let the train go on.

The sheriff and McDaniel were about to leave the cafe and go check on Clay when the telegraph operator came in the door and handed the sheriff a telegram.

The sheriff gave the operator a dime, then opened the telegram and read it. He got a disgusted look on his face, and handed it to McDaniel.

McDaniel read it then shook his head. "So, once more he slipped away from the long arm of the law. My guess is they changed into a different disguise and walked off the train free and clear, or, sat there and brazened it out, then left with the train. And I'll bet he was laughin' at us the whole time."

McDaniel raked his fingers through his hair. "He's got ta make ah mistake sometime and when he does, I just hope I'm there ta bring him down."

They headed for the doctor's office to let Clay know he was probably no longer in danger, at least for now.

-

To Clay's delight, the doctor said if they used a wagon so Clay could ride laying down, and if Clay promised to stay down for another two weeks, he could go home right after the hanging.

Clay agreed and with the help of the sheriff and the doctor, he was able to sit in a wheel chair, and was pushed by the young cowboy who had saved his life.

The cowboy pushed the wheelchair down to where Clay could see the gallows from the sidewalk.

When Clay wondered who the cowboy was, McDaniel told Clay about the attempt on his life and how he had been saved by the cowboy who had come along just in time.

Clay looked up and asked, "You lookin' for work?"

"Yes sir, I am," the cowboy said.

"Can you punch cows?" Clay asked.

"Punch cows, break horses, do ah bit of blacksmithin', run fence, whatever you need done," the cowboy said with pride. "Even tend the line shack durin' the winter."

"You got ah name?" Clay asked.

"If I tell ya, ya gotta promise not ta laugh and promise ta call me by my nickname," the cowboy said.

Clay looked at the sheriff who shrugged his shoulders, then back to the cowboy. "Fair enough," he said.

The cowboy looked at his feet and said, "Eggbert. Eggbert Tiggleoff - but those who don't want ta get knocked down or shot, call me, Randy. I picked out that name for myself. Randy Brown, which ta me seems like ah lot better name than what my ma and pa stuck me with."

Clay and the sheriff readily agreed Randy Brown was a much better name.

"Well, Randy Brown, welcome. You officially went on the payroll last night."

"Thank you, Mister Brentwood, you won't be sorry," Randy said, grinning from ear to ear.

"You interested in how much I pay?" Clay asked.

Randy looked off into the sky, then said, "No sir. I reckon you'll be fair."

Clay grinned. His gut was telling him Randy would make a good hand.

For the rest of the afternoon and most of the following day, Clay, along with half the town, watched solemnly as nineteen men were brought out to the gallows and hung, then carted away to be buried with no fanfare in the graveyard just outside of town.

What a waste of manhood, Clay thought as he watched the trapdoors open and the men drop through. It made Clay sick, but the law was the law and each one of them knew the consequences for what they were doing if they got caught. The only one to complain right up to the end was Carlyle. The others went quietly with no last words.

When it was over, both Clay and McDaniel signed papers for the sheriff as a witness.

Clay was even allowed to go to the hotel restaurant for supper, which made quite a scene because of all the well-wishers.

Clay was bombarded with questions coming from all directions. Two widow women openly said he could stay with them until he was back on his feet.

Embarrassed by the chuckling all around him, Clay thanked the ladies but turned them down. "I truly do need ta get back ta my ranch. And thank you again for the offer."

It was the doctor who finally broke it up so Clay could finish his meal and go back to his room at the doctor's office, where he would spend the night and get a clean bandage.

CHAPTER TWENTY

-

The following morning, Clay was still moving very slowly, but was able to stand up with the help of the doctor and the sheriff.

Outside, he was about to be helped into the back of a rented buggy and lay down on a mound of hay, covered over with a blanket, when Riley rode up and stepped down from his horse.

Clay was still standing at the end of the buggy and grinned when Riley walked up and looked at him with a puzzled expression on his face.

"Well, hello, Riley. What're you doin' in town?" Clay asked kinda casual like.

"Come ta see what was takin' ya so long ta get back," Riley said, pulling off his hat and scratching his head as he eyed his boss and the two men supporting him. "We was gettin' ah mite worried. What happened to ya, you get throwed or somethin?"

The doctor spoke up. "He was shot three times in the back."

Riley's eyes went wide and he swallowed. "I don't understand. Why would somebody want ta shoot Mister Brentwood?"

It was the sheriff who spoke, this time. "We're still tryin' ta figure that one out, but..."

Clay butted in. "You'll hear all about it, right along with the others when I get home, but right now, I need ta get in this buggy and lay down."

As the sheriff and the doctor helped Clay into the buggy, Clay said, "Oh, I almost forgot, this is Randy Brown," he said, nodding toward

Randy who was sitting on the buggy seat, holding the reins. "Hired him on two days ago."

Clay looked up at Randy and said, "This is Riley. You'll be workin' for him."

Riley looked at the cowboy, then leaned out of the saddle with his hand stretched out. "Welcome ta the BR. I'm one of the two ramrods. Give me just a second and I'll tie my horse ta the back of the buggy and ride on the seat with ya. I'm bettin' you can fill me in on what happened on the way back."

Randy glanced at Riley and liked the look of his face. "Sure, be happy to."

Riley was just climbing onto the buggy when two men came crashing through the doors of the saloon and marched out into the street. Both men were staggering from already having too much Who Shot John. From the looks of things, there had been an argument and one of them had challenged the other to a gunfight. Both had pistols hanging at their sides.

Before they drew on each other, the sheriff yelled, "Hey there! Don't nobody move!"

Both men looked in his direction then went for their guns. At the same time their guns went off, three pistols answered.

The sheriff whirled and saw Riley and Randy standing just to the side of him. Both had pistols in their hands and both barrels were smoking.

As they slipped their pistols back into their holsters, the sheriff noticed a bloody spot on the side of Randy's left arm and walked over to him.

"You've been hit," he said, inspecting the wound. "Looks like just ah scratch, but we'd better have the doc take ah look at it anyway."

"Ah, it ain't nuthin'," Randy said, trying to make light of his gunshot wound that stung like a dozen bee stings.

The doctor took him by the arm and led him inside, calling over his shoulder, "This won't take but a minute, then you can be on your way.

McDaniel walked up next to the buggy and said, "I think you've got yourself a good hand who rides for both the brand and the law. Think I'll have a talk with him. He'd make ah good ranger, that is if you think you can spare him."

"I reckon he's old enough ta make his own decisions," Clay said, laying his head back down.

Before they left town, McDaniel called Randy aside and they talked for a few minutes. Randy shook his head, no, then shook hands with

McDaniel, saying, "I'm right honored, but I think for now I'll stick with what I know best and that's punchin' cows. But if I get bored with it, I just might show up in Austin, knockin' on your door."

"You do that," McDaniel said.

After thanks and goodbyes were said all around, Randy tapped the reins lightly on the rump of the horse and with directions given by Riley, pointed the buggy in the direction of the ranch.

McDaniel, the sheriff and the doctor had lunch together and discussed the chances of the assassin following or finding his way to the ranch for another try at Clay.

The doctor looked at his two lunch companions and said, "I stopped by the ranch a month or so ago on my way back from somewhere, don't remember where right off hand, but the point is, that assassin fella wouldn't stand a chance of getting inside. That place has got a thick wall all the way around it. It's like a fort. He told me that after what happened with the Beeler gang, he wasn't taking any more chances."

"A fort, you say," McDaniel said.

"I was out there for supper right after it was built and yeah, that's what I'd call it," the sheriff said. "Wouldn't take more than ah few men to stand off an army, and he has more than just a few men out there, and all of them tough as nails."

"Well," McDaniel said, "then I won't worry about leavin' and goin' back ta Austin."

"I'll be making my way out there next week to have a look see at his wounds and to make sure he's staying down like I told him, which I'm sure he will be. I took Riley aside before they left and told him to relay a message to his housekeeper, Mrs. McIntyre, to keep him down," the doctor said.

"Well you can bet she'll be watchin' him like ah prison guard. He won't be able ta get away with nuthin'," the sheriff said, grinning.

"That's good to know," McDaniel said. "But if there's any trouble... any trouble at all, you get word to me."

"I'll see to it personally," the sheriff said.

McDaniel stood up and before he left, he shook hands with both the doctor and the sheriff, assuring them he would make himself available should there be any more trouble.

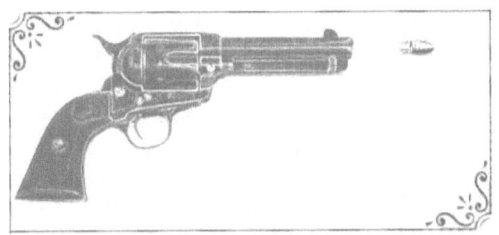

CHAPTER TWENTY-ONE

-

When the train pulled into Austin, the town was bustling with people, which suited Horace and Luella just fine. There was no law enforcement staring at them as they walked down the street looking for a hotel.

Still dressed as ranchers from western Texas, they checked into a hotel that had a sign,

'Cleanest rooms and finest restaurant south of Dallas.'

When Horace signed the register, he looked at the clerk and said, "My ranch fringes on two towns; Hartley, Texas and Logan, in the New Mexico territory – get mail at either address, but most of the ranch is north of Tucumcari, New Mexico, so which address do you want?'

The clerk was a man in his mid-fifties and looked like he'd been around the block a time or two. He was beginning to go bald on top and had brown, curly hair around his ears and on the back of his head and neck. He was wearing glasses and had put on some weight around the middle since taking this job.

While still studying the register, the clerk said, "Doesn't matter much. Several years back, twenty or so would be more like it; I came down out of Colorado and spent a few days in Hartley. Nice little town if you like one that goes to bed with the sun. Didn't find any work there, so I kept on traveling."

Looking up, the clerk continued. "Swain. Not a common name. Can't recall hearing that name or the Bar Slash S ranch when I was there. I did hear of a ranch east of there called the Waggoner ranch. They say it's the biggest one around - over five hundred thousand acres. That true?"

Being an actor who was always prepared to pick up lines dropped by one or more of the other actors, or adlib when he needed to, Horace said, "Haven't seen the place myself, but I have heard the same story. About my ranch, I don't reckon you would have heard about it cause I didn't have it yet. Found me a tidy sum of gold up in Colorado a little over ten years ago; and like you I found myself in Hartley. Was a couple of ranches for sale that bordered each other, so I up and bought both of'em and turned'm inta one good sized ranch – close ta ah hundred thousand acres."

Luella was standing a little behind Horace and wished he would shut up, but he kept blabbering on like everything he said was true.

"You out here buying or selling cattle?" the clerk asked.

"Neither," Horace said, feeling primed and enjoying this pretend game. "The little misses and me are goin' down ta Galveston on ah honeymoon. Didn't get much of ah chance nine years ago when we got hitched – what with buildin' up the ranch and all. Hear they got themselves a purty little island just off the coast where a man can sit out in the sun every day and watch the ocean. Never seen the ocean before. I hear it's big."

The clerk stifled a chuckle and reached behind him and pulled a key off its peg. "Yes, it is," he said, remembering seeing the ocean for the first time. "You'll be in room 106, just down the hall there. Faces the street," he said, pointing toward the hall.

Horace took the key, touched his finger to the brim of his hat and said, "Much obliged."

As Horace and Luella picked up their bags and headed down the hallway, the clerk inhaled Luella with his eyes and wished it was him going to the room with her. She was fine to look at and his imagination was running rampant. When his heart rate slowed down, he called out, "Congratulations, ma'am."

Luella, keeping up with the pretense, turned her head toward him and gave him a smile that would melt an iceberg. "Thank you," she mouthed, which left the clerk weak in the knees.

In the room, her attitude changed. "Are you crazy? We need to attract the least amount of attention we can and you stand there running off at the mouth with some made up story like you're performing on stage."

"I was just having a little fun," Horace said, disliking the feeling of being chastised.

Luella looked at him and softened. "I know you were, Horace, but now we'll need to check out of here tomorrow, pretending to be on our way to Galveston, then change disguises and find a different hotel where we can check out our victim and figure a plan."

"Guess there's no use unpacking if we're moving tomorrow," Horace said, feeling sorry he'd gotten carried away and put them in such a bind. "I'm really sorry. I'll try to behave myself, all right?"

Luella looked at his sad eyes and gave in. "Alright," she said, kissing him lightly on the lips.

Now that he was back in Luella's good graces, he patted his stomach and said, "How about some dinner, I'm starved."

The restaurant was only about half filled when they arrived. The room was very nicely appropriated with wine colored drapery and black onyx tables and chairs. The tables were covered with white tablecloths and the place settings were real china and fancy silverware. The few people that were already there were some of the town's more affluent, and all dressed for dinner. Lit candles adorned each table, giving the room a comfortable atmosphere.

A man in a black suit ushered them to a table and gave them each a menu, asking if they would like something to drink before their meal.

Horace, still playing the Texas rancher, ordered whiskey for himself and Luella ordered a bottle of champagne.

"We're on our honeymoon," Horace declared. "So, I want the best of everything."

The waiter bowed at the waist and said, "Congratulations. I'll see that you have the best we have to offer."

When the waiter left to get their drinks, Luella hissed, "Horace! I thought you were going to back off."

"I will, I will," Horace said picking up her hand and kissing it. "But tonight, we're on our honeymoon!"

Luella looked across the table and smiled. "Horace Libersky, what am I going to do with you?"

"Enjoy yourself to the fullest, my dear, enjoy yourself to the fullest," Horace said, smiling broadly. "We can afford it."

Suddenly, the room was filled with activity as waiters and waitresses went rushing around, pulling tables together to make one long table – placing chairs under the tables, while others put out place settings with their finest china and silverware. Another man was placing glasses and bottles of champagne on the long table every couple of feet.

Horace and Luella looked around to see what all the excitement was about and saw a beautiful woman in her thirties, standing near the entryway, bored to distraction by their slowness. You could tell by her attitude she was used to being catered to.

She was dressed to the nines in a red satin dress and her hair flowed down her back in large ringlets. A fancy little hat was perched at a tilt on her head that had an ostrich feather sticking out of it. The diamond on her finger was the biggest Luella had ever seen and she wanted it. Behind her were a dozen or so other well-dressed men and women, but none to equal the woman being catered to.

Finally, the waiter rushed up to her and said, "I'm sorry we took so long Mrs. Thompson, but we didn't know you would be with us this evening."

At that, he bowed and said, "If you will follow me."

Without a word, she followed him to the table and allowed him to seat her, then watched as he poured her a glass of champagne - the look of impatience exploding from her eyes.

Several other waiters stood behind the chairs to be occupied by the men and women in her small group. After seating them and pouring champagne, they disappeared, hoping not to garner the woman's wrath.

Luella studied the woman carefully. "So, this is our next victim," she said to herself.

"What? What?" Horace asked - mesmerized by the woman's beauty and the power she commanded over the waiters just by her presence.

Luella reached across the table and patted Horace's hand. "Down boy. That's your next victim."

Horace looked at Luella with astonishment written all over his face. "Why... why would someone want to harm a woman as beautiful as she is?"

"Money speaks volumes and is the primary reason," Luella whispered to herself.

Luella looked at her again and saw the harshness in her eyes - the holier than thou attitude as she looked down on anyone not in her tight little circle. She had money and power and knew how to use it to control people. Men only saw what they wanted to see, but Luella could see the real woman beneath the stunning exterior and understood why her husband wanted her dead. She was the one with the money. There was no doubt that she pulled the purse strings and made him dance like one of those puppets in a kid's show. But if she was six feet under the ground he would be free and all she had would be his, money, property, power, everything.

Luella turned back to Horace, and after taking a sip of her champagne, she said, "Take a deeper look, my sweet. Look beyond what your eyes see. See the real person and you'll come away with a different point of view. Besides, it's not for us to question, we took money to do a job and we've already botched the first half of it, so don't go soft on me now."

Horace looked toward the ceiling. "The ranger," he whispered. That was a black mark on his record he hoped to rectify as soon as he got rid of the woman sitting across the room from him.

Horace shook his head and chuckled as he remembered all the plays about beautiful women with black hearts. The woman sitting across the room was no different - sitting there like she owned the world, causing people to cringe with just a look. She reminded him of a deadly black widow spider.

Horace looked at Luella and said, "Have no fear my darling. I see her only as, twenty thousand dollars."

One of the men at the table stood up with his glass of champagne raised in the air. "To you, Mrs. Thompson. May your trip to England be all you wish it to be."

The rest of the group sitting at the table raised their glasses and said, "Here, here."

Neither Luella nor Horace could believe their bad luck. First, it was the ranger and now their second victim was about to leave the country before they had a chance to do the job they were paid to do.

The woman sitting closest to Mrs. Thompson said, "I understand you're leaving in the morning."

"That is correct. I'm leaving on the morning train for Galveston where I will catch a ship to England," Claire Thompson said.

"But what about Shiloh, darling?" the woman asked.

"What about him?" Claire Thompson asked, her eyes turning hard.

"Isn't he running for re-election?"

"He is. But what has that to do with me? I don't get involved with his politics; they're such a bore," Claire said, waving her hand to dismiss the discussion of her husband.

"How long will you be gone?" a heavyset woman down near the middle of the table asked.

"I'm not sure. Probably until I get bored. I may also go to Paris. I understand the men there all pride themselves at being the world's greatest lovers."

"Oh Claire!" one of the women exclaimed. "You say the most outrageous things!"

Several chuckles filled the air, but all were merely polite courtesies.

Luella looked at Horace and said, "We need to book seats on the morning train bound for Galveston."

"I will see to it as soon as we finish our supper," Horace said as he watched their meal arrive. There were oysters on the half-shell, two giant lobsters, two large steaks with several kinds of vegetables, and of course, more champagne.

"I hope this will be to your liking, sir," the waiter in the black suit said, bowing slightly at the waist.

"As good as I could get in New York or San Francisco," Horace said, sticking a ten-dollar bill into the waiter's lapel pocket.

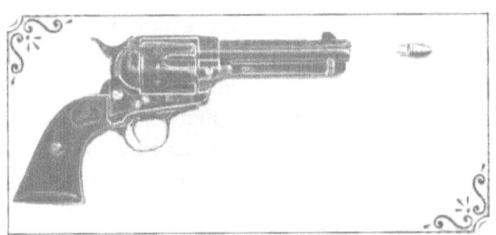

CHAPTER TWENTY-TWO

-

The following morning, Horace and Luella quietly boarded the train bound for Galveston at the same time Claire Thompson made her boarding a grand excursion with at least fifty well-wishers; mainly women dressed in high fashion and part of societies upper crust.

"Make the most of it, my dear," Luella whispered as she watched the affair. "It will be your last grand performance."

Luella still wasn't sure how they were going to do it, but when the train pulled into the Galveston station, if not before, it would be carrying a dead, Claire Thompson.

When Horace and Luella entered the dining car looking for a vacant table so they could have breakfast, there were only two vacant tables – and one of them had a reserved sign in the middle of the table with Claire Thompson's name on it.

"She sure does like to flaunt her money and power, doesn't she?" Horace said with a bit of envy in his voice.

"But not for much longer, my dear – not for much longer," Luella hissed. Her attitude toward the rich woman's influence was much different than Horace's. She found the woman to be rude and overbearing, belittling her stature in life, where Horace only saw the painted exterior.

Watching Claire Thompson taught Luella a thing or two about being rich and presenting herself. When they could finally travel, she would in no way be anything like this woman. When they decided to retire from the assassin business, she would conduct herself like a benevolent queen, gracing her subjects with kindness, yet staying aloof just enough to gain their approval and adoration.

Throughout the day, Luella watched and planned how they would get rid of miss high and mighty – along with possibly picking up a tidy sum of extra money by stealing her money and jewelry during the murder, making it look like a robbery gone bad.

By evening time, Luella had her plan in place and when they watched Claire retire for the evening, she began to put her plan together.

In their sleeping quarters, Luella made Horace up to look like Bill McDaniel, head of the Texas Rangers, based on a newspaper picture of him and her remembrances of him in Seymour. When she was satisfied, she had Horace walk through the train from one end to the other, glancing at the passengers, as though he was looking for someone - his badge in plain sight.

Later, in the middle of the night while the train labored to climb a steep grade, Horace, still dressed as Bill McDaniel broke into Claire Thompson's private quarters and stabbed her in the chest, then rummaged through her things and found a large amount of cash and a small, leather covered box with a fortune in jewelry inside, along with the ring Luella made him promise to get, even if he had to cut her finger off.

After putting the money and jewelry in his coat pockets, he talked loudly, almost yelling - as though they were arguing and then when he thought the other passengers had been fully aroused, he shot her in the same spot where he'd stabbed her earlier so the stab wound would not be easily noticed.

Leaving her stateroom – with his pistol in his hand and pointing to the star pinned on his vest, he motioned for the gawkers to get back inside their sleeping quarters as he made his way down the aisle to the end of the car.

Stepping outside, he found Luella waiting for him with their bags, ready to depart the train.

As the train topped over the rise of the steep hill, they easily stepped off the slow-moving train and slipped into the darkness; watching from the cover of the trees as the last car disappeared over the top of the hill.

Just before daylight, they exited the trees and saw a small ranch a short distance away.

The house was still dark as they slipped inside the barn and saddled two of the horses in the stalls. They led the horses out the back door of the barn and walked them a short distance away before mounting them and riding away.

Horace was still disguised as Bill McDaniel just in case anyone woke up and saw them.

Two days later, they rode into the thriving city of Houston. The town was bustling with activity and no one paid any attention to the new arrivals.

Horace and Luella rode up to the backside of the livery barn and turned the horses into the large corral through the back gate, then walked away. The hostler would find them at some point later that day and wonder how they got there, but that was no concern for Luella or Horace. The horses carried the owner's brand and they would eventually be returned to him.

Between two buildings, they quickly became a bible carrying couple who attracted very little attention as they entered the crowded sidewalks of Houston. A few blocks down the street, they rented a room at a small hotel not far from the train station, from a jolly fat man who paid scant attention to them. He was more interested in the story he was reading in one of those dime novels. Horace looked at the front cover and shook his head. Why do people get caught up in such gibberish, he wondered, secretly hoping someday they would write stories about him, wondering whose picture they would put on the pages. Maybe they would just leave it as a mystery face; after all, weren't the newspapers calling him The Chameleon? Or maybe they would call him, the assassin with a thousand faces.

The room was small and worn from years of use, but at least it was clean and allowed them a short reprieve from the past two days. After a short rest, they headed for the train station.

At the train station they purchased tickets to Oklahoma City, which wouldn't be leaving until late that same afternoon. Outside, they walked down the street until they saw the sign they were looking for. It was swaying gently in the breeze.

GRETA'S RESTAURANT
Best food in town

They smiled at each other, then hurried down the sidewalk.

They had had very little to eat during the past two days – only what Luella had been able to steal from the dining car on the train before they made their hasty exit after killing Mrs. Thompson.

The rich smell of food almost overwhelmed them as they entered the eatery.

The gray-haired woman who owned the place smiled as they took their seats, placing their bibles on the table.

"Good morning, I'm Greta Hardcastle and I own this fine establishment," she said, waving her arms wide.

Looking directly into Horace's eyes, she asked, "You a preacher?"

Horace was almost caught unawares until he glanced down and saw the bible laying on the table in front of him, and remembering how he was dressed. He smiled, allowing the actor in him to take over.

"I am the reverend Walter T. Barnes, minister of the word of God and salesman of the finest book ever written, the teachings of Jesus. Do you own a bible, sister?"

Greta swallowed hard and uttered, "I always wanted one but..."

"Have no fear for I believe this is why God led us to this fine establishment," Horace said in his best preacher's voice. "For the paltry sum of ten dollars, and breakfast for the missus and me thrown in, I can have, no... I will have shipped to you, your very own personalized bible from our headquarters in Chicago. Your name will be embossed in gold letters on the cover for all to see! Think about it, sister; it will be the best present you can ever give yourself, for nothing is better than the word of God!"

Greta was so caught up in Horace's enthusiasm that she readily agreed, and when they left, she held the bill of sale, written on a piece of brown paper, tightly against her chest.

According to Walter, as he had asked her to call him, they had completely sold out of all the bibles they had with them along with running out of receipts. But he had assured her receipt on the piece of brown paper was just as legal as anything she could get.

Greta had bought his lies, hook, line and sinker. "If I can't trust a man of God, who can I trust?" she had said to him as he pocketed her ten dollars.

Even while they ate their large meal, Luella was still having a hard time not bursting out with laughter. Not only had Horace gotten them a free breakfast, but also ten dollars in cold, hard, cash.

Back at the hotel, they sat down at the small table in their room. In the center of the table was the money and jewelry Horace had stolen, along with a bottle of whiskey they were taking turns drinking from. Since leaving the train, they had been on the run and hadn't taken the time to count the money or look at the jewelry Horace had taken.

Horace put the money on the table in stacks according to bill size.

Luella, who could no longer contain herself, burst into laughter.

"What's so funny?" Horace asked.

"Oh Horace," she said between bursts of laughter. "If Macklyn Arbuckle could have seen you at the restaurant, he would have had to take off his hat and bow."

Horace grinned and nodded his head. Up until the time they purchased the theater in Kansas City, Macklyn Arbuckle had been his biggest competition. He was the rage of the east coast and they'd heard he'd been offered a job in one of those new motion picture films people were talking about.

"Thank you, my dear. I wasn't half bad at that, was I?"

"You were superb! And right out of the blue!" she said, wiping the tears from her eyes.

Still smiling, Horace counted the stacks of money and said, "We have a little over twelve thousand dollars here. What do you estimate her jewelry is worth?"

Luella calmed herself and studied the necklaces, rings and bracelets in front of her, marveling at their beauty. "I'm no broker, but my guess is these hunks of rocks are worth more than thirty thousand dollars."

Horace let out a low whistle. "We hit the jackpot this time. We can go back to Kansas City - lay low for a while then slip back down and finish our work, this time making sure that ranger meets his maker, and then off to Europe."

Luella looked at Horace and nodded her head in agreement as she fingered the jewels that would somehow find themselves into her private stash.

In a few more days they would be back in Kansas City where she could prepare a plan to go back to Texas and finish the job of disposing of the Texas Ranger.

As she thought about it, maybe this would be their last job; after all, by all accounts, they now had enough money to retire, and with the sale of the theater, they could disappear before any more close calls. Yes, she thought to herself, it was time to quit the assassin business and maybe become a princess or some other title, like, baroness, while they toured Europe or South America.

CHAPTER TWENTY-THREE

-

The sun was shining brightly, a warm breeze wafting across the land brought little relief to the climbing temperature.

Clay stirred and opened his eyes. The sudden breeze had awakened him from a very tantalizing dream. Standing up, from the rocking chair on the front porch of his hacienda he felt a slight twinge in his back, but knew he was healing nicely and would soon be his old self again. He could hardly wait.

"Boss." He heard the voice coming from the yard and looked over to see Running Coyote headed his way.

As Running Coyote stepped under the shade of the porch, he said, "We got company coming."

Clay looked through the open gate and saw a plume of dust rising in the sky. Indeed, a rider was headed toward the hacienda, and riding hard.

"Well, let's go see who it is," Clay said, slapping his foreman on the shoulder.

They stopped next to the well in the center of the yard and Clay drank a cup of water from the bucket sitting on the edge of the wall surrounding the opening to the well. The water was wet, but not cold like a fresh bucket would be, but all things considered, it did quench his thirst.

When the rider got close, he slowed his horse down to a trot and came through the gate and stopped just in front of Clay and Running Coyote.

"What ah pleasant surprise," Clay said, extending his hand. "To what do we owe this unexpected visit?"

"Mornin', Clay... Runnin' Coyote."

Bill McDaniel handed the reins of his horse to the small Mexican boy who came to take the sweating animal to the barn for something to eat and a rubdown.

As the boy walked away with his horse, McDaniel turned back to Clay. "How are you feelin'? Good I hope," he said, slipping past Clay's question.

"Healin' right nicely," Clay replied, but still wanted an answer to his question. "Now I don't reckon you rode all this way just ta check on my well bein'. So... why did you come ridin' inta my place like ah pack of wolves was hot on your tail?"

Bill McDaniel walked over and got himself a drink from the bucket, then turned back and stared at Clay for what seemed to be an eternity. "I need ah place ta hide for a while."

Clay looked at Bill McDaniel and asked, "The head of the Texas Rangers needs ah place ta hide? Now that's gotta be one whale of ah story. Let's go inside and I'll have Mrs. McIntyre fix ya somethin' ta eat and you can fill me in on all the details while ya fill your belly.

While Mrs. McIntyre prepared something to eat, Clay and McDaniel sat at the kitchen table, drinking coffee. "So, what's the big mystery?" Clay asked.

"I'm sure you remember that assassin fella that the newspapers are callin', The Chameleon," Bill said.

"I do," Clay answered. "Think about him ever time I get ah pain in my back. Why?"

"He's the reason I'm here," Bill answered matter of factly.

Clay took a cheroot out of his shirt pocket and took his time lighting it, then said, "I'm all ears."

Leaving nothing out, Bill McDaniel told Clay the whole story as he knew it – the killing of the senator's wife, Mrs. Thompson, on the train, the stolen horses, the bible salesman who probably wasn't a bible salesman and the old couple who bought a ticket from Houston to Oklahoma City.

"Practically ever man, woman and child, on that train said they saw me struttin' up and down the aisles, and twelve people on the sleeping car swears it was me that killed the senator's wife," Bill said, shaking his head. "Now, ever gun slick in Texas is looking to make a name for himself by killin' me for the five-thousand-dollar reward money the senator put on my head. So, I guess you can understand why I need a place ta hide until I can get this thing figured out."

"Sure, sure," Clay said. "And you can't prove you weren't on the train? No one who could verify that you were someplace else?"

Bill shook his head back and forth. "That's the rub. As fate would have it, I had taken a few days off ta go fishin'. I was camped down along the river south of town during the time the senator's wife was killed and nobody saw me. First I knew anything was wrong was when I come ridin' back into town and some damn fool took a shot at me.

Jake, the hostler, told me what was goin' on and even showed me ah wanted poster."

Bill pulled the wanted poster from his shirt pocket and laid it on the table.

"Whew," Clay said, staring at the poster. "Sure didn't take the senator long to put you between ah rock and ah hard spot, did it? Makes ah man ah mite suspicious."

"I kinda got the same thought," Bill said, "but I couldn't stick around ta investigate, now could I?"

Clay shook his head, no, and was about to say something when he looked up and saw Mrs. McIntyre bringing in a large tray of food that was emitting wonderful smells.

As she sat a plate in front of each of them, she looked at Clay and said, "I'm thinkin' you wouldn't want your friend ta be eatin' alone."

Bill looked at her and said, "Thank you, ma'am."

She gave the head of the Texas Rangers a smile and a quick curtsy.

"Eat," she said, "afore it gets cold," then turned and left the room.

When Mrs. McIntyre was gone, Clay said, "Five thousand, you say. That's ah nice piece of change."

Bill McDaniel looked at Clay and grinned. "Don't be getting any ideas, my friend. Besides, you don't need the money."

That night, the two rangers sat up late talking about this assassin who it seemed, could look like most anyone he wanted to, leaving someone else to carry the blame for the murders he committed, which left the law without much to go on.

"How do you track down someone when you have no idea what he really looks like?" Bill asked.

Right before they decided to turn in, they finally came to the conclusion, that possibly, the old bible carrying couple who kept turning up, was the closest thing they had to an actual lead to being able to identify the killer. But that would mean catching him or them, dressed as an elderly couple who carried bibles – which, these days could mean any of a multitude of couples since there were a lot of itinerate preachers roaming the country these days.

"And what if they decide to change disguises? How do you recognize them then?" Bill asked.

Clay lay awake long into the night, thinking about this man who thought so little of life that he could shoot someone down in cold blood and never seem to waste any time feeling the consequences for what he'd done – along with the fact that he always left some innocent person accused of the crime he'd committed.

He was also bothered by the fact that he was more than likely still on this man's hit list. The man hadn't accomplished his job the first time, or as he understood it, the second time, either. Would the third time be a charm?

"Whoever paid him ta do the job, is more than likely asking why I'm still alive," Clay mumbled to himself. "And that's another thing. Who wants me dead bad enough to hire somebody ta kill me?"

By morning, Clay had come to a decision, and at breakfast he informed Bill McDaniel and his ranch hands that he would be going to try and track this man down and bring him to justice before anymore innocent people were killed or falsely accused of murder.

Without being asked, Mrs. McIntyre who as usual, had been eavesdropping, said from the kitchen door, "I'd not be thinkin' that would be such ah good idea; at least not yet. You've still got ah wee bit of healin' ta be doin'. Maybe ya'll be ready in another week or so, I'm thinkin'."

Bill McDaniel lowered his head, suppressing his grin, while all the hands turned to look at Clay, nodding their heads in agreement.

Clay stared at Mrs. McIntyre for a moment and then cleared his throat. "After taking your medical opinion into careful consideration and after having given your words a lot of thought, my answer is, no, I will not be waiting another week or even another few days. This man is like ah crazed animal who needs ta be put down before he kills again."

"But boss, you sure you're strong enough ta go traipsin' all over the country lookin' for only god knows who? Where will ya start? Does anybody even know what the killer really looks like? Have ya considered how long it's gonna take just ta find out who this here mysterious feller is? And then catchin' him might not be too easy, either. That could make for ah lot of saddle sores." Riley said, turning to look at the rest of the ranch hands who nodded their heads in agreement.

Clay grinned and lit a cheroot, then blew a long stream of smoke into the air before deflating their argument.

"You all seem to forget that I don't have to go gettin' saddle sores anymore while chasin' some no good half way across the country. I now own my own train, and I can get all the rest I need during my trip ta Oklahoma City, which is where I will be startin' the search," Clay said with a smirk.

"And I'll be along with him to see that he takes things easy," Bill McDaniel said, glad Clay was willing to help track this madman down.

Clay indicated he needed more coffee and while Mrs. McIntyre was filling his cup, he said, "Sorry Bill, but you need ta stay outta sight for awhile. Ever gun-slick in the country would like ta take ah crack at you and I might catch ah stray bullet. Besides, I can't be lookin' after you and searchin' for him at the same time. No, it's best if you stay here while I do some snoopin' around."

Bill got a deflated look on his face. He was not a man who allowed other men to do his work for him, but realized what Clay said was true, and nodded his head in concession.

Running Coyote, who had been sitting, until now, quietly observing the proceedings, spoke up. "There's one other little thing you forgot to mention, boss. You're more than likely high on this man's list of people to kill. He missed you twice, and I think if you give him a third chance, he's going make sure he does the job this time."

The room suddenly became silent as they all sat, staring at Clay.

"That surely is ah good point - one that I've given some thought to and I agree, I will need to be careful – plus, I just may have a trick or two up my sleeve," Clay said.

At this, Bill McDaniel raised his head and asked, "What are you sayin'? What's that devious mind of yours up to now?"

Clay grinned and looked over to He Who Bites and said, "Ride inta town and tell the engineer I'll be needin' the train by late this afternoon, and be ready for possibly an extended trip. Have him stock up on some food, too."

Clay reached into his pocket and pulled out a small wad of bills and peeled off several and handed them to He Who Bites. "This should take care of things until I get in there."

Clay could feel his adrenaline beginning to rise. He would no longer be sitting on the porch day after day, wishing he could get up and do something. Bill McDaniel's arrival had come just in time. Maybe he wasn't totally healed up yet, but he was close enough.

He turned and looked at Mrs. McIntyre and asked, "Could I see you in my office?"

She gave him a strange look, but said, "Of course," and headed toward her boss's office to find out what he was up to.

Clay excused himself and followed her.

Inside Clay's office, he walked around behind his large mahogany desk and sat down,
gesturing to Mrs. McIntyre, indicating her to take a seat in one of the chairs in front of his desk.

Clay took his time, mulling things over in his mind, then smiled at his housekeeper and said, "I hope you won't think I'm crazy, but I have an idea about how ta keep the killer from recognizing me if and when the situation arises."

Mrs. McIntyre sat; staring at Clay, waiting for him to reveal whatever he had on his mind.

Clay swung his chair around and looked out the window for what seemed to Mrs. McIntyre, a long time before he continued. Turning back, he asked, "Do you think you could help me change my appearance so I don't look like myself – maybe teach me how ta make myself look older – gray hair, eyebrows, and maybe a false mustache? I don't think I'd go much for a false beard, but somethin' I could do quick like, myself?"

Suddenly her eyes began to gleam as she realized what Clay was talking about and smiled. She stood up and paced around the room, looking at him from different angles.

"Tis ah devious man ya can be when ya set yer mind to it," she said, grinning. "And ta answer yer question, aye, I did ah wee bit of theater back in Ireland and I reckon I can teach ya ta make yerself look so different yer own men won't recognize ya, but it will mean delayin' yer trip until tomorrow. Do ya really think ya can pull it off?"

Clay made a grimace and said, "I don't know. I do know it's been workin' for him, and I'm thinkin' if the man who's been tryin' ta kill me doesn't recognize me, he won't be tryin' ta put lead in me, which will give me ah better chance ta figure out who he is and how ta bring him ta justice."

Mrs. McIntyre walked up to him and studied his face for a moment, then ran her fingers through his hair before saying. "I'll be needin' ta go ta town fer ah few things you'll need. Cindy can take care of things here while I'm gone. By tomorrow when you leave, you'll be ah a master at disguises."

Clay stood up and smiled down at her and said, "That sounds fine, but I won't be waitin' for tomorrow. I'll ride inta town with ya, and you can come ta the train and show me what ta do and how ta do it. And by the way, I don't want the men ta know about this."

Mrs. McIntyre looked at Clay with a wide grin spreading across her face and said, "No I don't suppose ya do. They might think ya'd gone daft, n off yer duff."

"And, well, I'm not so sure they wouldn't be right," Clay said, scratching his neck. "I'll be ready ta leave in about an hour."

With everyone wanting to know what his plans were and how they could stay in contact with him, Clay was barely able to get packed.

He called the men into the dining room and addressed them all so there would be no misunderstanding.

"I won't be gone any longer than I have to, and I'll send word when I get the chance, if there is anything ta tell. Otherwise, work goes on just like I was here."

Then, as an afterthought, he said, "Bill, if ya find yerself gettin' bored, I'm sure the men can find somethin' for ya ta do."

CHAPTER TWENTY-FOUR

-

Horace and Luella stepped off the train and had to steady themselves. A cold wind, driven by dark clouds overhead was causing people to scramble for the safety of the depot. Both men's and women's hats were flying off to who knew where. One woman was down and two men were trying to get her back on her feet, again.

Horace and Luella locked arms and leaned forward against the spitting rain that was mixed with sleet, accompanying the wind, as they made their way into the crowded depot.

"This is just not acceptable," a rotund woman of around sixty with hair sticking out from her head in all directions, said to the porter carrying her six suitcases.

"Yes'um," the porter said, looking around for somewhere to set her heavy luggage.

"Go this minute and find a taxi, or whatever kind of transportation this god forsaken place has to offer. Tell them I want to be taken to the hotel immediately."

"Beggin' yer pardon, ma'am, but which one?"

"Don't be impertinent, young man. The one I'm registered with, of course. Why they ever freed you people is beyond me."

The porter stood there, staring at the floor, wondering what to do.

Before she could continue with her tirade, a man stepped inside the depot and called out, "Mrs. Constance Hildebrand, hotel transportation for Mrs. Constance Hildebrand!"

"That would be me," she said with an arrogant tone. "Boy, take my luggage to the taxi and be quick about it. The sooner I get to the hotel the better."

"I think I'd shoot her for almost nothing," Horace whispered to Luella as the woman followed the driver from the depot.

Luella chuckled, nodding her head in agreement.

Looking through the window, she watched as a heavy gust of wind slammed into Mrs. Constance Hildebrand and drove her off the platform where she landed face down on the siding next to the engine and was immediately covered with black soot.

Loud chuckling filled the room and a man's voice was heard, saying, "Serves the old biddy right. Now maybe she can see what it feels like to be black. Hope it don't come off for weeks."

This got a loud round of laughter as Horace and Luella made their way to the train directory hanging on the wall and studied it.

"Well, what do you want to do?" Luella asked. "Do we keep going on the next available train, or spend the night and leave tomorrow?"

Horace looked around the room and then back at Luella. "Neither. I'd like to spend a few days here. I can't abide going back to Kansas City with that ranger mishap hanging over my head."

"You can't be serious!" Luella said, hoping she could change his mind. She was more than ready to get back to the safety of Kansas City. "Maybe we should just forget about him. We have enough money to retire on. We could give it all up right now and travel the world, free as birds."

Horace ground his teeth together and exhaled a long sigh. "It has nothing to do with the money. It's about my reputation. I have never failed fulfilling a contract and I'm not about to start now."

Luella was becoming agitated and it showed in her speech. "Reputation be dammed! No one knows who you are! The papers are calling you a chameleon - the man of a thousand faces. We can quit and disappear right now and no one would know or care."

"Well, my dear, I think the law would care. Yes, on one hand they would be happy if I were to disappear as you suggest, but on the other, they would be disappointed that they weren't able to slip a noose around my neck. And of course the man who paid out good money to see the ranger dead, would be most unhappy."

"Who cares?" Luella said, filled with frustration. "He doesn't have a clue as to your identity. He can rant and rave all he wants, but that's all he can do. Horace, there's something about that ranger that gives me the creeps. He's been far too lucky. I say we just forget him and move on with our lives."

"I wish it was that simple, my dear, but it isn't. I don't know how I know it, but he will be coming to Oklahoma City and I will be here waiting. I'm told these rangers stick together and he will come looking for me for making his boss the accused... and for shooting him in the back."

Luella was stunned. This was not like Horace. Normally he wanted to get the job done and hurry back to his precious friends and theater.

"I guess we'd better get a hotel room then," she said, "If you're bound and determined to go through with this, we'll need a plan.

Once she got him in the hotel room she would change his mind – it had always worked before and she hoped it would this time.

For some reason Luella didn't understand, Horace rented a suite instead of just a room as he normally did. He couldn't be serious about staying here and facing the ranger if he showed up as Horace felt he would, could he? It was insane.

Luella tried every seductive move she could think of, but Horace had only one thing on his mind – killing the ranger.

At dinner that evening, Horace laid out his plan. They would take turns watching the train station for he was sure that's how the ranger would arrive.

"How do you know this?" Luella inquired.

Horace took a sip from his coffee cup, then looked at Luella and said, "I'm not sure. Call it premonition, a nagging thought in my head, how I would do it, maybe? – I just know he will be coming and we need to be ready for him."

CHAPTER TWENTY-FIVE

-

Clay sat at the table in his private car, drinking coffee and listening to the clickity clack of the train wheels. He was about to begin the search for this chameleon as the papers called him, and still didn't have a clear plan on how to go about it.

He'd gone over what little information he had, at least a hundred times, and still had very little to go on. Bill had said an elderly, bible-carrying couple who had been seen at several of the killing sights, had purchased train tickets to Oklahoma City. Not much to base his plan on, but he had to start somewhere.

Mrs. McIntyre had purchased everything she could find in the way of theatrical makeup in the small town of Seymour, but told him he might need to seek out someone from a theater in Oklahoma City, if they had one, and get better instructions.

Clay still wasn't entirely convinced disguising himself was his best option, but he would at least have that to fall back on if things didn't go right. At least he hoped he would.

His next problem to overcome was the fact that, according to the sheriff in Seymour, the only way he could carry a gun openly in Oklahoma City, was to declare himself as a lawman, which would be like hanging a sign around his neck if the assassin happened to be in town and saw him.

Clay had gone down to the local gunsmith in Seymour and purchased a belt holster that would allow him to carry a pistol concealed at his waist, under his coat. It would mean, to draw it, he would have to open his coat and do a cross draw, which, he guessed was better than not having a weapon in case he needed to protect himself. The gunsmith assured him this was where the card sharks carried their guns, which didn't impress him much since a lot of card sharks got themselves killed.

With everything he'd had to take care of, he'd gotten a late start, but the engineer had assured him they would be in Oklahoma City around breakfast time; so, with nothing else to do, Clay pulled off his boots and dropped down on his bed and in minutes was sound asleep.

The slowing of the train brought Clay awake and he swung his legs over the side of the bed and sat up. Through the window he could see the passing landscape, dotted with a light dusting of snow. Winter was coming early this year. Smoke was coming from the chimneys of the houses. Oklahoma City was growing on a daily basis.

By the time the train pulled onto a sidetrack where it would stay while he was in town, he'd washed his face, shaved, combed his hair and put on clean clothes.

After a brief conversation with the engineer who said he would be at a nearby hotel until he was needed again, Clay stopped by a small restaurant not far from the train station, and when he entered, he immediately spotted the sheriff sitting at the counter, joking with the waitress.

The sheriff looked to be in his mid-forties and in decent shape. His hair had no gray in it and there was no paunch protruding over his belt. He was dressed in a dark, somewhat worn suit, and a forty-four pistol hung against his right leg.

As Clay entered the restaurant, the small bell over the door made a tingling sound. The sheriff turned and let his eyes take in the newcomer.

Clay walked directly over to the sheriff and stuck out his hand. "Clay Brentwood, Texas Ranger."

"Sam Hargrove," the sheriff said, shaking Clay's hand.

"What brings a Texas Ranger to my neck of the woods?" the sheriff asked amiably.

"Lookin' for an old man and woman who are carrying bibles. The man claims ta be ah bible salesman."

"What did they do, steal money from the collection plate?" the sheriff asked with a grin.

Clay took the stool next to the sheriff just as the waitress sat a cup of coffee in front of him.

"I'll have some breakfast. Whatever the house special is," Clay said with a smile.

"Steak and eggs, coming up," she said and turned toward the kitchen.

While Clay was waiting for his breakfast, he explained about the assassin and how he operated, and his reason for being in Oklahoma City.

The sheriff let out a slow whistle. "I've read about that fella. And you think he might be here in town?"

"Ta be honest, it's just ah hunch," Clay said as the waitress set his breakfast in front of him.

"You don't want folks to know you're a lawman in case he is here which would make it easier for him to spot you, but you want to carry your pistol in a belly holster in case there is trouble. Is that about right?" the sheriff asked.

"That sums it up right nicely," Clay said after swallowing a mouthful of steak and egg.

"Stop by the office and I'll give you a permit to carry a gun in case you need to use it," the sheriff said as he stood up and turned toward the door.

"Fifteen or twenty minutes from now be alright?" Clay asked.

"I'll have it ready for you," the sheriff answered as he opened the door and left.

-

Horace had been on his way down to a spot near the train depot where he could see who came and went without himself being seen and almost had a heart attack when he saw the ranger coming down the opposite side of the street, walking leisurely from the direction of the depot.

Stepping behind a pile of crates sitting on the sidewalk, he watched until the ranger entered the restaurant, then hurried back to the hotel. In their suite, he grabbed a case leaning against the wall near the bed. The case held a thirty-caliber rifle that could be broken down into two pieces and carried in the case, along with ammunition.

Luella was not in the suite so he had no chance to inform her that his suspicions had been correct, but she would know soon enough. Once the ranger was dead, they could disappear, never to be heard of again – unless they needed more money that is. Then, the chameleon would temporarily reappear, then disappear again when the job was completed.

Standing in the shadow of the alleyway across the street from the restaurant, Horace was dressed as a workman so he looked much like many other men here in town. From his hiding place he could see through the window of the restaurant and thought about taking his shot through the window, but after remembering his last attempt at shooting through a window, he decided to wait for a better opportunity – one he would be sure of making.

Besides, he would have to shoot the sheriff, too, and he had no contract on him.

When the sheriff left the restaurant and headed for his office, Horace looked around to make sure he was still alone, then picked up the case that was leaning against the building and opened it, smiling at his cleverness. No carrying of weapons was allowed inside the city limits, but no one would question a workman carrying a case filled with tools.

He very quickly assembled the rifle and loaded it with thirty caliber shells, then cocked it and waited. He wished Luella could be here to witness his final triumph. He knew she was anxious to be done with the assassination business.

The excitement of the moment was causing his adrenaline to run full speed. His hunch had been right. The ranger had come to town just as his gut told him he would and another opportunity was presenting itself.

From the shadow of the alley he would kill the ranger and be gone before anyone realized where the shot had come from. His contract would finally be fulfilled and he and Luella could retire from the assassin business once and for all and live in comfort the rest of their days.

The tingling of the doorbell brought Horace back to the task at hand. He watched as the ranger walked out onto the sidewalk and stood looking around. He pulled a cheroot from his pocket and lit it, blowing smoke off into the air.

"A final smoke before leaving this world. Enjoy it while you can," Horace whispered to himself as he hefted the rifle in his hand.

Horace took a deep breath and lifted the rifle to his shoulder and sighted down the barrel, aiming at the center of Clay's chest. The ranger was standing there, giving him a perfect target. There was no way he could miss, this time. Horace put his finger against the trigger and took a deep breath, then began the gentle squeeze.

Just as Horace squeezed the trigger and heard the loud boom close to his ear, Clay stepped off the sidewalk and into the street.

Before he heard the report of the rifle, Clay heard the bullet as it whizzed past him and embed itself in the wall of the restaurant.

Reaction kicked in and he threw himself forward into the street - rolling to his side, while at the same time, grabbing for his pistol, only to realize his pistol was not hanging against his leg where it normally was, but hidden inside his coat.

He continued to roll while he reached inside his coat and drew his pistol from the belly holster. During this evasive action to give the shooter a hard time for a second shot, his eyes searched the opposite side of the street. Nothing was left out from the ground to the tops of the buildings, but he saw no one to shoot at.

Still looking for movement, he came to one knee just as the sheriff came running up, pistol in hand and looking around.

"You all right?" he asked, helping Clay finish getting to his feet.

"Other than bein' embarrassed for bein' ah damn fool, yeah, I'm alright."

"You think it was this assassin fella?"

"Don't know of anybody else who would be takin' ah shot at me," Clay said.

"What I don't understand," the sheriff said, "is how he knew you were in town? You just got here a little over an hour ago."

Clay studied the alleyway across the street, then turned to the sheriff. "That's ah right good question. They say this fella is uncanny and I'm beginn' ta believe'm. How he knew I was comin' in the first place is beyond me, but somehow he must'a, and musta been watchin' the train station. It's the only thing that makes sense."

"I think the shot come from that alley over yonder," Clay said, pointing toward the space between the two buildings where Horace had been standing.

As they walked across the street toward the alley, Clay said, "He knows what I look like, but I still wouldn't recognize him if we was ta walk down the street side by side, and that disturbs me ah good bit."

In the alley, they saw tracks where someone had been standing and shoe prints of someone running down the alley. But when they got to the sidewalk of the next street, the prints disappeared.

-

Clay took his time, circling around and came up on his train car from the rear and only when he was sure he hadn't been followed or being watched, did he climb aboard.

Clay pulled the shades down to cover the windows. Now that the assassin knew he was in town, he didn't want to give him another chance at killing him.

Clay made a pot of coffee and sat at the table, drinking three cups, slowly calming his nerves as he went over in his mind what had taken place since coming to town.

Once again, he had cheated death, but how many more times would he be lucky?

Would the man hang around, trying to get another shot at him or would he and his female companion grab the next train out of town? And if they did, how would they be dressed? Surely not like an old couple again, he couldn't be that lucky. As he sat there, a plan began to form in his mind.

Half an hour later, Clay Brentwood, Texas Ranger, left by the rear of his private train car and circled around and approached the train depot looking like a businessman in his seventies. He had a stylish gray mustache and wore round glasses. He wore a wig that matched the mustache, and colored his eyebrows to match both his hair and mustache. He walked with an old man's shuffle, which took a little practice. He was wearing a long coat to cover the pistol hanging once again against his hip, plus the belly gun. In one hand he carried a small valise and in the other, a walking stick.

Before leaving the train car, he'd looked at himself in the full-length mirror and grinned. If he hadn't known better, he would not have recognized the man staring back at him.

When he entered the depot, which he'd decided before leaving the train, was the best place to do his surveillance from, the man standing behind the counter looked up and said, "The train headed for Wichita will be pulling in... in about an hour, if that's your destination, if not, there's no other train until morning."

Clay shuffled up to the counter and purchased a ticket to Wichita, only nodding his head yes or no, when the ticket taker asked a question.

The ticket taker watched as the old man shuffled over and sat down on the bench to wait, wondering who the man was? He was sure he hadn't come in on any of the recent trains and he knew he'd never seen him before. The old man had not uttered a word about himself or why he was going to Wichita, which was unusual because older folks mostly jabbered on like magpies.

Being the curious type, he was about to go over and try to find out more about the old man, but as he turned to leave his station behind the counter, the clickity, click of the telegraph machine began to chatter at him.

He sat down at the machine and picked up a pencil and began to jot down the message coming through.

When the machine stopped its clatter, the ticket taker read the message and shook his head. Standing up he walked over and stood in front of the old man.

Clay, who had been sitting quietly, listening to the Morse code and deciphering the message, already knew what the ticket taker was going to say, but sat quietly, looking up at him, waiting for him to divulge the message.

"I'm sorry to inform you, mister..." he said, trying to get a name from the old man, but frowned when the old man just sat there staring at him with a blank look on his face.

Finally, the ticket taker gave up and said, "The train will be delayed for a couple of hours due to some kind of difficulty. You're welcome to sit here and wait, or you can come back later."

Clay continued to stare at the ticket taker for a few moments, knowing the man hadn't told him the whole story. The tracks had been torn up and when the train stopped, a gang of robbers had boarded the train and held up the passengers. Not that it mattered because the result would be the same; the train would be delayed.

Without a word, Clay stood up and shuffled toward the door, where he stopped and pulled out a pocket watch to check the time against the large clock on the wall behind the counter, then nodding his head, he exited the depot.

The ticket taker watched as the old man shuffled along, going in the direction of town, confused by the old man's reluctance to talk.

"Maybe he's got something wrong with his voice box and can't speak," the ticket taker said to himself as he went back to his desk and wrote out a report to take to the sheriff.

A short distance from the depot, Clay moved into the darkness of a small stand of Maple and Chinese Elm trees between the depot and town. He could still watch the depot without being seen. He still wasn't comfortable, dressed as he was, walking around like one of them actors on the stage.

CHAPTER TWENTY-SIX

Luella entered their suite with a few packages in her hand and stopped short. Horace was sitting at the table next to the window, holding the bottle of whiskey to his lips. She could see his hand was trembling and some of the whiskey was spilling down his chin and dripping onto his shirt.

Horace sat staring out of the window and when he turned to look at her, there was a wild glaze to his eyes.

"What's wrong?" she asked, knowing immediately something had happened and Horace had been shaken by the ordeal.

With a trembling hand, Horace sat the whiskey bottle on the table and said, "The man has more lives than a cat."

"Who has? What cat?" Luella asked just before realization settled on her and a chill ran through her, making her shiver.

"He's here, isn't he?" Luella asked, knowing what the answer would be.

Horace sighed and said, "Not only is he here, but I missed him, again."

"You what? How? When?" she asked as her memory recalled hearing gunshots while she was in the mercantile store, never realizing Horace might be the one doing the shooting.

After taking another drink to help calm his nerves, Horace related everything that had happened. "I was sure I couldn't miss this time, and instead, I was barely able to escape before I had to come face to face with both the ranger and the sheriff.

Luella took this to be a sign and said so. "Horace, I know you don't believe in signs and omens, but I do and this is a sign for us to get out of town immediately. We have to put as many miles as we can between us and that ranger, and we have to start now."

With that, Luella pulled their bags from beneath the bed and began throwing their few possessions in them.

"No!" Horace yelled as he stood up and took Luella by the shoulders. "No, we cannot leave before I kill that ranger. I made a contract, and by damn, I mean to see the job done."

"Horace, please," Luella pleaded, knowing it would do no good. Horace was obsessed with the challenge of killing the ranger and would not give up until either, the ranger was dead, or he was, and maybe her too.

"Think, honey," Horace said, more calm now from the whiskey's influence. "You're smart, much smarter than some Texas Ranger. You've always planned our jobs with the cunning of a fox. So, all I'm asking for is one more chance at that ranger. Come up with a foolproof plan. You can do it. I know you can. If you do this for me, we can go away with our heads held high; knowing we'd never failed a job. Just this one last time, please."

Luella took a deep breath to calm her nerves. The look on Horace's face was more than she could endure. Even though it was against her better judgment, she nodded her head, assenting to his request.

"That's my girl," Horace said pulling her close, kissing her, long and passionately.

CHAPTER TWENTY-SEVEN

Clay's back and feet were hurting and in general, he was tired of standing behind the tree watching everyone who came past, especially couples. The train to Wichita had come and gone, and still he'd waited, but no one even closely resembling what he thought they might look like had boarded the train.

Circling through the stand of trees he passed behind the depot and finally climbed back onto his private train car. Inside, he made a fresh pot of coffee and while he was waiting for it to brew, he paced back and forth. He knew he would be hard put to continue with the farce any longer. He knew he would be safer wearing the disguise, but it just wasn't in his nature to pretend to be somebody he wasn't. Besides, not having access to his pistol without pulling back his long coat slowed him down and could get him killed.

When the coffee was ready, he laced it with a strong dollop of whiskey and sat down at the table to think. He knew the sheriff would back his play, but he had no idea what that play might be. He still had no clue to the man's identity, or his partners for that matter. He felt like he was between a rock and a hard spot. There was no doubt, the man would be waiting for another chance to shoot him if he showed his face in town, but on the other hand, he couldn't just sit back and wait for the man to turn himself in.

He was on his second cup of whiskey-laced coffee when a knock on the door brought him to his feet. Pulling his pistol, Clay eased down to the door and peeked around the edge of the shade, then relaxed. Harold, the engineer was standing patiently waiting for him to answer his knock.

Clay dropped his pistol back into its resting place, then opened the door and said, "Come in."

The engineer stepped inside, then stopped and stared at Clay for a moment. He looked around the inside of the train car, then back to Clay.

"Who are you and where's Mister Brentwood," he asked, drawing a small caliber pistol from his pocket.

It took Clay a moment to realize he was still in his disguise, which made him chuckle.

"You think this is funny?" the engineer asked, waving the pistol in Clay's face.

"No. No, not at all, and you can put your peashooter back in your pocket, Harold. It's me, Clay - Clay Brentwood, your boss," he said, seeing the shocked look on the engineer's face.

The engineer stepped back, still holding his pistol pointed at Clay and said, "Mister, I don't know what you're trying to pull, but you for damn sure, aren't Clay Brentwood."

Clay held up both hands, palms foreword and said, "Hold on ole timer. Just hold on," and with that he reached up and pulled off his hat and wig, then removed the mustache and the rest of his disguise.

"Well, I'll be horn-swagled," the engineer said, slapping his hand against the side of his leg. "You sure had me fooled. Why are you wearing that git-up?"

Clay poured Harold a cup of coffee and when they were seated at the table, Clay told him the entire story and when he finished, Clay said, "So this was the only way I could figure to get into town without being recognized, but I can't continue with this disguise. It's too cumbersome."

"So, what do you plan to do? Surely, you're not thinking of going back into town looking like yourself, are you? This time you might not be so lucky," the engineer said with a stern look on his face.

"I don't see that I have any other choice," Clay said, shaking his head.

The engineer got up and poured himself a little more coffee, then said, "You say you want to be able to be free enough to draw your weapon to protect yourself, right?"

"That would be correct," Clay answered, not knowing where the conversation was going.

The engineer walked back and forth down the aisle of the train car for a full three minutes without saying anything, then stopped in front of Clay and said, "Then go into town dressed in a disguise that will allow you the freedom you want to defend yourself, yet not be recognized."

"And pray tell, just what might that be?" Clay asked.

The engineer grinned and said, "Why a gambler, of course. They always carry a gun in case of trouble, don't they?"

Clay nodded his head and answered, "And what am I supposed to do about the no gun law? If you're not a lawman, you're not allowed to wear or carry a gun inside the city limits of Oklahoma City."

The engineer frowned. "I did not know that. That would put a big wrinkle in the idea, wouldn't it?"

"Even if the sheriff went along with it, which he couldn't do without a doing a lot of explaining to the city council, it would look mighty suspicious to the people of town."

The engineer scratched the stubble of beard on his face and after a minute, Clay saw his engineer's eyes light up.

"What if you were ah new deputy? They can carry guns can't they? And of course he wouldn't look like you," Harold said with a big grin spreading across his face.

At the same time Harold, the engineer, was explaining his plan to Clay, Luella was explaining her new plan to Horace, and when she finished, Horace smiled and said, "See, I knew you could come up with something. You always do.

That night, both the hunter and the hunted slept peacefully, each believing tomorrow would bring the results they hoped for.

Around ten pm, a southbound train made its regular stop in Oklahoma City and among the passengers leaving the train was a very pretty, fiery redheaded woman whose name was Loralie Benson. She was from Tennessee and was in Oklahoma City to deliver six of her Morgan horses to a buyer, never expecting the events that were about to unfold; would land her right in the middle.

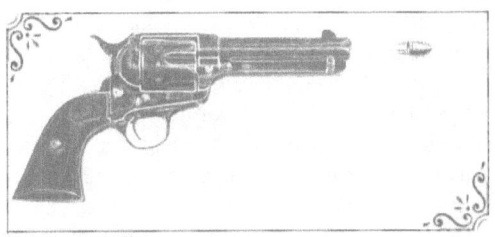

CHAPTER TWENTY-EIGHT

-

As promised, Harold kept an eye on the three trains that had come and gone during the night, with only departing passengers - none boarding, so there had been no need to awaken his boss. If things came to a head like they thought they would, Clay would need to be well rested and alert.

Over coffee the following morning, the old engineer, who turned out to be quite the artist at changing people's appearances, smiled and handed Clay a mirror. "What'ya think?"

Clay looked into the hand mirror and shook his head. The face looking back at him had absolutely no resemblance to his own.

"You could have been in the theater instead of bein' ah train engineer," Clay said with a grin.

"Just what makes you think I wasn't?" Harold asked. "Six years --- makeup man to some of Broadway's biggest stars," he said, nodding his head in a slight bow. "But the railroad gave me a chance to travel and see the west."

"Well, Broadway lost a star," Clay said, nodding his head up and down.

"Let's go see if we can put our plan into action," the engineer said, standing up – pleased with Clay's reaction.

-

The restaurant was packed with morning diners when Clay stepped inside and looked around.

At the back of the room, Clay found what he was looking for, the eyes of the sheriff, who was staring back at him.

Clay walked back to the sheriff's table and indicated the empty chair with his hand, not trusting himself to speak, yet.

Without replying, the sheriff looked him over from head to foot and then stared at the forty-four pistol hanging on Clay's hip.

"There's ah no gun law here in Oklahoma City, mister, and we take it real serious like, so why don't you just unbuckle your holster and leave your gun with me. I'll give you ah receipt for it and you can pick it up when you leave town. How long you planning to be here?"

Clay noticed the frown on the sheriff's face as he pulled the empty chair back and sat down without unbuckling his gun belt. Instead, reached into his shirt pocket and pulled out a cheroot and was lighting it when the waitress walked up with a coffee pot in her hand, but before she could pour a cup for Clay, the sheriff said, "None for him, he won't be staying that long."

Clay turned his head to look at the sheriff and found himself staring down the barrel of the sheriff's big forty-four.

"You're under arrest for carrying ah gun inside the city limits. Now get up. We're gonna to take ah walk over to the jailhouse.

As Clay stood up and turned toward the door, he felt his pistol being lifted from his holster, and still, he said nothing; he was having too much fun.

As they walked across the street and entered the jail, Clay was enjoying himself and nodded his head at the men and tipped his hat to the ladies.

Inside the sheriff's office, the sheriff said, "The cells are through that door," indicating a door on the far side of the office.

Just before they entered the cell area, Clay stopped and very slowly turned around, not wanting to spook the sheriff. He didn't want to get himself shot or clubbed with the barrel of the sheriff's pistol before he let him know who he was.

"How's it gonna look, you throwin' your new deputy in the hoosegow for carryin' a gun?" Clay asked with a Texas drawl.

"New deputy? Are you nuts, I don't have ah new deputy? Is this some kind of ah prank? Who the hell are you, mister?"

"You really don't recognize me, Sam?" Clay asked.

The sheriff looked at the man standing in front of him and tried to remember if he'd ever seen him before, but drew a blank.

"Mister, I ain't never seen you before. Now you'd better tell me what this is all about cause I'm starting to get ah mite riled."

Clay doffed his hat and said, "Please allow me to introduce myself. My name is Clay Brentwood. I'm ah Texas Ranger here in town huntin' ah killer the newspapers call, The Chameleon. I was hopin' ta pretend ta be your new deputy so I could move around town without bein' recognized. I need ta be able ta pack my gun in case I get ah chance ta apprehend this hombre, cause he's ah right dangerous fella."

The sheriff stepped back and stared at the man standing in front of him. The man he was looking at had no resemblance to the man he knew as Clay Brentwood. This man had unruly, dishwater blond hair that hung down to his shoulders. There was a long scar down across his left eye that ran almost to his jawbone. His skin was sort of pasty, like he hadn't spent much time out in the sun and his clothes could use washing. He'd been so caught up with the man not turning over his weapon that he'd not even considered it might be the ranger in disguise.

Clay grinned and said, "Sam, I thought you'd recognize my voice, that's why I didn't say anything over at the restaurant."

"Well I'll be ah ring-tailed rattlesnake. You sure had me fooled. Where'd you learn to do that – change yourself to look and sound like somebody else?"

"Let's just say I had ah little help from ah friend. Now, do I get the deputy job, or not?"

Sam Hargrove walked over to his desk and withdrew a deputy badge from the middle drawer and tossed it to Clay.

"Of course you do; but on one condition," the sheriff said.

"And what might that condition be?" Clay asked as he pinned the badge on his vest.

"That you keep me informed as to who you are, in case you change identities again," the sheriff said, grinning from ear to ear.

"You have my word on it, Sam," Clay said, looking down at his deputy badge. "Although, and no offense intended, I'm hoping this will be a temporary job."

-

Loralie was up early. She was excited about the sale. Six of her Morgan horses would bring her enough money to live on for close to a year.

Back on her ranch in Tennessee, she wore long pants and a man's shirt, along with boots and a wide brimmed hat to work and train her horses, but today, she wanted to look womanly and took a long, hot bath, enjoying the luxury.

After toweling herself off and applying powder to herself, she got dressed in the new clothes she'd brought with her.

Standing in front of the mirror, she was pleased at what she saw. The dark green skirt fit her nicely and the light green blouse flattered her red hair and green eyes. She pinned up her hair, then changed her mind and decided to let it hang down over her shoulders.

The only thing she wasn't comfortable with was her shoes. She'd worn boots most of her life and these women's shoes just didn't fit quite right. Otherwise, she knew she looked good and hoped to impress the buyer. This sale was very important to her and she wanted no hitches.

On her way down to the livery stable where she'd left her horses overnight, men smiled and tipped their hats: she even got a few whistles, which pleased her to no end.

The only thing that would make this trip better would be to run into Clay Brentwood. She hadn't had a letter from him in some time and she was worried that some other woman may have already dragged him in front of a preacher. Although, in all fairness, he wasn't aware that she hadn't married the young lawyer who had courted her for awhile until she informed him of her feelings for Clay.

As she approached the corral next to the livery barn, the hostler was just closing the gate and smiled when she stopped in front of him.

"I've seen ah lot of horses come through here during the past fifteen years, but these are some of the best I've ever had the pleasure of taking care of," the hostler told her when she walked up to the corral fence and looked at the six shiny coated and well curried Morgans who were parading themselves around the lot.

"Thanks. I'm kinda proud of'em, too. Any chance ah mister Wallace Masters has been by this mornin'?" Loralie asked.

The hostler, a long, lean man of around sixty, in bib overalls spit a stream of tobacco juice into the dirt, wiped his mouth on his shirt sleeve, then said, "Bout fifteen minutes ago. Looked'm over and said to tell you he'd meet you in the hotel restaurant. Said he was buying breakfast and that you'd know what he meant."

Loralie smiled, knowing that meant the man was happy with what he saw and agreed to buy the six horses she'd transported all the way across several states.

As she turned to leave, the hostler pulled his hat off and pressed it against his chest, and said, "Begging your pardon, ma'am, and I ain't meaning no disrespect, but I gotta say I reckon you're the finest looking horse breeder I ever had the pleasure of laying my eyes on."

Loralie felt the heat rising on her cheeks as she made a slight curtsy and said, "Why, thank you kind sir. That's the finest compliment I've had in ah long time."

Wallace Masters had a large ranch down in southern Texas and over the past year had taken a particular interest in harness racing. During one of the races he'd attended and had won a considerable amount on a horse he later found out came from a woman breeder back in Tennessee, he decided he wanted to get involved with harness racing. He sent her a letter asking her to meet him in Oklahoma City with a few of her best horses. He went on to tell her if they were as good as the one he'd seen, he was very interested in purchasing several of them to be used in harness racing.

Masters arrived in Oklahoma City late and had been informed by a note left at the desk that Loralie Benson had arrived and her horses were down at the livery barn, should he want to see them.

It was late and he was tired, but he intentionally got up early and went down to the livery to inspect the horses without the owner being there, just in case he didn't like what he saw.

He introduced himself to the hostler and asked to see the horses. The hostler turned all six out into the corral, where Wallace Masters walked among them rubbing their necks and checking them over.

Each one stood fourteen hands and appeared to be in excellent condition. He was impressed and eager to make the deal.

Back at the hotel restaurant, he sequestered a table so he could see anyone coming or going and when Loralie walked into the room and looked around, Wallace Masters got a lump in his throat. The woman was beautiful with her flaming red hair and green eyes. If this was the horse breeder he'd come to see, he wanted to know a whole lot more about her.

When the headwaiter pointed in his direction and she started toward him, Masters stood up and pulled out a chair for her.

Loralie smiled as she came close and stopped in front of him, then held out her hand. "Loralie Benson and you must be Mister Wallace Masters."

"Yes ma'am, that would be correct, and I must say, you're not quite what I expected," Wallace said, indicating the chair.

Loralie took her seat and stared at the rancher. He was tall, maybe six feet, and would weigh close to two hundred pounds she guessed. He looked to be around forty, with wavy brown hair and brown eyes, not at all unpleasant to look at.

Once she was seated, she asked, "What did you expect, someone in dirty buckskins with long, stringy hair and ah wart on her nose?"

Masters grinned and said, "Something like that. And I must confess I might have been able to deal a bit easier with someone like that."

Over breakfast, Masters found her very businesslike, but also, easy to deal with and by the time they'd finished eating, he found himself the proud owner of six Morgans.

She had also informed him that she was cross breeding the Morgans with other breeds to develop horses to work cattle. Some folks were calling them quarter horses.

Wallace Masters said he would be interested in seeing them also and she had invited him to come to her ranch in Tennessee so he could see for himself.

Although he was a bit disappointed when he'd asked her to dinner that evening and she had declined, stating she had to get back to Tennessee, he did promise to visit her ranch soon. He could always use good cattle ponies and if they were anything like the Morgans, he would be interested.

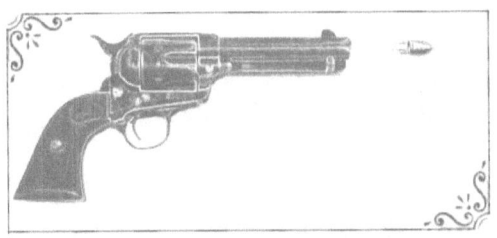

CHAPTER TWENTY-NINE

-

Horace and Luella stood on the sidewalk, dressed in simple clothes and each holding a bible. Inside each bible, the pages had been cut out to hold a thirty-six-caliber pistol.

The plan was simple. They would watch for the ranger to come walking down the sidewalk, then approach him and entice him into the alley where she would distract him while Horace took his pistol from the bible and shoot him. Luella could also remove her pistol in case it was needed. He would be dead before he had any inkling as to what was happening.

They could slip away without being seen and once again walk down the street with no one suspecting a man and woman carrying a bible of being killers.

-

Loralie left the bank with the money from the sale of her horses in her purse. She was headed toward the train station to make arrangements for leaving on the next available train headed east when she saw two men exit the sheriff's office. One was the sheriff and the other had a familiar look to the way he walked, but nothing she could put her finger on.

As she got closer, she heard the one with the scar on his face say, "I'll be wanderin' around town, checkin' ever place I think he might be. If I see'm, I'll try ta get word ta ya before I do anythin', but if I can't and you hear gunshots, come ah runnin'."

If the sheriff answered, Loralie would not have known for she was rooted in place by the sound of the man's voice.

"No, it can't be," she whispered to herself. This man in no way looked anything like Clay Brentwood, yet it was his voice she heard. That she knew for sure.

As she got closer, he turned and looked directly into her eyes and the surprised look he got on his face was enough for her. Even though this man looked nothing like Clay, she knew without a doubt, it was him all right.

"Loralie!" he said, his eyes wide and a big grin spreading across his face.

Loralie was very confused. "Clay Brentwood, is it really you? I...? What?"

Before she had a chance to say anything else, Clay took her by the arm and guided her down the street toward his private train car. The sheriff followed along behind wondering who this very attractive redhead might be and what her association with Clay Brentwood was?

Unbeknownst to Clay or the sheriff, Horace and Luella were standing directly across the street and had heard Loralie's surprised voice when she called out Clay's name.

After following them down to the side track and watching them board Clay's private car, Horace looked at Luella and said, "Well, I have to give credit where credit is due. The man is a lot smarter than we thought. He's using our own tactics against us. I would have never recognized him in that getup."

Luella smiled and said, "No matter. We can use that to our advantage."

-

After introductions, and while the sheriff made coffee, Clay told Loralie the story of the killer called The Chameleon and explained his reason for being in disguise.

"I can't believe you recognized me..." Clay said, shaking his head.

After accepting a cup of coffee from the sheriff, she took a sip, then said, "I wasn't really sure at first. It was your walk that first attracted my attention, but then when you spoke, I knew it had to be you, only, it sure didn't look like you. But when your eyes got big when you recognized me, well, that's when I was sure. How'd you learn ta do that, make yourself look different, I mean."

About that time, Clay's engineer, Harold came in the far door and stopped abruptly, taking in the people in front of him, then relaxed when he saw his boss and the sheriff, but especially appreciating the red headed woman sitting across from Clay.

"That's the culprit," Clay said, pointing toward Harold. "He's the one that made me up ta look like this."

Loralie stood up and walked over to Harold and stuck out her hand. "Well, you sure did ah Jim dandy job of it. I'm Loralie Benson. Clay and I go back some. He saved my bacon ah few times."

After some discussion, it was decided Loralie and Harold would go back to the hotel and get Loralie's things and bring them back to the private train car, and wait for Clay to get his business tracking down the assassin finished.

"When this is over, I can take ya back ta Tennessee, if you don't mind ridin' on ah private train," Clay said, grinning like a young schoolboy.

"I don't reckon I would mind that ahtall," Loralie said, her mind racing ahead to them being alone during the long trip between Oklahoma City and the small town close to her ranch just outside of Cinch Mountain, Tennessee.

Horace and Luella, well hidden in the trees next to where Clay's private train sat, watched as Loralie and Harold left the train and headed toward town.

"I wish they would raise the shades so I could get a clear shot," Horace said.

It was bright daylight so there was no need for lamps being lit inside the train car, which would have at least given Horace a shadow to shoot at.

Twenty minutes later, Clay and the sheriff left the train, but on the opposite side where once again, Horace couldn't get a shot at him. By the time he could, Clay was too far out of pistol range.

"Well, what do we do now?" Horace asked as the ranger and the sheriff disappeared beyond the train depot.

Luella thought for a moment, then said, "We wait for him, inside the train car."

Horace looked at Luella and grinned. Once again she had come up with a solution to their problem. Just before easing from their hiding place, Horace reached over and kissed Luella on the cheek.

CHAPTER THIRTY

-

Back at the sheriff's office, the sheriff stood looking out the window for what seemed to be a long time. Finally, he turned and looked at Clay, who was watching from the other window, on the opposite side of the door.

"Oklahoma City is growing bigger ever day. It's no longer ah one horse town and a man has his choice of hotels, saloons or a hundred other places to hide in. The best we can hope for is, that you spot him somewhere, but where to start looking is beyond me."

Clay was still in his deputy disguise and said, "I guess my best bet would be ta just walk up and down the streets, lookin' inside the stores and saloons, and such. Maybe I'll get lucky."

"That sounds like a lot of walking. In the old days, before the city got so big, a man could sit on a stool out in front of my office and see most everbody coming and going. But not today."

Clay nodded his head in agreement. It would help if he knew what the man or woman looked like. Maybe this disguise business wasn't the right way to go about it. Maybe he should just go back to being himself and take a chance the man would see him and try to kill him again.

Just then, the door opened and Harold and Loralie came in, Harold carrying Loralie's one and only carpetbag.

"Any luck, yet?" Loralie asked.

"No," Clay answered. "And the truth is, I feel like I'm chasing ah ghost. He knows what I look like, but I don't have ah clue as ta what he looks like. I feel like ah cat chasin' his tail."

Loralie placed her hand on Clay's arm and said, "I wish there was somthin' I could do ta help."

Clay patted her hand and said, "The best thing you can do right now is ta go back ta the train, where you won't be ah distraction or get yourself in harm's way, and wait.

"Is that what I am, a distraction?" Loralie asked with a coy smile.

Clay looked down at his boots and said, "You know what I mean. If trouble comes, you'd want ta be right in the thick of it and help, and, well... yes, I reckon you would be ah distraction, cause I'd want ta make sure you was safe instead ah concentratin' on the job at hand, which might wind up gettin' both of us killed, and I sure wouldn't like that."

Loralie smiled, then reached up and kissed Clay on the cheek. "Alright, since ya put it that way, I'll go back ta the train and wait, but I don't have ta like it; and you hav'ta promise me you'll not get yourself killed."

Clay smiled and said, "I'll do my best."

-

Luella was watching through a small crack between the train car window and the pulled down shade when she saw Harold and Loralie coming toward the train.

"Here comes the woman and the engineer," Luella said, taking up her pistol that was laying on the table.

Horace moved quickly to stand to the side of the door so he wouldn't be seen until they were inside the train car, his pistol gripped tightly in his hand. Killing the ranger was getting to be more complicated each time they tried.

When Loralie and Harold entered the car, they saw Luella standing down near the far end, holding a bible in one hand, the other hand behind her back, holding her pistol out of sight.

Harold sat Loralie's bag down and lifted his hat. "Ma'am, this is a private train car and folks aren't allowed to come in without being invited. I'm afraid I'm going to have to ask you to leave."

Loralie looked at the woman and a cold chill ran down her spine. She remembered Clay telling her about one of the assassin's disguises, a bible salesman, and this woman was holding a bible.

The door behind them closed with a bang. Harold and Loralie turned around. Standing with his back to the door, a pistol in his hand, Horace stared at them, smiling.

He had a nice face and looked like the gentle type, Loralie thought, except for his eyes. He had some of the coldest eyes Loralie had ever seen and she knew instantly they had walked into a trap.

"You're that killer the newspapers call, The Chameleon, ain't'cha?" Loralie said to him, watching his eyes light up. She turned to look back at the woman, who now, also held a pistol in her hand.

"And you're his woman, I reckon," Loralie said, staring at the woman with defiance in her eyes.

Luella nodded her head and said, "And you, my dear, are the bait to lure the ranger to his deathtrap," Luella said with a cynical smile on her lips.

"Now see here..." Harold said just before he felt the barrel of the man's pistol poke him in the back.

"Just shut up and sit down if you want to see the sun come up tomorrow," Horace said with a growl in his voice.

Harold complied without any further words being spoken. He needed to think, knowing he wouldn't be of any help to his boss if he was dead.

Luella saw the engineer touch his coat pocket with his hand as he sat down and she looked at Horace and said, "You might want to search him. I think he has a gun in his coat pocket."

Horace gave a sigh, angry with himself for not thinking of searching the man before ordering him to sit down.

"Stand up and raise your hands above your head," Horace ordered, pointing his pistol at the engineer's head.

After a thorough search and finding only the one small caliber pistol and a few shells, Horace ordered the engineer to sit down, again.

Once again, Harold complied without a word, wondering what he was going to do now that he had no weapon. At least with the pistol, he might have stood a chance, but...

Luella shoved Loralie into a seat at the opposite end of the train car so she couldn't communicate with the engineer. She was taking no chances.

Fortunately, Loralie was still dressed in her fancy clothes and could feel the pistol strapped to the lower part of her leg. She had learned long ago to never go anywhere without her pistol.

Ever since her parents had been murdered, she'd carried a gun and had had to use it on several occasions. Truth be known, she hated violence and killing, but there were people out there who could care less that she was a woman and would never lose any sleep over killing her. Times were hard and if a body wanted to survive...

Thinking Loralie was a city girl, Luella hadn't had the forethought to search her.

Approximately half an hour later, Horace was beginning to pace back and forth, peeking through the narrow space between the shade and the window, from time to time.

"Where is he?" he asked Luella, who could only shrug her shoulders.

Horace was anxious for this to be over. He and Luella needed to get away from this god-forsaken country. He missed the theater and his adoring fans and the fancy night clubs.

Luella watched him and knew he was becoming nervous, which she knew from past experience, was not a good thing. He might do something stupid, like trying to find the ranger to shoot it out with him, which she knew he could never hope to win. The ranger would kill Horace before he could get off a shot.

Luella walked over and looked down at the pretty redhead who sat quietly staring at the door. "When's he due to come back?"

Loralie stared straight ahead, uttering not a word.

"I asked you a question, Red, and I want an answer," Luella said, as she reached out and slapped Loralie across the face. "And I'm not going to ask you a second time."

Loralie bit back the tears forming in her eyes from the sting of the woman's hand, then slowly turned to stare up at her with eyes flashing daggers and a defiant set to her jaw.

"Even if I knew, which I don't, I wouldn't tell ya. But, I will tell ya this – Clay Brentwood will live ta see the two of ya put six feet under the ground where the maggots can feed on yer rotten corpses."

For her response, Loralie received a fist to her jaw that made her head reel. The woman was seething with anger almost to the point of shooting her, which is what Loralie was trying to do without actually getting shot. If she could get them riled up, they wouldn't be thinking straight and maybe, just maybe she could get to her pistol, or take away the one the woman was holding. If she could somehow get off a shot, or cause one of them to fire their pistols, maybe Clay would hear the noise and be alerted.

Unfortunately for all concerned, at this point in time, Clay was at the north end of town, wishing he could sit down and rest his aching feet. Cowboy boots were definitely not made for walking long distances and today he'd done ah whole bunch.

He'd looked into and checked every hotel and saloon in town, plus as many other stores as was open. The man had either, left town by some means other than the train, or was holed up somewhere, waiting for Clay to show himself.

By now, it was late afternoon and his throat was dry, along with his stomach moaning and groaning about not having anything since breakfast.

He didn't want to go to the restaurant without Loralie, but since he was standing in front of a saloon, he could grab a quick beer to quench his parched throat, then head back to the train and take off this ridiculous disguise, then the two of them could go into town and eat at one of the better restaurants, that is, if that assassin didn't spot him and begin taking pot shots at him, again.

As he stood at the bar, sipping on a cold beer, he reflected on things. That assassin fella had stayed here in Oklahoma City just like he thought he might. The man had built a reputation and he was the only flaw, which Clay figured would rankle the man's pride. He wouldn't leave until he'd done what he came here to do, which was to kill him or be killed. He doubted the man would consider giving up.

Then, there was Loralie Benson showing up all of a sudden here in Oklahoma City. He knew it was purely coincidence, but still, it was a mystery. They seemed to run into each other whenever there was trouble.

The truth was, Clay was glad to see her and he thought she felt the same way. It would be nice to sit across the supper table from a pretty face and talk.

Clay grinned. It really was good to see her again. Dressed up in city clothes, she was even prettier than he'd remembered her being when he'd first seen her in her buckskins and toting a pistol on her hip – shooting it out with outlaws.

Suddenly, he got a funny feeling in his stomach when the thought of her not being married to that lawyer fella. Was that what her last letter hinted at, he wondered?

Trying not to dwell on that, he moved on. She said she was raising and training Morgan horses and doing well for herself. He was proud of her. She had come a long way and had faced more hardships than most women would endure.

Suddenly, Clay wanted to hurry up and get the business with this assassin killer done and over with. The thought of the long train ride all the way back to Tennessee, with Loralie, sounded mighty good to him and he got the impression she was looking forward to it, too.

Clay left the saloon, walking briskly toward the far end of town, his thirst quenched and the thought of having supper with Loralie, made him quicken his step.

CHAPTER THIRTY-ONE

It was getting late and Horace was feeling the effects of waiting, which he wasn't good at, even in normal times.

Horace motioned for Luella to join him at the far end of the private car, and when she got there, he spoke in a low voice so the engineer and the woman couldn't hear.

"I don't like this waiting. It will be dark soon and that means trouble in my book. The ranger and his cohorts could sneak up on us and shoot us through the window."

"We could turn the lamps off so he couldn't see our shadows," Luella said.

"No, that won't work. He'll be expecting to find the woman and the engineer here and they would have the lamps lit."

"What do you want to do?" Luella asked in a frustrated tone.

Horace had been thinking for some time now about the situation they were in and had come up with a plan.

"We leave here and get out of town and wait for him there. Make him come to us in a place where we can see all around for at least half a mile. That way he can't sneak up on us with the sheriff and god only knows who else."

"You mean, move the train out away from town?" Luella asked, surprised that Horace should come up with such an ingenious plan.

"That's right," Horace hissed back at her. "It's too crowded here. We need to be out in the middle of nowhere."

"But couldn't he sneak up on us during the night?"

Horace thought for a moment and said, "Not if we send him a note stating he should come alone tomorrow morning at say, seven. That way the sun will be up and we can see for a long distance in all directions. If we see anybody else, we put the train in high gear and pull away."

"And how do you propose to get this note to him?" Luella asked matter of factly.

"I'll sneak over to the depot and tell the man there to deliver the message after we've gone."

And just how do you know he will do as you say?" Luella asked.

Horace thought for a moment, then said with a sneaky grin, "He'll be afraid not to do as I tell him to, that's how."

Luella wasn't sure what was going on in Horace's brain, but the way he was keyed up, there would be no use arguing with him; besides, it sounded like a good plan. After they killed the ranger, they could take the train and keep going until they got far away.

Loralie watched as Horace and Luella stood at the far end of the car, speaking in low tones - too low for her to hear what was being said, but she knew whatever it was, it had to be bad for Clay.

Then, without warning, the man turned and left the car. With the shades still drawn, she couldn't see which direction he went.

"He goin' out ta get us some supper?" Loralie asked, trying to be glib.

The woman ignored her and sat down, staring at her and Harold. She still held her pistol in her hand and the look in her eyes said she would not hesitate to use it.

Loralie wished the woman would be distracted by something long enough for her to pull her own pistol from where it was strapped to the lower part of her leg, but the woman never took her eyes off either her or Harold.

There was a coldness about the woman that told Loralie she was probably the brains of their little assassin business, and pulled the strings.

The only thing Loralie could do would be to bide her time, knowing at some point, her chance would come. She just hoped it wouldn't be too late to help Clay.

-

The telegraph operator looked up as Horace came in the door and walked up to the counter.

"Yes sir. You looking to buy a train ticket or send a telegram?" he asked.

"Neither," Horace said, pulling his pistol from his pocket and pointing it at the man behind the counter. I want you to write a note for me and then deliver it."

"But, I..." the telegraph operator said with a gagging noise in his throat.

"Shut up and do as I say," Horace hissed, "or I will shoot you. Are you ready to die?"

"Yes sir. I mean, no sir," the operator said, grabbing a pencil and piece of paper. His hand was shaking almost too violently to write.

"Write!" Horace demanded, then began dictating the message to the ranger.

"Tomorrow morning, a little before seven, follow the train track east. Come alone. When you see the train, raise your hands in the air. If I see a weapon of any kind, or anyone with you, the girl dies."

When the man said nothing else, the telegraph operator looked up, his eyes wide with fright, and asked, "Will there be a signature, sir?"

"He'll know who the note is from," Horace said.

"And who do you want me to give this note to, sir?" the operator asked.

"Clay Brentwood. He's the Texas Ranger pretending to be the sheriff's deputy. And I want you to deliver the note no sooner than thirty minutes after that private train out there leaves. I'll have a man hiding out there, watching and if you leave this depot before the thirty minutes are up, he has instructions to shoot you. Do you understand?"

The operator swallowed and blinked his eyes. "Yes sir. I understand perfectly," he said, feeling a wet spot begin to grow in his pants.

"Fine," Horace said with a slight grin – then pulled a dollar from his pocket and dropped it on the counter. "A little something for your help."

The telegraph operator stood silently while the man made his exit, then looked up at the clock and noted the time.

When he was sure the man was gone, he turned back to his desk where he kept a bottle of whiskey hidden in the bottom drawer.

Back at the train, Horace told Luella everything had gone smoothly and he would be up in the engine with the engineer until he found a place to stop.

Next, he ordered Harold to come with him and they left the private train car.

Once they had climbed up in the engine, Horace ordered Harold to fire up the engine and head east.

Harold shook his head and said, "We can't go anywhere without my tender, that is unless you want to shovel coal into the belly of this beast.

Once again, Horace berated himself for not realizing the engineer would need help operating the engine.

"Where is he?" Horace asked.

Harold took his time, like he was thinking about an answer, then said, "Not sure. Maybe at the hotel. He might be having supper at the restaurant, or he could be playing cards at the saloon. Then again, he could be laying with some woman in her room."

"Well you'd better guess right or you might find a bullet in your brain, mister engineer."

Harold sat on the seat he used when driving the big engine and said, "I seriously doubt that. If you kill me, who's going to operate this engine? You? I think not."

Horace nodded his head. "Well, maybe you're right. I won't kill you. But that won't stop me from shooting you in the leg or the foot – somewhere that will give you a lot of pain but still allow you to run this train."

Harold was convinced the man would do exactly as he said he would, which prompted him to go find the tender.

Horace and Harold were walking down the sidewalk when Harold saw the tender come out of the restaurant and approached him.

Thoughts about trying to make a break for it, here on the crowded street, crossed Harold's mind, but after consideration, decided not to endanger innocent people. He looked around, hoping to see his boss and possibly figure a way to signal him, but saw no one resembling the deputy he'd made him up to look like.

As the train left town, Horace leaned out and looked back along the track in the growing dusk, but saw no one following them.

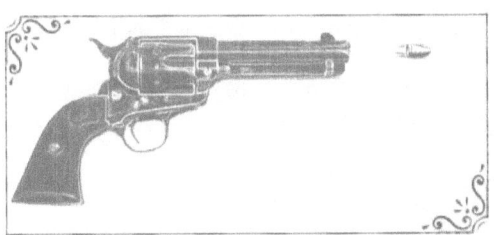

CHAPTER THIRTY-TWO

-

Clay was still a long way from the depot when the train left the sidetrack and headed east. Although Clay heard the shrill whistle coming from the engine, he didn't associate it with his train, but he did find it strange. He'd read the train schedule so he could keep watch in case the assassin tried to leave town and didn't recall a train coming through at this time of day. But that didn't mean a whole lot since train schedules were only hopeful arriving and departing times, what with outlaws and the Indians tearing up the tracks, causing long delays.

The sun was closing in on the western horizon when Clay rounded the depot and came to an abrupt stop. His train was gone! "What the..." he said, turning and heading back to the depot and entered.

The telegraph operator looked up and saw a man come in with anger on his face, then moved his eyes to the clock. It had been well over an hour since the man forcing him to write the note had left – closer to two hours.

"Where's my train?" the man with long hair and a scar down across his face, yelled"

Garnering his strength, the telegraph operator asked, "And just who might you be?"

"Clay Brentwood, Texas Ranger, owner of the train that used ta sit on that side track out there," he said, pointing in the direction of the sidetrack.

The telegraph operator felt his courage returning and said, "I'm sorry sir, but I've met Mister Brentwood and you look nothing like him. Who are you and what are you trying to pull?"

Clay realized the telegraph operator had never seen him in disguise and felt foolish. He reached up and pulled off his hat and wig, then peeled the scar from his face.

The telegraph operator's eyes went wide and Clay heard a gasp escape from lips. "I... I don't understand. Why are you dressed this way; trying to look like someone else?"

Clay sighed, "It's ah long story and I don't have time ta explain it right now. Now where is my train?"

The telegraph operator coughed to clear his throat and said, "A man came in waving a gun in my face, demanding I write you a note, and said not to give it to you until you came in. He also said he had someone waiting out there and if I left before you came in, the man had been instructed to shoot me."

He knew this was a lie, but he also knew it sounded better than he'd been afraid to go looking for him just in case there really was someone out there.

Clay could tell by the nervousness in the man's voice that he was not telling the truth, but at the moment, that wasn't important.

"Well, where's the note?" Clay asked, holding out his hand.

The telegraph operator reached under the counter and pulled out the note he'd written and handed it to Clay.

Clay read the note, twice, then looked at the operator and asked, "How long ago did my train leave."

The telegraph operator looked up at the clock and said, "Over an hour ago."

Clay's mind went back to the train whistle he'd heard earlier and he gritted his teeth.

Clay left the depot and headed for the sheriff's office and sighed a sigh of relief when he saw the sheriff still at his desk doing paperwork.

The sheriff looked up and saw the anger in Clay's eyes along with the fact that he had removed part of his disguise.

"What's up? Did you find him?" the sheriff asked.

Clay walked over and poured himself a cup of coffee, blew on it, took a sip and then said, "Not like you're thinkin'.."

Clay walked over and dropped the note on the sheriff's desk, then sat down in the chair in front of the desk and waited while the sheriff read the note, twice.

"There's only one place where he can go without worrying about another train coming through and running inta him," the sheriff said, standing up and walking over to the coffee pot to refill his cup.

"Bout six miles east o' here there's some stock pens where the local ranchers load their cattle to go ta Wichita, or Kansas City. There's ah sidetrack where the train sits while they load. My guess is that's where he'll be. I can round up ah posse and we can be out there when you show up. When he sees he's outnumbered, he's sure ta give up."

"Not so sure about that," Clay said as he went on to explain more about the man he was chasing.

"The man is crazy. He has no conscience and to my way of thinkin', he won't be taken alive. I got the feelin' he'll kill everbody he's got out there before he goes down, if nothin' else but ta spite me."

"Well what do you propose to do, then?" the sheriff asked.

Clay thought for a moment, then asked, "You got ah map of this part of the country?"

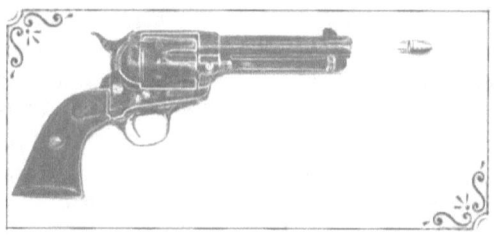

CHAPTER THIRTY-THREE

Darkness had settled over the land by the time Clay's small train was parked on the sidetrack next to the stock pens.

Loralie was told, with a pistol pointed at her, to fix something for them to eat. Luella watched over her shoulder every minute.

Horace stood on the back steps of the train car and surveyed the area. For the most part, the landscape was flat and as long as the moon stayed out from behind the clouds, he could see for a good distance all around. He was nervous. The ranger would come after the woman and him, no doubt, but would he bring the sheriff and a posse along?

He wanted a drink, but was afraid to chance it for fear he wouldn't be at his best when the ranger showed up. It had been a long, trying day and he was tired. He needed sleep and wasn't sure he could stay awake until morning. He started to light a cigarette, then changed his mind. The glow from a lit cigarette could be seen from a long way off, and make him an easy target for a sharpshooter.

Suddenly, he began to shake; realizing he was already a target, standing here in the moonlight.

Turning, he went back inside the coach and immediately lit a cigarette to help calm his frazzled nerves.

"Isn't that food ready, yet?" he barked.

Luella took one look at Horace's eyes and knew he was on the brink of a breakdown. This ranger and his damn luck was the cause of it all.

Turning, she reached out and slapped Loralie across the face, causing her to lose her balance and fall onto one of the seats.

Quick as a cat, Loralie was on her feet, fists balled up and ready to fight, but stepped back when the barrel of Luella's pistol met her oncoming charge.

"What was that for?" Loralie asked, rubbing her stinging cheek.

"I don't know. Maybe because you're that ranger's woman and I hate him and can't wait to see him dead."

Being called, that ranger's woman startled Loralie for a moment. Oh, she'd had hopes and even dreams, but didn't realize her affection for Clay was that apparent. But why not? she pondered. Every time she got anywhere close to him she felt tingly all over and got butterflies in her stomach. Suddenly, she wondered if he felt the same way?

Once again, she felt the sting of Luella's hand slapping her across the face and came back from wherever she'd been.

"I'm talking to you, miss high and mighty!" Luella yelled.

"Will you stop doin' that!" Loralie yelled back.

Luella saw something in the woman's eyes that caused her to take a step backward. It wouldn't take much more for the woman to attack her. The only reason she hadn't so far was the fact that she had a gun, but much more abuse and the pistol wouldn't stop her.

"Horace is hungry and wants his supper!" Luella said, trying to speak in a commanding voice. "Now, move!"

Loralie walked over and dumped some of the stew she'd made from the few supplies in the pantry, into a bowl, adding some last minute ingredients she'd seen in the cupboard, like, curry powder, mustard powder and paprika. She dumped in a heaping quantity of each spice, hoping it would be enough. After stirring in into the stew, she set the bowl on the table in front of Horace, along with a loaf of uncut bread.

"And mine?" Luella asked.

After setting a second bowl of stew on the table, also laced with the spices, Luella instructed Loralie to sit down across from them and stay quiet.

"What about us?" she asked, pointing toward Harold and the tender, knowing what the woman's answer would be, but making her say so.

"You'll eat when we're finished, and not until. Now, get Horace another bowl of this gruel you call food."

Loralie was amazed that he'd wolfed down the first bowl so fast and more than likely didn't even taste it, which in this case, was good.

She did as she was told and as she set the bowl of stew on the table, she was tempted to throw it in the woman's face and grab her pistol away from her, but wasn't sure she could get it before the man would be on her, so she waited.

Loralie sat down and watched as they ate. The man sure was hungry, along with being strung out and nervous as a calf at branding time. But the woman was like an iceberg. Nothing seemed to penetrate her nerves.

Luella took only a few bites then shoved the bowl away and said, "I can't eat this slop. Isn't there anything decent to eat in that cupboard?"

Loralie frowned. She had intentionally put those spicy ingredients in their bowls of stew, hoping they wouldn't taste them, but in the next hour or so, feel the effects. It was too bad the woman hadn't eaten more.

"There's some tins of caviar and oysters up there, if you like that sort of thing," Loralie said, shrugging her shoulders. "Never acquired the taste for it myself."

"Yes, get them down and put them on a plate. I don't eat out of a tin can. And see if there are any crackers."

"Yes ma'am," Loralie said, rising, the glimmer of an idea growing in her head.

On the top shelf, she found a tin of crackers and made the plate up real special like, with the caviar piled high on each cracker, the oysters in a small bowl, along with a small fork to eat the oysters with – and of course some of her special ingredients mixed into the caviar.

Loralie watched as the woman ate with relish.

Later, while she, Harold and the tender were eating their stew, Loralie couldn't help but chuckle a few times, drawing a whispery query from Harold. "What in the world do you find that's funny? We may only have hours to live and you're laughing? Tell me so I can go to my death, laughing as well."

As quietly and quickly as she could, Loralie whispered what she'd done to the stew, then glanced up at the clock. "It shouldn't be long now."

Both Harold and the tender fought their desires to laugh out loud.

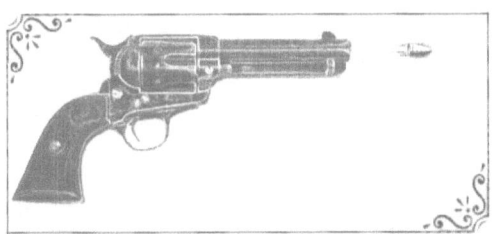

CHAPTER THIRTY-FOUR

-

During the time when everything was coming to a head in Oklahoma City, in the dining room of Clay's house, everyone was nearly finished eating supper when Mrs. McIntyre noticed that Bill McDaniel's plate still had most of his food on it.

"What's the matter, Mister McDaniel, is my cookin' not up ta yer likin'?"

Bill McDaniel looked down at his plate and noticed he had eaten very little of what had been put in front of him. Steak, potatoes and beets, along with some green beans, was some of his favorite things to eat, but right now, his mind was somewhere else. The last thing on his mind was food.

"It's not the food or your cookin', Mrs. McIntyre. You're ah wonderful cook. I guess I'm just not in the mood ta eat right now."

"Well, what is it then, I might be askin'? Are ya worried about Mister Brentwood? If that's what it is, yer not alone. So are the rest of us," she said, waving her hand around the table, "but we eat ta keep our strength up."

Bill McDaniel looked around the table and noticed for the first time, worried looks on all their faces.

"Why haven't we heard somethin'?" he asked. "You'd think he could take ah minute or two ta send ah telegram, couldn't he?"

Running Coyote swallowed the last mouthful of food from his plate, took a sip of water, then said, "We all are concerned, Mister

McDaniel, but I for one am not worried about the outcome. Mister Brentwood will get the job done, then send word when he gets his business finished and he's headed home. Like you, we all wish it would be sooner than later, but... right now, he's probably got his hands full."

"Well, maybe that's good enough for the rest of you, but it's not good enough for me. I want to know first hand what's goin' on and if he does in fact... have his hands full, well... I need ta be there ta help him out. I should never have let him go alone and I plan on rectifyin' that situation right now."

With that he scooted his chair back and stood up. "If someone will see ta saddlin' my horse, I'll get my saddlebags packed."

Brave Eagle stood up and called after McDaniel who was heading up the stairs, "I think it would be better if you waited for morning."

Without hesitating or looking back over his shoulder, McDaniel said, "There's ah full moon. I can see just fine."

When Bill McDaniel came down the stairs, Mrs. McIntyre handed him a package of food to take with him.

McDaniel smiled, put two fingers to the brim of his hat and said, "Thank you."

Outside, McDaniel found Riley sitting on his horse, holding the reins of McDaniel's horse in one hand and a lead rope in the other, with Clay's black stallion attached to the end of it.

"You plannin' on escortin' me inta Seymour?" McDaniel asked.

Riley grinned and said, "Nope. I plan on goin' all the way. The way I figure it, three guns are better'n two, wouldn't ya say?"

Bill McDaniel grinned as he put his foot in the stirrup and swung a leg over and settled onto the saddle.

"Can't argue with that kind of logic," he said as he touched the sides of his horse with his heels and they headed east, following the moonlit trail to Seymour, hoping to get some information from the sheriff, then catch a train to Oklahoma City and in the process, find Clay and lend him a hand if he needed it.

Bill McDaniel, head of the Texas Rangers was definitely not the type to let others do his fighting for him and admonished himself for letting Clay go alone.

As far as Riley was concerned, if his boss was in trouble, well... he rode for the brand and besides, he liked a good fight just as well as the next man.

The sheriff in Seymour hadn't heard anything but said he'd wire the sheriff in Oklahoma City that they were coming.

They got lucky and was able to board a train within a couple of hours of getting into Seymour, which suited both McDaniel and Riley just fine even though they'd had no reply from the sheriff in Oklahoma City.

"Don't mean anything," McDaniel said as the boarded the train.

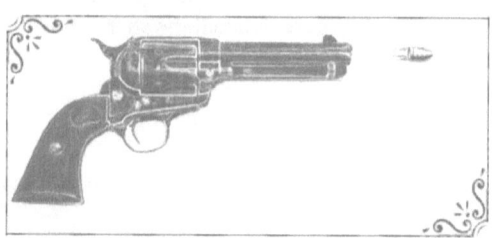

CHAPTER THIRTY-FIVE

-

Sometimes fate has a way of working things out.

When the train pulled into Oklahoma City, McDaniel and Riley stepped off the train so they could unload their horses and when they stepped down from the train, they ran slap dab into Clay and the sheriff as they were about to board the train.

Clay shook his head and asked, "What are you two doin' here?"

Riley grinned and said, "We got worried about ya, you bein' out here all alone and all. So... we decided ta come keep ya company. Ain't'cha glad ta see us?"

Clay grinned and said, "Of course I am. Now turn around and get back on the train."

"Why? We goin' somewheres?" Riley asked.

"We are," Clay said. "I'll tell you all about it when we get on the train."

McDaniel looked around and asked, "Why are we ridin' this train when we should be ridin' on your train? And by the way, where is your train?"

Once they were seated, Clay brought them up to date, and finished up by saying, "So, here's the plan. This train will pass right by the stock pens and we can see if my train is parked there. If it is, there's a spot about a mile on up the track where the train can stop and let us off."

The porter brought them a pot of coffee and some cups and Clay waited for him to leave before he continued.

"Now the way I see it, this assassin fella will be lookin' for me ta come ridin' up the track around seven in the mornin' and we ain't gonna disappoint him."

"We ain't?" Riley asked, scratching his neck, wondering how Clay was going to be in two places at the same time.

"No, we ain't," Clay said. "One of Sam's deputies will be dressed like me and come ridin' up the track, keepin' his head down like he's lookin' for somethin'."

"And you're not afraid of him gettin' shot by the assassin?" Bill McDaniel asked.

"That's the beauty of the plan," Clay said with a grin. "He's gonna stop, just out of rifle range and sit there like he's tryin' ta decide whether ta come on up toward the train or what?"

Remembering how his half-brother, Walks Tall liked to build drama in his stories, Clay took a sip of coffee while the suspense grew in their minds.

"Ok, so this assassin feller is standin' there on the train, watchin' and waitin'. So, what happens next?" Riley asked, his Adams apple bobbing up and down.

Clay sat his cup down on the table and was about to continue when he saw the twinkle in Bill McDaniel's eyes. McDaniel could see what Clay was up to and was enjoying ever minute of it.

"What happens next is, while this assassin fella is tryin' ta decide what ta do, we slip up from the other direction and take'm by surprise," Clay said with a grin.

"Well, I'll be hog-swallered," Riley said with a grin. "That's ah Jim-dandy plan."

"Not to throw a wet blanket on the idea or anything, but what do we do if this assassin fella suspects you might do something like this and has someone, like maybe his woman, watchin' the other end of the train?" McDaniel asked.

"Damn," Riley said, looking at Bill McDaniel, then over at Clay waiting to hear Clay's answer. "That's ah right good question. What about that, Mister Brentwood?"

"Thought about that," Clay said. "By the time the sun comes up, we'll be hidin' in the cattle pens. If he's got her lookin' for us ta be comin' from the east for ah blindside attack, then she'll have her attention on the railroad tracks and not the cattle pens."

Riley was nodding his head, his mind going a mile a minute. "If he's watchin' the track, lookin fer you ta come from that direction, and his woman is watchin' the track in case we try ta sneak in from the other direction, then who's watchin' the prisoners? You know, the engineer and the tender feller – oh, and that woman friend of your'n?"

Clay took a drink of coffee, then took his time lighting a cheroot and blowing the smoke into the air, making a smoke ring.

"Knowin' Loralie Benson the way I do, we may not have ta do anything atall... She just might have'm captured by now and just waitin' for us ta show up. That is unless they was smart and tied her up good and tight, sometime back."

"She ah hell cat, is she?" Riley asked.

Bill McDaniel grinned and said, "Worse than that, if the stories Clay here has told me is true."

"Oh, they're true alright," Clay said with a grin. "That girl's got sand and you can bet your last dollar she's not gonna take bein' kidnapped, lightly."

The porter, a tall black man with graying hair and a bit of a limp, came up to them and looked down at Clay and said, "The cattle pens is comin' up soon and thet train you is lookin' for is sittin' there, jest like you said it might be, Mister Brentwood."

Clay thanked him and gave him a dollar, and when he'd gone, Clay said, "The sheriff and I need to stay out of sight, but the two of you can sit in the seats, lookin' out the window like your regular passengers watchin' the landscape."

Horace heard the train coming and jumped up and watched out of the window of the back door of the train car.

As the train went by, he could see the passengers inside the passing cars, but saw no one who resembled the sheriff or the ranger, and gave a sigh of relief when the train finally passed by.

Even so, he wanted to take no chances and held his gun on the prisoners while Luella tied them up with rope taken from the window shades, then shoved them back into the seats, where they were warned to stay quiet.

Loralie thought they might do something like this, so, while she was making stew for their supper, she rubbed fat from the meat on her wrists and hoped whoever tied her up wouldn't notice.

Luella had been so intent on what the ranger might do that she did a poor job of trussing them up. Another mistake.

Satisfied she'd done a good job, she picked up her pistol and looked at Horace, who nodded his head and said, "You watch the other end of the car in case they circle around and try to come at us from that direction."

The three prisoners watched as Luella went one direction and Horace went the other. At first, both of them stayed inside the car, looking out through the windows until Horace said, "I'm going out on the landing so I can see better."

Luella nodded her head and did the same thing at her end of the car.

As soon as both of them were gone, Loralie began moving her hands back and forth, easily sliding her hands out of the soft rope material used to hold the shades back.

Harold turned so Loralie could untie his wrists. Loralie looked at both doors before bending down and untying Harold.

While Harold was freeing the tender, Loralie lifted her foot and raised the hem of her dress up high enough to reveal the thirty-two caliber pistol and holster strapped to her leg.

Both Harold and the tender had surprised looks on their faces – and not just from seeing the pistol. Loralie had shapely legs and saw both of them gaping at her bare skin. When she turned her head and looked directly at both of them, they each got embarrassed looks on their faces. She quickly dropped her skirt back down, covering her leg, smiling inwardly. Men could so easily be distracted.

Both men looked away, with Harold mumbling, "Sorry."

"Don't be," Loralie said. "I took it as ah compliment."

She looked at the tender and asked, "You got ah name? I've only ever heard you called, Tender."

"That's my nickname, he said with a grin. My name is Charles Richfield, but nobody's called me by that in more'n a coon's age."

Harold looked at him and said, "I didn't know that. I thought your name really was, Tender and you just happened to be one."

Loralie noticed the door of the car begin to open and she, along with the two men, sat back in their seats putting their hands behind their backs.

Luella glared at them and said, "I heard talking. No talking!"

The three prisoners stared at her without making a sound.

After a moment, Luella made a disgusting sound and went back out on the landing to keep watch, while holding her stomach.

Harold looked over toward Loralie and mouthed, "I think it's working."

Loralie raised her hand with her fingers crossed.

Loralie wasn't sure what to do next, but decided to wait to see what happened, take things as they came. She knew Clay wouldn't just walk into a trap; but she also knew he would not just sit around and do nothing. Knowing she could possibly die at the hands of these two lunatics he would come after her, just like he always did.

CHAPTER THIRTY-SIX

-

A little over a mile beyond the cattle pens, the train topped over a small rise and on the far side, slowed to a stop, giving the four men time to get off and unload their horses.

"Didn't you bring any horses?" Riley asked as Clay walked up and put his arms around the black stallion's neck.

"Figured we'd ride back on Clay's train," the sheriff said shrugging his shoulders.

"Thank you for bringin' Midnight," Clay said, "but we can't use any horses on this raid. We can stake'm out in that stand o' trees, yonder," he said, pointing toward a small group of trees a short distance south of the tracks, "until this thing is over, then we can come pick'm up."

"That would make sense if we're to hide in the stock pens. They'd see us comin' if we were on horseback," McDaniel said.

"Riley," Clay said, "you won't be comin' with us."

"Aww, com'on, boss. I didn't come all this way ta miss out on the fightin'. Sides, the horses don't need no babysitter," Riley complained.

"I don't recall sayin' you'd be stayin' here," Clay said with a grin.

"Then what am I gonna be doin'?" Riley asked, his eyes lighting up. "Somethin' excitin' I hope."

-

An outhouse sat not far from the stock pens and had been occupied by both Horace and Luella, several times each during the last few hours.

Holding her stomach, Luella confronted Loralie and yelled, "What did you put in our food you little tramp?"

Loralie looked up at Luella and said, "Well now, let me see. Nothin' we don't normally put in our stew; ah few spices, that's all. Why? Did it upset yer delicate nature?"

"I should shoot you right now!" Luella spit out, holding her stomach even tighter as she turned and ran for the door.

Halfway to the outhouse, Luella met Horace on his way back.

"We've been poisoned," he said as they passed.

"No," Luella shouted back. "Just a cruel joke by those hillbillies. She put something in our food to give us the forty-yard trots.

Unbeknownst to anyone on the train, Clay, Bill McDaniel and the sheriff had sneaked into the cattle pens to wait for the sun to come up.

By the time Clay and the other two were safely inside the cattle pens, the visits to the outhouse were over, so they wouldn't be seen running back and forth, which might have brought this whole matter to a close much sooner since both Luella and Horace were drained of energy and not in any condition to put up a decent fight.

Clay figured since they weren't planning on doing anything until daylight, he might as well catch a nap and suggested the sheriff and McDaniel do the same.

-

A few minutes before daylight came creeping over the horizon, Luella was sitting on one of the back steps; her was head hanging down, her eyes nearly closed and her breathing labored. The pain in her stomach had subsided some, but the rest of her body felt drained. It was all she could do to stay sitting upright.

When the door of the coach opened, Luella looked in that direction and tried to raise her pistol, but a foot came down on her wrist and a hand jerked the pistol from her fist.

"You don't look none too good, Missy," Loralie said with a grin. "I wonder if it was somethin' ya ate?"

"Oh, go to hell," Luella spat out at her as she leaned forward and began to heave.

Grinning, Loralie went back inside and gave Harold the pistol she'd taken away from Luella.

As luck would have it, at that moment, Horace glanced inside just as Loralie handed Harold Luella's pistol and in a moment of panic, jerked the door open and fired at Harold, his bullet hitting him in the shoulder, causing him to drop the pistol.

Loralie swung around and fired at Horace, who had already jumped back to the side, but reached his hand around the doorsill and fired another round in their direction.

The tender had by then, picked up Harold's pistol, shoved him down behind the seat and fired at the back door.

Clay, the sheriff and Bill McDaniel came to their feet, McDaniel saying, "What the..."

"I think Loralie just may have started the dance for us. Com'on,'" Clay said, jerking his pistol from his holster as he climbed through the railing and ran toward the train.

Just before reaching the train, Clay, along with everyone else, heard what sounded like gun shots and the yelling of a wild Indian charging from somewhere off to the side of the train.

As Clay had instructed him, Riley had ridden off to the side and waited until he heard gunfire or yelling, whichever came first. Then he was to come riding toward the train, like he was a band of Indians, yelling and shooting his pistol in the air, which is what he was now doing.

Clay grinned. They could board the train while Riley held their attention.

It seemed like everything was happening all at once. Horace guessed Luella was either dead or captured and when he looked down the track, he saw a rider coming toward them.

Assuming it was the ranger, he figured he could still fulfill his contract. Without giving Luella another thought, Horace jumped down from the train and ran toward the deputy. Raising both arms in the air, yelling, "I surrender. I surrender."

When Horace got close and saw it was not the ranger, anger seized him. It had been his plan to catch the ranger off guard and kill him, then steal his horse and make his getaway. Either way, he needed that horse.

He lowered his right hand, which still held his pistol, and shot the deputy, hitting him a glancing blow to the head, knocking him from his saddle.

Horace ran over and grabbed the horse's reins so it wouldn't run away, as he bent down and pulled the deputies pistol from his holster. He stuck the gun in his belt, then swung aboard the horse and rode back in the direction of town, hoping he could get back to Oklahoma City where he could disappear among the throng of people until he could find a way out of town.

But first, he needed Luella's carpetbag, which held their money and bank account books. He felt if he could get back to Kansas City, he would be all right. He could clean out the bank accounts and disappear. He would go to London, or Paris, one of the large cities in Europe where no one would ever find him.

When the shooting started, Clay, McDaniel and the sheriff stormed the train and climbed aboard, pistols in hand, ready for whatever was happening.

When Clay came crashing through the door, looking for Horace or the woman, he found Loralie tending to Harold's shoulder. She looked up at him and said, "Sure took ya long enough ta get here."

"Are you all right?" Clay asked, seeing his answer before she said anything.

"Couple of small bruises, but nothin' I can't live with," she said, then grinned. "Sure am glad ya came."

About that time, the door opened and Clay swung his pistol in that direction. McDaniel and Riley came in, carrying the deputy, with McDaniel shouting, "Don't shoot!"

As Loralie ran toward the injured deputy, Riley informed them, "He ain't dead, but he took ah glancin' blow ta his head and he's in bad shape."

"And the man we came out here ta get?" Clay asked.

"Stole the deputies horse and headed back ta town," McDaniel said, shaking his head.

Clay rubbed his face, then turned and asked the tender, "Can you run this train?"

"Sure, in a pinch, but I'll need somebody to shovel coal. I can't do both."

By now, Loralie was fussing over the unconscious deputy and Riley walked up and said, "I can shovel coal."

Clay looked at Riley and said, "Thanks."

Turning back to Riley and the others, he said, "I'm gonna take Riley's horse and head for town while you go on up the tracks and pick up the other horses. I'll see you back in town."

As he started to leave, Loralie stood up and stepped in front of him.

"You be careful. I don't want ta have ta come and pull you outta another mess," she said with a twinkle in her eyes, then she reached up and kissed him on the mouth.

When she finished the kiss, she stepped back and said, "Now get outta here and go find that lunatic afore he kills anymore innocent folks."

As Clay disappeared out the door, the sheriff looked around and asked, "Where's the woman?"

Loralie looked over at the sheriff, then ran for the door of the coach and looked out. Luella was gone.

Loralie stepped out onto the back steps and looked out across the flat, desolate countryside.

A good quarter of a mile in the distance, Loralie saw someone hobbling across the prairie and knew it had to be Luella.

"I found her," Loralie yelled over her shoulder as she leaped from the train and began running toward the struggling Luella.

The men watched through the windows of the train car as Loralie raced after the lone figure in the far distance.

McDaniel looked at the tender and said, "Maybe you should start gettin' the train ready ta go. Loralie will be bringin' that woman back, right shortly, and we need ta be gettin' back ta town."

-

Luella heard Loralie coming and turned to make a fight of it, but Loralie didn't break stride as she ran headlong into the tired and dragged out fugitive.

Loralie sprang to her feet and grabbed Luella by the hair of her head and yanked her to her feet, slapping her across the face. "That was for slapping me just because you was mad at Clay."

Then she slapped the woman again, on the other side of her face and said, "That was cause you slapped me ah second time."

Luella staggered backward, but stayed on her feet and in defiance, tried to take a swing at Loralie, but missed.

But Loralie didn't miss as she stepped in close and with her fist balled up, slammed it into Luella's face, knocking her to the ground.

Blood was flowing from Luella's nose as Loralie dragged her back onto her feet and shoved her in the direction of the train. "Get ah move on. We're burnin' daylight."

CHAPTER THIRTY-SEVEN

-

Horace rode up to the back of the hotel and jumped off the horse who stood with his head hanging down from the hard run all the way back to town.

Horace raced up the back steps, down the hall and entered their room.

Inside the room, he quickly checked Luella's bag and found the money, jewelry, and bank books. He sighed with relief, then quickly packed his own bag and hurried back down the hallway and down the steps.

He'd just reached the ground and was about to head down the alley when he saw a rider coming his way. He knew it was the ranger and drew his pistol and fired in his direction, then turned and ran down the alley, ducking behind an outhouse, his breath coming in short gulps.

The bullet had missed Clay by a wide margin.

"Hey, you, Mister Chameleon, or whoever you are. Stand where you are. I'm Texas Ranger, Clay Brentwood and you are under arrest on ah whole bunch of charges."

As Clay stepped from the saddle, Horace stepped from behind the outhouse and fired at Clay, then ducked back behind the outhouse.

Clay felt the bullet sting his ear as it drove a hole through the lobe. He swore. "I'm gettin' damn tired of that man shootin' me."

Clay drew his pistol and began to walk slowly toward the outhouse, his eyes watching for movement of any kind.

Clay saw movement just beyond the outhouse wall and turned in time to see Horace race across the small space between the outhouse and the back of the saloon, firing his pistol as he ran.

Clay sidestepped the barrage of bullets coming his way as the zing of two of them came dangerously close to his head.

Feeling wetness on his shoulder, Clay pulled off his neck kerchief and put it against his bleeding ear, then ran around the side of the saloon and raced toward the front.

As he rounded the front of the saloon, Clay saw Horace come barreling out through the batwing doors.

"That's far enough," Clay yelled.

Startled at seeing the ranger, Horace lifted his pistol in the ranger's direction. "Damn you! I'll see you dead if it's the last thing I do!"

Horace's bullet missed its target, but Clay's didn't and he saw the small hole appear in Horace's forehead.

For a few seconds, Horace stood there, a bewildered look on his face, then he toppled over backwards.

Suddenly, Clay heard a voice say, "Hold it right there, mister."

Clay dropped his pistol back into his holster, then, very slowly, pulled his coat back to reveal the ranger's badge.

One of the sheriff's deputies pushed his way through the crowd, and when he saw Clay, he said, "It's alright, men. He really is a Texas Ranger."

Then he turned to Clay and asked, "Is this the man you've been looking for?"

Clay nodded his head and said, "It is. When I tried to arrest him, he threw down on me."

The deputy looked around and then back at Clay. "Where's the sheriff?"

"He'll be along directly," Clay said. "He's bringin' my train back."

-

During the ride back into town, Luella learned that Horace had left her to fend for herself and felt betrayed. In order to save her own neck from the hangman, she promised to give McDaniel the names of every person who had ever paid them money to do their killing for them, on the condition that she would get life in prison and not executed.

McDaniel said he thought that could be arranged, but the final decision would be up to the judge.

When the train pulled onto the sidetrack, they found Clay waiting for them.

Loralie was excited to see him and jumped from the train before it had come to a complete stop. She rushed over and kissed him right in front of everyone.

"Is it over?" she asked. "Is that awful man in jail?"

Luella was coming down the steps and heard Clay say, "He's dead. I tried ta arrest him, but he shot at me and I had no choice."

"You're bleedin'! Let me have a look at it." Loralie said as she pulled Clay toward his private train car.

As Luella walked past Loralie and Clay, her eyes shot daggers at them, all the while, knowing Horace had made the right decision. A bullet was better than a hangman's noose, even though for herself, life in prison had to be better than dying. Maybe after a few years...

After a long talk with McDaniel, the judge announced at Luella's trial, that because she had turned over evidence that would eventually bring to justice the culprits who had initiated the killings, instead of hanging, she would spend the rest of her life in prison without a chance for parole, and may God have mercy on her soul.

The judge then went on to say, the money, jewelry and bank books had been turned over to the court. The judge also decided to trace down the relatives of the dead victims and give them some of the money, at least the ones that could be found. The rest would go to the state for schools and hospitals and other such places that needed money.

McDaniel went to arrest the senator and found him slumped down on his desk, a bullet in his brain.

McDaniel came back and talked to the judge again and he agreed to turn a sizeable amount of money over to the town of Waco, to help build their college.

Clay and Loralie spent the better part of two weeks getting back to Tennessee and the experience was very pleasant for both of them.

Over supper at the only restaurant in Cinch Mountain, they agreed to find a way to see each other more often, if possible.

As the train headed west, toward Texas, Clay sat in his private car, staring out of the window. Loralie had pulled no punches when the talk got around to marriage. She was all for it, but would wait for Clay to come to terms with the idea.

Leaning his head back, he closed his eyes and thought about the fiery redhead he'd just spent time with. She was a handful, of that, there was no doubt, and he had no illusions about her answer if he should ask her hand in marriage but was he ready? He would need some time to think things over.

Clay dozed off, his mind swirling with thoughts of what would happen if he married again.

While Clay was resting and dreaming of the future, things were going on he wasn't aware of.

The state of Oklahoma had no facilities for women prisoners of Luella's crimes, so the judge sent her to the Kansas State Prison, in Lancing, Kansas, which meant sending her by train, with an escort – a young deputy who had no experience with this sort of thing, but was willing to make the trip.

In Topeka, an opportunity presented itself that Luella couldn't resist. During the two-hour layover, a woman from one of the churches came aboard and the deputy allowed her and Luella time alone to discuss Luella's future while he went to the dining car for a cup of coffee.

A short time later, Luella, dressed in the woman's clothes, her bonnet shading her face, exited the train and escaped, with one thing on her mind --- revenge.

THE END

MEET THE AUTHOR

JARED McVAY is a four-time award-winning author. He writes several genres, including - westerns, fantasy, action/adventure, and children's books. Before becoming an author, he was a professional actor on stage, in movies and on television. As a young man he was a cowboy, a rodeo clown, a lumberjack, a power lineman, a world-class sailor and spent his military time with the Navy Sea Bees where he learned his electrical trade. When not writing you can find him fishing somewhere or traveling around and just enjoying life with his girlfriend, Jerri.

THANK YOU FOR READING!

If you enjoyed this book, we would appreciate your customer review on your book seller's website or on Goodreads.

Also, we would like for you to know that you can find more great books like this one at

www.SixGunBooks.com

Stories so real you can smell the gunsmoke.™